PRAISE for *Out of the Shadows with Catherine the Great*

The author's impeccable command of the history of the period, combined with superlative knowledge of the workings of the court of Catherine II (the Great), guarantee the accuracy of her portrayal of this special time in eighteenth-century Russia. Readers are simultaneously drawn into the adventures of not only the newly crowned empress, but her best friend Maria, whose own circumstances harbor an enormous secret. In a sense, author Judith Rypma makes Time Travelers of us all.

Edward A. Cole, Ph.D.
Professor Emeritus of Russian Intellectual History

This compelling historical narrative of vivid characters draws readers into the newly crowned Catherine the Great's inner circle. In the sparkling imperial court of the Enlightenment, Russia is almost immediately transformed by expansion, dissension, murder, and war amidst the high-stakes game of European power politics.

Meanwhile, Maria—one of Catherine's closest confidants—continues to feel estranged and haunted by a tantalizing secret. Will she ever get back to the future that she left inexplicably and unwillingly 250 years ahead? Caught between two worlds in ways she never could have imagined, she faces a fascinating tension between eighteenth-century traditions and turning points, personal dilemmas, and one woman's loves and attachments to both eras. Rypma's epic saga about love, power, and ambition in Catherine's Russia may have something to say about our own twenty-first-century dilemmas.

Scott Van Lingenfelter
Author, *Russia in the 21st Century*

Out of the Shadows *takes us back to the glorious early reign of Catherine the Great seen through the eyes of not only the world's greatest stateswoman but her spunky and engaging maid of honor, Maria—a young woman transported from the end of the twentieth century.*

Rypma's mastery of all aspects of prose fiction shine as she presents well-drawn characters, an enthralling story, a tightly motivated plot, and meticulous manipulation of time. Once you begin the novel, you will have difficulty in putting it down to return to the twenty-first century. History buffs who immerse themselves in Catherine II and Maria's world will savor this book.

Christine A. Rydel, Ph.D.
Professor of Russian Language, Literature, & Culture,
retired former Editor, Ardis Publishers

This novel is intended as a stand-alone sequel to be enjoyed even if you haven't read its predecessor. Book One—*In the Shadows with Catherine the Great*—explores Catherine's first 32 years leading up to her coup. It also covers Maria's portal into the past and her evolving relationships with Catherine and Igor.

PRAISE for *In the Shadows with Catherine the Great (Book One)*

"Couldn't wait to turn the pages!"

"A book written with love—and made to be loved."

"Pushkin's *Captain's Daughter* meets Gabaldon's *Outlander*."

"I couldn't wait for the sequel."

Other Novels by Judith Rypma

Baba Yaga and the Stepmother: A Retelling of Snow White

In the Shadows with Catherine the Great

Mrs. Fleeney's Flowers

The Amber Beads

Details plus links to all novels and 10 collections of poetry appear on her website:

www.rypmabooks.com

OUT OF THE SHADOWS
WITH CATHERINE THE GREAT

JUDITH A. RYPMA

Published by Leonora Books

Author of *In the Shadows with Catherine the Great*

ISBN: 978-1-7367311-6-1

Leonora Books

Cover design by Shelley Savoy

Author photo by R. Materson

Back cover painting: Eriksen, Vigilius. *Catherine II in Front of the Mirror*. 1762-4, Hermitage Museum, Saint Petersburg, Russia.

Interior design by Booknook.biz
New River, AZ

"Ultimately the scales come down in Catherine's favor, and posterity, while taking into account her weaknesses and failures, her prejudices and her pride, justly calls her Great."
Virginia Rounding

TABLE OF CONTENTS

Out of the Shadows

With Catherine the Great

CHAPTER 1

(MARIA) JUNE 30–EARLY JULY 1762

The noise outside reaches a crescendo. It is a celebratory racket, like you'd expect on New Year's Eve. Yet this is early summer.

"It's happened!" Igor shouts, ducking into our jewelry shop after a survey of St. Petersburg's packed streets.

Although I don't tell my husband "I told you so," I imagine the dazzling smile he wears as a partial apology for any doubts he might've had about my predictions that this day would truly come. He also shares my pure relief that the recent nightmare—beginning with Empress Elizabeth's agonizing, drawn-out death and culminating with the insidious six-month reign of her nephew Peter III (toppled this morning by his wife Catherine) is over.

"We must go to the city gates!" Igor urges. "They say Her Imperial Majesty Catherine the Second is on her way to Petersburg."

Igor's Aunt Gina, too weary to attend morning mass, nevertheless wants to come with us to witness this day of marvel. It falls to her nephew to dissuade her. "Too many people," he insists to his beloved aunt, who immigrated from Italy to Russia before his birth. "Do you mind preparing us a feast instead? And pull out some of the best chianti that Uncle Giuseppe left us. After we return, we can all celebrate!"

She agrees reluctantly, and we embrace before Igor and I merge onto the wide, crowded Great Perspective Avenue that I alone know someday will be renamed Nevsky Prospekt.

Empress Catherine II makes her triumphant entry in a captain's uniform, riding majestically at the head of her troops. In the nearly two decades that I've known her, she has never looked so handsome and so stately. The overjoyed crowd is obviously in love with this dark-haired vision atop a stallion. Those who cannot squeeze into the mass of people climb balconies and rooftops, hang out windows, sometimes swing from trees. It is an ocean of bright and cheering faces fully supporting a successful, bloodless coup.

Igor and I find a spot in the archway of a fan-maker's shop near the original Kazan Cathedral, where richly garmented members of the Holy Synod have trailed the procession all the way from the city gates. Jubilantly hoisting signs and icons, the people and clergy have come together to bless their new empress. Military bands strike up instruments, and constantly ringing city bells mingle rather than compete with drums and trombones.

"Although Her Majesty dislikes music, I think today will be an exception!" I shout to Igor over the cacophony. He squeezes my hand while steering me back through the crowd.

Wine merchants and tavern-keepers have been persuaded—or perhaps ordered—to open their shops this Sunday, and as the festivities proceed merrily throughout the morning and well into afternoon, more than a few celebrants down glass after glass of spirits.

Rather than follow the procession to the palace, we make our way back home. There will be time enough, I surmise, to see our newly anointed Gracious Sovereign. Catherine undoubtedly will be bursting with energy and orders, with no time for us: one of her ladies and Igor, her favorite jeweler. For nearly two decades, first I and then Igor have served her not only in our official capacities, but as friends and finally spies. Eventually I will be privileged to speak with the woman I alone realize will someday be known as Catherine the Great.

"We must," I muse later, setting out the antipasto Aunt Gina made, "start thinking of jewels for her coronation!"

Igor laughs uproariously. "Of course, my efficient business partner. Our entire nation has just experienced a *coup d'état*, and my beloved yet apparently mercenary wife is worrying about how much money we can make off it."

"You know that's not what I meant," I start to apologize, and then he leans over the table and kisses me.

"I know it well, my precious opal. You are not wrong. At some point there will be a coronation, and before and after

JUDITH RYPMA

that endless balls and countless demands for jewels for all the nobility from Petersburg to Moscow."

"Not to mention the empress," Aunt Gina adds. "Did you not tell me, Maria Sergeievna, that the horrible woman with whom the emp—the former emperor—shares a bed has raided most of the empress's jewels?"

"She did. Peter ordered many of the state jewels taken from Catherine Alexeievna's possession and given to that horrible Vorontsova."

"Don't worry," Igor assures us, adding, "I've accumulated a small stash of her gemstones and pieces now hidden at Countess Praskovia Bruce's home. Her Majesty will not lack for jewels."

I am stunned. If I ever doubted my husband's faith in my mysterious foretelling of events, this confirms he has believed me. Knows I really *do* come from the future. For how long he's thought so, I have no idea; it is enough. Rising from the table, I wrap my arms around him. "Is your nephew not the most wonderful man in the world, Aunt Gina?"

"Just like my brother-in-law: his father. Both with hearts of gold and the courage and faith of soldiers."

"Speaking of soldiers," Igor says after we finish dining. "I hope you don't mind if I slip away to one of the barracks and get some news."

"You'd be better off to go to a tavern," I suggest. "I fear most of those on military duty may be taking advantage of a full day of drinking establishments being open."

Igor stretches, grins, kisses us both, and disappears.

I do not see my husband that night but am not too worried after a messenger stops by late to confirm Igor is fine.

The worst that could happen, I suppose upon awakening alone, is that he has overindulged and is sleeping it off someplace.

So when someone arrives at noon, I fully expect it to be Igor. Instead, my old friend and fellow lady-in-waiting Tatiana—elevated to countess upon her recent marriage—stands outside.

"Let me in, my dear." Dressed in a mint-colored tea gown, she sweeps in dramatically, startling our apprentice George into dropping a magnifying glass.

"Isn't it marvelous?" exclaims Countess Tatiana, her pale skin aglow with excitement as George bows hastily and then scurries next door to continue preparing for stacks of orders Igor expects. "Well, it's not so marvelous that the police have now shut down all the wine shops. Perhaps the situation *had* become rather wild. A group of soldiers broke into one cellar and stole gallons of Hungarian wine. When they didn't have glasses, they drank out of their hats!"

Having just left the winter palace, Tatiana is so full of similar news she ignores the coffee, bread, and gooseberry preserves Aunt Gina has served. "My husband is delirious with joy! He has struggled for months to tolerate Emperor Peter's disrespect and disdain for the Russian guards, not to mention being forced to wear that awful Holstein uniform. He said we can burn it now!"

"And you may remain at court?"

"Most definitely. Things are much too interesting to leave now. Much safer with the emperor in custody. Plus, a mes-

senger arrived from Count Stanislaus Poniatowski with word
that he expects to return from Poland!"

"No doubt he *wants* to return," I muse, thinking fondly
of Catherine's second lover and the man who sired her now
deceased baby girl.

"No doubt. I don't think he knows about Grigory Orlov,
so I would hate to have to handle that reply!" Grigory, Catherine's lover and partner in the coup along with his military
brothers, must be even more ecstatic than the Polish count.
Still, there is no room in the newly elevated empress's kingdom—or bedroom—for two lovers.

"What else have you heard?"

"Well, they say the *former* emperor is at his country estate
in Ropsha, and that he is making all sorts of silly demands."

"Such as?"

"He begged for his Oranienbaum Palace bed, for one."

"Why?"

"Have you ever seen that thing, Maria?"

I admit I have not.

"It is huge, with four posters and all of the trappings, from
a white satin coverlet and pink and silver brocade curtains to
plumes of feathers decorating the top. I cannot believe Alexis
Orlov would retrieve it for him."

"What else did he want?"

"Well, Her Imperial Majesty has granted some of his other
requests. He pleaded for his blackamoor Narcisse, his dog
Mopsy, and his violin. Not his entire violin collection, just the
one he plays the most. He also asked for *das Fraulein*."

"Vorontsova? No, that is just too much kindness. Why

would Catherine—Her Majesty—permit him to share his arrest with his mistress?"

"She did not grant that one. They say his mistress has been sent to her family in Moscow. And my husband has been getting all kinds of news about the abdication."

Finishing off thick slices of brown bread slathered with preserves, I listen carefully as Tatiana recounts how Peter dispatched Prince Golitsyn to meet Catherine on her way to Peterhof. "Peter had the audacity to offer to share the crown with her. Ah, too little, too late," she laughs. "After that, the tiny tyrant offered to immediately abdicate in return for safe passage to his precious Holstein."

"Her Majesty declined, did she not?"

"*Da*, of course. She ignored both letters and waited until she received news of his unconditional surrender."

I laugh, half to myself. "All those years of mock warfare, of toy soldiers, of excessive staged drills, and when it comes time to enact it all, to actually take control, he could not."

We continue to chat until Tatiana must leave to check on her toddler. "How is your little boy?" I ask politely.

"Still crying all the time. The nurse seems not to hear him. I have not reached that point. Oh, my dearest, did I tell you I am with child again?"

"No! Congratulations!" I stammer, almost immediately aware I am experiencing a sense of jealousy. In the span of just a few years, Tatiana will have had two children in comparison to my childlessness. I dread the thought of mentioning it to Igor.

The subject of pregnancy is one my husband and I rarely discuss—he because he lost his own mother giving birth to him, and I because . . . *Because I was born in 1982*! Having been inexplicably and terrifyingly transported two hundred fifty years into the past after touching a marble goddess statue in the Hermitage in 1999, I still—after eighteen years here—have doubts about becoming *that* assimilated into this era. The whole process of childbirth, not to mention the sometimes ridiculous, dangerous eighteenth-century habits that precede and accompany it, for a long time kept me religiously taking herbs to prevent that possibility. And then there's the other niggling and terrifying risk: that somehow, someday I might end up back in the future and have a child left in the past!

Only recently have my fears somewhat dissipated.

Tatiana, as unaware as everyone else about my unprecedented situation, looks at me sympathetically. Perhaps noticing my discomfort, she hastily changes the subject back to Catherine's coup and her husband Peter III's short, unpopular reign.

Barely does Tatiana depart, promising to send a messenger if Her Majesty has need of me, when another visitor shows up.

"How did you manage?" I ask Anya, now a great friend. She was once my fellow seamstress when Empress Elizabeth banished me to the sewing staff for marrying Igor without royal permission. It is a surprise to see her on a Monday.

A huge grin spreads across her delicate features. "Madame has fled! Resigned, I believe."

"How is this possible? She is the head of the atelier!"

"I always suspected Madame Vorahov favored His Majesty—I mean, the former emperor—over the new empress.

I'm guessing she feared some kind of retribution, and so she simply handed her keys to one of the senior seamstresses, gathered some possessions, and left the palace! Several groomsmen saw her working her way swiftly in the opposite direction of the crowds."

"What a relief. For you, I mean."

"It is. I do not believe she ever intended to advance me up the ranks. Notice, though, that *no one* is working right now. Everyone's either disappeared or gone to join the celebrations in the streets. It is a holiday, Maria! And who needs a seamstress during such a momentous event?"

"Who indeed," I laugh, putting up my hand to stop Aunt Gina from heading for the kitchen. "No, Aunt Gina, I will get us something."

Most food markets are closed due to the coup. At least we have the makings of a meal. "Do not protest," I overrule Anya as she rises to depart. "I've seen the diet on which you subsist—and recall that I once did so, as well. We will celebrate with blini and caviar. Perhaps even pickles, marinated mushrooms, and vodka!"

My entreaties to convince Anya to stay with us longer, at least for a few days of rest, are unsuccessful. I do manage to get her to spend part of the afternoon relaxing.

"I must go and see my father to find out how he fares," she explains. "There's always a risk that at such times people will vandalize his brewery. I'll stay there a couple days and by that time, things might be normal again in the palace."

"Especially with a coronation to plan!"

"Especially that."

Igor confirms all Tatiana's and Anya's news when he

arrives after I've cleared the plateware. "It was chaos that first night. I could not leave, my dearest."

"What happened?"

"Someone started a rumor that the emperor was on his way with thousands of Hussars to reclaim the city. The Izmailovsky guards believed the plans included capturing Her Majesty—and that perhaps one plan had already succeeded."

"My God!"

"Just after midnight we all marched to the square. After the guards insisted upon seeing her Imperial Majesty, she emerged dressed in a military uniform. Everyone was pretty drunk, and they started cheering when she reassured them all was well, she had not been dethroned, and the empire was safe. She had to ride out to one of the barracks! Then," he grins, "everyone went back to the taverns and wine shops to resume celebrating. They are even toasting the traditional boon of a lowered price on salt."

Knowing how much we need the seasoning, I cannot resist asking for details.

"Ten kopecks per pood."

"Terrific," I complain. "We would have to eat a ton of salt to save any money. Well, I am certain there will be more and better benefits under the new reign."

"At least no one is preparing for war anymore, which may be why all the soldiers are so busy drinking."

"Tatiana tells me the taverns are closed."

"This is true, but I assume only temporarily. The bills have been sent to Her Majesty, and heaven knows how much it will all cost. Things are calm now, however, and I'd like to get back to work."

"You need some sleep first," I admonish.

"Fine. But I don't intend to sleep alone."

I return his smile, and we climb upstairs hand in hand, prepared to celebrate. After nearly two decades living in the eighteenth rather than twenty-first century, not to mention awaiting Catherine the Great's rise to power, I scarcely can believe that it has come to pass.

CHAPTER 2

(CATHERINE) EARLY JULY 1762

"Catherine showed herself even more spectacular in her magnanimity to her enemies than her generosity to her friends; her refusal to enact any of the penalties a conqueror might be expected to impose upon the vanquished is unparalleled in history."
—Gina Kaus

"Schlüsselburg was only forty miles from the capital and [Peter] would become the second deposed emperor imprisoned in this bastion. Sending him back to Holstein had been ruled out. But if not to Schlüsselburg or Holstein, where was he to go?"
—Robert Massie

The newly anointed autocrat—Gracious Sovereign of all the Russias—was elated. Catherine (now Catherine the

Second) had only moments, though, to pause and examine her joyful feelings. In these nascent hours and days of her reign, she slept only briefly and reluctantly. She had too much to accomplish. Too much to do to secure the fragility of the power she now wielded. Too many ideas she'd harbored for so long and yearned to implement. Her imagination galloped ahead, despite her realizing in these early days that she had to corral it with common sense.

She summoned Grigory Orlov, the only person in whom she dared confide and could trust implicitly. Alas, Princess Catherine Dashkova, who often needed to be kept at arm's length despite her loyalty, had fumed when she discovered that her idol Catherine and the man the young princess considered a common oaf were more than merely her co-conspirators: they were in fact lovers. Incensed, she had departed the palace of Peterhof in the middle of the coup.

"Do not worry about Little Catherine," Grigory reassured her now. "She will recover, especially after the generous promotion you gave her husband. And you know she loves you, albeit not as much as I." He knelt in front of the divan and kissed her hand.

With a mere look, Catherine dismissed the ladies and servants hovering in her sitting room.

"I am not certain of that."

"That I love you?"

"No, that she will forgive me for our perceived sin. Don't forget that not only were we best of friends and intellectual partners for the past couple years, but that she played a key role in the coup. She actually rode out with me in uniform to demand Peter's abdication. I'm certain she feels betrayed."

"She'll forgive you. And she craves power."

"Which could also transform her and convince her to change sides. I worry that she may turn from best friend to a potential enemy. One of many!"

Grigory waved his hand as if in dismissal. "Your life in Russia has always been plagued by enemies. The difference is that now you have plenty of allies to keep an eye on them. Most importantly, how do you feel?"

"Relieved might be the appropriate term. Nervous for another. And I am jubilant at all we have accomplished!"

Grigory laughed, daring to take her in his arms. "All will be well."

She might have made time for love-making—at least for an hour—yet talking and planning seemed much more essential than yielding to physical desires. Currently she could not afford the leisure, and wondered idly if that were a precursor of her new life.

It turned out Grigory had something totally different on his mind.

Noting the anguish behind his eyes, she motioned him to sit beside her. "What is wrong, my dearest?"

He exhaled deeply, as if preparing for battle. "Katinka, I believe what I am to suggest is best for you, for the kingdom."

"Let me be the judge of what is best for me and for Russia," she chided gently.

This man who'd so often stared death in the face without blinking, and most recently risked his life for her to effect the coup, suddenly appeared uncharacteristically helpless albeit resolute.

"No, Your Imperial Majesty. This is crucial. I beg leave to retire to my country estate."

Aghast, she could only stare at him. "Why would you say such a thing?"

He seemed to struggle with words to make her understand. Deep down she *did* comprehend his doubts. Regardless of all his strength of body and character, this was not a man made for court life. And he knew it. In fact, it was a generous offer in many ways, particularly as it would quell any gossip about their relationship if he were far away.

"I am afraid, for one," Grigory explained sadly, "that in gaining an empress, I have lost a mistress and all of her love."

"Never, my darling. You will stay. Will you not?"

It was more of a command than a request, and they both realized it.

Catherine was in love, with no intention of punishing this man—who, along with his brothers, had done so much to elevate her to the throne—by sending him away for the sake of her reputation. She would not give up his companionship or his talents just to maintain appearances of piety.

"We will not speak of this again," she said firmly, and rested briefly in his strong arms until one of her ministers was announced.

Over the following days Grigory appeared regularly to provide reports as if nothing had happened. She always stopped to hear him out, even when engrossed in writing a thoughtful, carefully worded letter to Frederick of Prussia on the vellum with gilded edges that she favored. This was an impossible task at best. She had no desire to resume war between the two empires.

Certainly she had always dreamed of expanding the Russian empire, but this was not the time. She must tread carefully lest Frederick sense any weakness and launch his own attack. Right now she needed a nation at peace, a delicate situation since not everyone had been disappointed when Peter allied with Frederick. Yet for six years this had been a country asked to shed its blood and its resources, and too many families had sacrificed too much. Let the other European powers fight it out if they choose. Still, she couldn't help wondering about Frederick's response when he heard—as he surely must have by now—of her accession to the throne.

Catherine had no idea how Frederick perceived her since the sole brief trip she and her mother Johanna had made to Berlin when he was an untried king and she a child. She vividly recalled that they had spoken about the arts, although in those days she must have seemed like merely an earnest, educated, and overconfident fourteen-year-old enroute to Russia. Years later his amused, condescending attitude toward her husband Peter III had been predictable, and before that he had detested Empress Elizabeth, going so far as to call her "an illiterate cunt ruled by pricks."

She yearned to believe that Frederick might be relieved. Russia had been on the verge of taking over his empire at the moment of Elizabeth's death. Peter immediately had withdrawn all troops from his beloved Prussia to make peace with the king he adored. Catherine would now have the power to resume that war.

And how would relations between Prussia and Russia unfold now with an always evolving cast of kings and queens who ruled over ever-shifting borders? It seemed as if the most recent Europe resembled a haphazard checkerboard that crowned new kings gleefully during every competition.

She forced herself to return to Grigory's report.

"I took care of the matter of the young guardsman who came forward during the coup to present you with a missing sword-knot, as well," he was saying.

"His name?" she asked idly, recalling the good-looking man.

"I believe it is Grigory Potemkin. He has been promoted, per Your Majesty's wishes."

"Excellent. And my orders regarding Prince Georg, my uncle?"

"He has not fared well, though is unharmed thanks to Your Imperial Majesty's orders for his rescue. A mob did plunder his house and possessions. As we speak, he is preparing to return to Holstein along with all the former emperor's regiments. This is where they belong and should remain for the rest of their days!"

"Again, well done. Perhaps I should worry that they will regroup and counterattack. However, I am not Peter and I believe they know that well. If I had to re-engage the military . . ."

"It would be done immediately." He stood straighter. "The troops are loyal to you, Your Imperial Majesty."

"And we are pleased that you have personally taken charge of recalling the exiled Chancellor Bestushev, as well."

"I will escort him into the city myself," Grigory promised. "As you commanded, I am restoring all Bestushev's titles that Empress Elizabeth stripped when she exiled him. He is also to maintain a suite of rooms here and a house in the city."

"It is the least that I owe him. If it were not for the chancellor's plans and ideas so many years ago, we might not sit here now. He was the very first to approach me right after Paul's birth about assuming power as sole ruler rather than Peter's consort. That was even before it had entered my mind, and his loyalty and discretion have always served me well. I do hope he is not too old now for a political function. At the very least I hope to call upon him occasionally for his wisdom and experience."

"He is most grateful for your beneficence, Katinka. He said as much in a letter to me, proclaiming repeatedly that at last Russia has a monarch who will always do what is best for the kingdom and its twenty million subjects."

Grigory then continued with a lengthy list of all those requesting favors until Catherine raised her hand, signaling she'd had enough. "I am compelled to do a thousand strange things and respond to a thousand requests," she sighed. "If I yield, they will all adore me. If not, then I do not know what will happen."

"You will be crowned, that is what will happen."

"Yes, there must be a coronation," she agreed firmly.

"The people already clamor for it. Your husband made a fatal error dismissing the idea."

"To be sure. And the event *must* take place in Moscow." At the last word, her eyes closed briefly as she mentally tried to shake off her distaste for that medieval city.

"Let us plan a date then," Grigory said enthusiastically.

"We must allow time to organize. I wish this to be an extravagant pageant for my subjects."

"It shall be." Grigory started to take her in his arms until she laughingly extricated herself.

"Then let the preparations begin. We shall have it this summer, or early autumn at the latest."

"May I suggest you summon Masha?" He used the nickname for Maria, but Catherine grasped who he meant immediately.

"Yes, we would very much like to see her. And to reward her." She instinctively stroked her bare neck, realizing she wore no jewels whatsoever. This would not do.

Her relationship with Maria Sergeievna Blukhova and her husband Igor Blukhov was not only professional; it was a matter of pleasure and satisfaction. She had few true friends. She valued Maria's friendship immensely and was cognizant that the Blukhovs had stood by her during these difficult, treacherous eighteen years. Maria had served both as a confidant and at times a secret messenger. As had her husband.

Catherine never forgot a good deed and rewarded her friends whenever she could.

"I shall summon Igor, too, if you wish it."

"Not yet. Igor is certainly a close friend, not to mention an extremely talented craftsman. At present, though, I will keep Pauzié in place as head imperial jeweler. If I am not mistaken, Igor Blukhov is an independent artist, and I do not wish to interfere with his creativity. He serves me well as it is, and I definitely shall see that he gets more commissions than he can handle."

She leaned forward to kiss him lightly. "Speaking of rewards, my darling, how does Adjutant-General Orlov sound?" she teased.

Grigory knelt before her, then stood to bow formally. "Thank you, Your Gracious Sovereign."

"Actually, I prefer the sound of *Count* Orlov rather than a military title like adjutant-general."

Grigory appeared stunned, especially when she added, "You may tell your brothers that this shall be taken care of for all of you at the coronation, if not sooner."

"We will be honored beyond compare."

"All well-deserved, of course. Without the five Orlov brothers, I undoubtedly would be languishing in a convent or a prison while that disgusting Vorontsova became empress."

"Your Imperial Majesty is too forgiving," Grigory chided. "Vorontsova is the one who should be imprisoned, not living a fine life in Moscow."

Catherine shook her chestnut curls. "I have no desire to begin my reign with revenge unless or until it is absolutely necessary. With Peter imprisoned, his mistress bears watching, but is no danger. And she has few allies and fewer brains. I do not wish my former enemies to suffer needlessly, especially those who merely followed my husband because they assumed he would award them power. Let all those have an opportunity to transfer their allegiance to me, or they may choose to live out their lives far away from us."

They kissed again briefly before Catherine returned to her letter.

She paused for a brief lunch while reviewing some of the voluminous reports she'd demanded from all the ministers, including those governing each province. Shortly thereafter, a letter arrived via messenger.

After quickly reading it, she sent for Grigory and ordered everyone else to leave the room.

"What is it, Katinka?"

"There is a letter from your brother."

"Which?"

"Alex—the one I left in charge of my husband." She pronounced the last word with slightly less distaste than usual. "Let me read this to you and see what you think." She put on her glasses and frowned at the hastily scrawled paper.

I fear that our monster has fallen very sick and might die tonight, but I fear even more that he might live through it . . . he is really a danger to us all, often speaking as if he still maintains his former position.

"My God! How is this possible?" Grigory said in a hushed, angry tone.

"I don't know. Overseeing a confinement should not be a big challenge. Peter has had tendencies toward illness all his life. I don't like this."

"It puts us all in danger!"

"Truly. He *must* survive. If anything happens to him, it is I who will be blamed. It is my reign that will topple. See to it immediately that doctors have in fact tended him. I presume, however, that he is simply being melodramatic at the thought of spending his life in Schlüsselburg Fortress. He hasn't even been sent there yet!"

Grigory wheeled on his knee-high black boots and hastily exited the room.

Two days later another note arrived while Catherine was meeting with Count Panin—another co-conspirator and her seven-year-old son's tutor. This letter proclaimed that Peter had been examined by his own physician and another staff surgeon. Both had declared him recovered and out of danger, and both had now left Ropsha with that conviction.

"Damn the man!" Catherine fumed, unaware how often she tapped her fingers rapidly on the mahogany desk. "Every day it is something else. Illness, recovery, requests for special items and concessions. Peter also claims he needs privacy to tend to his personal toilet."

Count Panin nodded grimly. "He will remain a problem."

"Unquestionably. And he continues to ask to be sent to Holstein, to the heart of the enemy's territory, and that I cannot condone. Frederick would not hesitate to help put him back on the throne, dangling him on a string as if he were one of Peter's own beloved puppets. In the meantime, my husband's life is to be as comfortable as possible. Within reason, of course."

There was much more she longed to say, but for now she must remain wary of Panin, who had always assumed that the coup's intent was to put her son Paul on the throne with Catherine acting as regent. Although he had not confronted her when it became almost immediately clear that she and her supporters had other plans, she could not completely trust him.

Nevertheless, she was immensely relieved the threat to Peter III's health appeared over. She stopped tapping and reached for her ministers' latest reports. "Let us continue. We have a Herculean task ahead of us."

Chapter 3

(Maria) early July 1762

In one of the empress's antechambers, I nervously await admittance to our Gracious Sovereign's presence.

I still cannot believe that at long last it has come to pass. Cannot grasp the fact that I am here to be received by Catherine the Great. For so many years she has awaited a chance to rule while I have awaited a chance to get back to 1999. To where—and when—I belong. I've lost track of how many times I've wondered whether the same number of years passed in the present or future. If so, my Aunt Roberta, who adopted me after my parents' deaths, must have long since resigned herself to my own demise.

A servant hands me a glass of wine, and I sip gratefully, feeling a bit of the dizziness that accompanied me on my unwilling time travel back to 1744 when I was just short of my seventeenth birthday. So many times I've re-lived that day, beginning with Aunt Roberta promising to meet me in the Hermitage's cloakroom without ever suspecting she'd probably never see me again. Me so overcome by curiosity that I'd touched a marble statue of some goddess half unwrapped in the antiquities section. The sudden shift and darkness hurling me inexplicably into another time. My terror, grief, and eventual acceptance of my new life well over two hundred years prior to my old one. Discovering that the lanky teen princess from Prussia sent to be examined by Empress Elizabeth's nephew and heir Peter as a potential bride eventually would become Catherine the Great.

Still reeling from the shock of what I didn't realize was time travel, I didn't know then who she was and what year it was. Had I known at that moment, I would have screamed. Wept. Wailed. Yet now I am happy—and madly in love with the husband with whom I at last risked sharing my secret.

All these years of living in the shadow of Empress Elizabeth and her idiotic heir (Catherine's husband Peter) have not felt carefree. The court remained a dangerous place, full of intrigue and behind-the-scenes wrangling over the throne— all inspired by an empress who thought as little about her empire as her short-term successor, Peter the Third, before he was dethroned by his wife.

Already the change since Catherine's accession is evident.

Rather than lounging around playing cards and gossiping, ladies scurry in and out on never-ending errands. Servants and lackeys move quickly and efficiently through the halls. The new empress's suite of apartments, not to mention the entire palace, has assumed the air of a business office rather than a living area.

Men in fancy frock coats—diplomats and ministers who once struggled in a stagnant court to appear busy or get anything accomplished—are obviously intent on a plethora of duties. They move briskly in and out of Catherine's chambers, tightly clutching stacks of paper rather than the silver vodka flasks that only months ago were common. Each time the door opens or closes I hear Catherine's voice, firmer and more assured than ever, issuing commands.

Princess Dashkova—Little Catherine—appears, as well, and she is wearing what is obviously a new gown and a neckful of jewels, unusual in that she is known for her preference for simplicity. Tatiana told me that not only has the princess's husband been placed in charge of the army's elite cavalry regiment, she herself has received thousands of rubles and a generous annual pension. In these early weeks she dines frequently with the empress, and I feel a little jealousy at their friendship. From what Anya and Tatiana have told me, however, the empress seems to be attempting to distance herself from her enthusiastic young co-conspirator.

An hour passes quickly as I overhear edges of conversations about everything from fishing rights to road conditions to potential population growth. Two finance clerks, heedless of eavesdroppers, discuss the necessity of taking care of an unpaid bill for 74,000 rubles. Peter III did not see fit, it seems, to pay Empress Elizabeth Petrovna's funeral expenses.

When I am ushered into the chamber where Catherine sits behind her favorite escritoire scribbling furiously, she stops and acknowledges my presence.

I drop into the deepest curtsy I can manage, bowing my head at the same time. "At your command, Your Imperial Majesty."

"At my command indeed!" she laughs, and as I raise my eyes to her sparkling violet-like ones, she grasps my hand and urges me to stand. "I believe, Maria Sergeievna, that you do not march to the tune of the legendary German pied piper. Most likely you probably would not follow him. You have a strength of mind that impresses me."

"Thank you from the bottom of my heart, Your Imperial Majesty."

"Now, let us discuss what must be done to make our physical appearance more . . ." she trails off.

"To make Your Imperial Majesty look as regal and powerful as befitting her rank as Autocrat of All the Russias?" The words come out before I planned to utter them.

"Exactly." She wriggles both hands in the air, demonstrating a lack of the usual heavy jeweled rings she favors. "What I need, Maria Sergeievna, is for you to select appropriate jewels for me to wear with whatever gowns I am being dressed in. However, someone else needs to deal with the chaos that has descended in matters of my wardrobe. I have no time to waste trying to coax or supervise recalcitrant wardrobe women!"

She sweeps an arm that takes in the paper piles and maps fanned across her desk.

"This is due perhaps to Madame Vorohov's departure?" I venture.

She frowns, obviously surprised. "Departure? To where?"

"I do not know. She left several days ago and has not returned. I understand that Madame may have left the atelier permanently."

"We did not grant her permission to do so," Catherine mutters. At first she seems angry, or at least disgruntled. Then, as her eyes return to the stacks of reports on her writing desk, she sighs. "Very well. We cannot fritter away time appointing a replacement."

I choose my words carefully. "If I might be so bold, Your Imperial Majesty . . . There is one unusually talented embroiderer who has been with the Imperial Wardrobe staff since childhood. I believe she could take charge most capably—and she is discreet."

"And does she possess exquisite taste?"

"Yes, Your Imperial Majesty. In fact, you have selected many of her previous designs. Perhaps you recall the peacock gown, for example?"

"Ah, yes. With much fondness. I do so each time I'm at Tsarskoye Selo and observe the peacocks strutting around with their folded tails trailing in the gravel." She smiles. "Then see to it that this is done, Maria Sergeievna."

"Immediately. Her name is Anya."

"Then I shall wait to meet this Anya. Meanwhile, I am ordering my chamberlain to spend up to twenty thousand rubles on my apparel. I do hope your recommended seamstress is up to such a task."

Catherine picks up her quill again, and I realize this is a

dismissal. We will always be friends; it's just that the boundaries of that friendship have shifted slightly out of necessity.

As I back out of the chamber with another deep curtsy, Catherine suddenly calls me back. "And Masha, you should go to Tsarskoye Selo and retrieve the few jewels I have hidden there at Catherine Palace. You will find them in the charge of my most trusted lady, Olga. She is the *only* one I trust there, so I would like you to collect them from her and deliver them here to me personally. If that beast I married hasn't ordered Olga to turn them over to Vorontsova, that is."

"Of course." My mind races ahead to the tasks I now have. First, locate Anya, and then return to the ladies of the wardrobe currently in charge of dressing the empress. Then I must obtain the key to the jewels that remain here before ordering a carriage to Catherine Palace.

For just a moment I regret not having the afternoon and evening to work on a brooch that I'm designing myself. I shrug it off. After all, I am serving a new empress. A soon-to-be great one.

I select the fastest carriage driver to take me roughly twenty-five kilometers south to Catherine Palace in Tsarskoye Selo, or Tsar's Village as the town surrounding it is named. Upon arrival, I can barely keep up with the servant striding ahead. Together we sweep through the gilded enfilade of portals connecting each elaborate room to the next, like a golden necklace culminating at its pendant: the breathtaking Amber Room.

I am permitted to sit in an elegant chair to await Lady

Olga. It is the first time I have ever been in here alone, and I recall Catherine telling me not long ago, "I feel lucky in there. Someday I hope to have card tables brought in this chamber so I can earn enough to pay off my debts!"

The chamber makes me feel more spiritual than fortunate. I recall my Aunt Roberta telling me it was—or would be—under re-creation because the Nazis had or would steal and hide it. To my knowledge the Amber Room hadn't been found when I left the present, but here I am beholding the real thing.

There is no way to prepare. The chamber is fashioned so much like a glittering, three-dimensional puzzle reaching about twelve-feet high that I imagine myself as the little ballerina inside a jewel box.

I try to count the shades of amber. There must be thousands of pieces ranging in hue from pear, lemon, banana, wheat, and sunflower to poppy, marigold, root beer, umber, and butterscotch. Lesser and rarer amber hues of green, red, white, blue, and black blend in subtly. The room also contains eighteen mirrored pilasters, numerous gilded carvings, lacquered paintings, candelabras, and murals. Surely if angels exist, this must be where.

The entire chamber was a gift from King Frederick of Prussia's father, Frederick Wilhelm I, to Peter the Great. His daughter Elizabeth inherited it after he left it neglected in crates. She ordered it assembled and reassembled, moving it from place to place almost as often as she changed and discarded her thousands of gowns. While serving both Catherine and the late empress for several years, I have only gotten quick glimpses of the chamber.

Despite the room having its own curator, apparently no one has done much to repair the damage from frequent moves and age. Not all the puzzle pieces are slotted or glued properly, some panels hang loosely, and a few chunks lie on the floor. I have a feeling much of the needed restoration will fall to Catherine, who will surely do so because she virtually worships her predecessor Peter the Great, even carrying around a portrait of him on one of her snuff boxes much the way her husband always wore a ring bearing the likeness of Russia's enemy, Frederick the Great.

I wish Igor could see the Amber Room, since he often works with the popular and treasured organic material. It might make up for his disappointment earlier this year when we attended the first ball Peter hosted at the newly built Winter Palace. I'd been trying to describe the Hermitage's fabulous Malachite Room to my husband—the one I saw on the day I left my own time.

He insisted such things were not possible. "There is not that much of the substance in the entire world to sheath entire columns and fashion large basins out of malachite, my darling. Look, see this piece?" He held up a chunk of the deep green swirled stone that I love so much. "It came from our own Russian empire, true, but is difficult to obtain."

I was equally as insistent, and it was only after we looked around the public areas and asked some ladies with access to the entire palace that I conceded: "Perhaps malachite will be discovered elsewhere or in a future century."

"I hope so," he muttered. Igor hoarded the stuff, using it once to make a snuffbox and a few times for earrings and a tiny green turtle.

The Amber Room, on the other hand, is ancient. Tens of millions of years ago the amber started to form. Knowing how popular it is now and will continue to be, I suppose we must someday run out of it. Now, regardless of the warping, the room shimmers from every angle, bathing me in streams of light. Somehow it is fitting that I am here surrounded by bits and pieces of flora and fauna trapped and then preserved forever in another time. Somehow, I no longer mind the thought.

CHAPTER 4

(CATHERINE) JULY 6, 1762

"So at last God has brought everything to pass according to His designs.
The whole thing was rather a miracle than a pre-arranged plan,
for so many lucky circumstances could not have coincided
unless God's hand had been over it all."
—Catherine II, letter to Count Poniatowski

The messenger admitted to Catherine's sitting room seemed out of breath, not to mention unusually nervous. He bowed almost to the level of prostration, and the strong odor of horse sweat indicated he'd galloped his animal too hard.

"I come from Monsieur Orlov," he stammered.

"Which Orlov?" she asked impatiently.

"Alexis, Ma'am. From Ropsha."

She felt an inexplicable sense of foreboding. She wanted no more news or demands from that place.

"My orders, Your Imperial Majesty, are to deliver this to you in private." He appeared embarrassed, and his frightened eyes wandered to two ladies settled on a corner divan.

Catherine took the letter and waved dismissal at the ladies.

Once totally alone, she tapped the paper on her hand before opening it. This would be another ridiculous demand or pathetic plea from the childish man she had married. The man she attempted not to think about. Or perhaps it was good news from Alexis, again reporting a recovery from whatever purported illness had ailed the former emperor. Most likely an injury to his pride.

Resigned, she opened the dirt-smeared letter and read the first few lines:

Matushka, *Little Mother, most merciful* Gosudarina, *sovereign lady, how can I explain or describe what happened? You will not believe your faithful servant, but before God I speak the truth,* Matushka. *I am ready for death, but I know not how it came about.*

Now what calamity had developed? Alexis *did* have a tendency toward the melodramatic, yet what had happened that was deserving of his own death? His scribbling, she noted briefly, was barely legible. The next few sentences, however, brought Catherine to her knees:

We are lost if you do not have mercy on us. Matushka, *he is no more. But no one intended it so. How could any of us have ventured to raise our hands against our* Gosudar, *sovereign lord. But* Gosudarina, *it has happened. At dinner he started quarreling and struggling with Prince Fyodor . . . before we could separate everyone, he was dead.*

Shocked beyond anything she'd ever felt, she read and reread the letter. *Peter was dead?*

It did not seem possible. Her husband, this man-child who had spent his entire life playing soldiers and obsessing over all things military, was gone. Would never realize his dream of an actual march. Had been incapable of mustering his own soldiers to lead a counterattack on her. At this moment, though, it mattered little that this was exactly what she had *not* wanted him to do.

She scanned the rest rapidly, looking for answers:

We ourselves know not what we did. But we are equally guilty and deserve to die. Have mercy on me, if only for my brother's sake. I have confessed my guilt and there is nothing further for me to tell. Forgive us or quickly make an end of me. The sun will no longer shine for me and life is not worth living. We have angered you and lost our souls forever.

The frantic, anguished letter provided no answers, only questions. She'd never known the confident, courageous Alexis to sound so desperate.

She did not know what to think or how to react. How could this thirty-four-year-old man who as a teenager had been so eager to meet her that he'd marked her and her mother's progress to Russia with two miniature toy dolls on a map be dead? If in one corner of her mind she sensed a minute strand of relief, she pushed it aside resolutely. True, the adult Peter had often functioned as the bane of her existence. Either an imprisoned Peter or a Peter safely in Prussia and in league with Frederick posed a danger to the realm. Would have. She knew that.

But not this. It was the last thing she needed. No matter which of the men most likely orchestrated the murder and why, all blame would inevitably fall on herself.

She studied the last phrase: *We have angered you and lost our souls forever.*

Our souls indeed, she nearly wailed.

"*My soul*, you idiot!" she wanted to scream and wondered when Alexis himself would arrive to tell her what really happened.

No one would believe this was some type of accident, as the letter implied it was. She should have known better than to entrust the charge of her husband to Alexis Orlov, a violent soldier who detested Peter. If such a fight had really occurred between Peter and the guards, Alexis himself was probably involved.

Nor would anyone believe she had not had a hand in this. No one.

She dared not ring for someone this soon. Not even Grigory.

Then she started to shake. First her hands, which had dropped the letter after a fourth reading. Then her legs.

She must have made a sound, perhaps a cry, because two ladies emerged from where she had sent them and started to fuss.

"Leave us!" Catherine managed to say sharply, relieved that she still had command of her voice. When they did, she sank onto the divan and held a handkerchief to her eyes.

Whether she shed a few tears or let them flow for a long time, she resolved that no one would ever know.

An hour passed. Then another. She rose, resolved that she had wept the last tears over Peter that she ever would. She kept a key around her neck. Moving slowly through her chambers to the small desk beside her bed, she carefully unlocked it. She folded the parchment with its offending, hideous news and placed it inside before turning the key.

There, she vowed, the letter should remain: unseen, unread, and unjudged by anyone. She did not wish to read it again. Perhaps ever. Nor did she wish to share it with anyone.

She rang for coffee, then changed her mind and ordered a cordial of brandy. Although she must have all her wits about her, first she needed to cease this residual trembling.

For a long time, she drummed bejeweled fingers on an agate table that held her quills and ink pots. There were decisions to be made. She held not only Alexis's future and that of the other parties involved in her hands, she was now the protectorate of the entire Russian Empire.

Feeling sufficiently collected, Catherine returned to her own papers. There was much to be done. First and foremost, she must order an autopsy, if for no other reason than to clear herself. Peter had in fact been ill that week, and she could only hope some other cause might have been a factor in his death. She could not—would not—call this murder, regardless of the unclear and mysterious circumstances.

She refused to have this awful and unexpected death shortening her reign. Whether or not she could maintain power after this, she had no idea. Regardless, the question of her involvement would haunt her and inevitably overshadow her place in history.

Ultimately Catherine decided to handle and publicize the death as if it were in fact medically induced. Just to be certain, she commanded that the postmortem examination include a search for less obvious causes of death, specifically for poisoning. Did she want to know the truth? Perhaps not, but she must.

When a dust-covered, sweating Alexis Orlov eventually showed up the night she received the letter, he babbled on and on about having no right to live. He offered no further explanations beyond that the death included a physical altercation. In both manner and the words in his letter, he exhibited all the angst of a man who had not *intended* such consequences. He also admitted that all dozen or so men in the house, including Peter, had been drinking heavily.

Certainly she was suspicious. She dismissed him without calling for his brother.

Grigory had been with her during the time of the tragic incident. However, if he were somehow involved—and she did not believe that he was—he should not be seen in her company now.

Over the next few days, she waited and planned, consulting frequently with Count Panin. When Princess Catherine Daskhova arrived, the new empress hugged the younger woman, admitting to her, "My horror at this death is inexpressible. It has been a blow that strikes me to the earth!"

"It is, Madame, a death too sudden both for your glory and for mine," the princess said firmly, picking up immediately on her distraught idol's obvious agony.

Catherine nodded in appreciation, at the same time realizing her mentee's concept of her own importance in events would need gentle correcting. For the past week, it had become obvious that Little Catherine envisioned herself as both a pivotal player in the coup *and* a permanent adviser to the new empress.

To Count Panin, however, Catherine listened carefully. With his assistance, she drew up a proclamation once she had received the hasty conclusions of the postmortem physicians:

On the seventh day of our reign, we received the news to our great sorrow and affliction that it was God's will to end the life of the former Emperor Peter III by a severe attack of hemorrhoidal colic.

This announcement followed the contention of those who conducted the autopsy that no evidence of poison existed and that this "colic" evidently had caused an apoplexy that impacted his brain.

There was more, of course. When she did summon Grigory, she told him, "The physicians also say that he had a healthy stomach, albeit a greatly inflamed bowel. His heart apparently was extraordinarily small and quite decayed."

Grigory grimaced. "I never believed he had a heart at all!"

"We shall not speak ill of the dead emperor. He is no longer in our lives."

"As long as he doesn't haunt them in death as in life."

"And as long as he does not become a martyr to my people!"

In truth she could not be certain whether the doctors had told her only what they believed she wanted to hear. Perhaps it *was* a natural death, no matter Alexis's claims. Catherine did not want to believe the worst possible scenario: that Peter's death was premeditated by at least one of the major players in her accession to the throne.

Curious as she might be, she did not wish to observe the body personally or see for herself whether any visible evidence of foul play revealed itself.

"He shall lie in State at the Alexander Nevsky Monastery. Entombed there, as well," she ordered Panin. By unspoken agreement, they believed it would be inappropriate for an unanointed emperor to lie beside Peter the Great and other anointed successors in the traditional Peter and Paul Cathedral.

"He shall wear his favorite blue uniform," she added. "It was his fondest wish to be Prussian, and Prussian he shall be to the end."

Unlike the weeks of pious obeisance she'd paid to his aunt, the departed Empress Elizabeth Petrovna, Catherine would not join the viewers paying their respects. Peter III existed no more, and any initial grief she'd felt was mitigated by the need to hold her kingdom together. Still, she doubted not that no matter how short or long a time she might reign, she'd never entirely quell her uneasiness over his death.

She had emerged intact from Elizabeth's shadow, and hopefully from Peter's. Now it seemed she might have to fight her way out of the darkness of his death, a darkness that threatened to eclipse her reign and her legacy.

CHAPTER 5

(MARIA) JULY–EARLY AUGUST 1762

She cannot go!" Igor insists, tapping his fingers on the new annex's worktable in the same way I've seen Empress Elizabeth and then Catherine do when upset.

"With the war over, it is now safe to travel through Prussia. And she has yearned for so many years for that to be so."

"I don't believe she truly desires to return. Any other relatives she and my mother had in Italy must surely be dead by now—or will be by the time she makes a journey that could last months."

Igor and I seldom disagree; however, just last week Aunt

Gina informed me privately in no uncertain terms that she planned to arrange for a carriage to go back to Venezia, where she grew up and where one brother still lived. Last year she'd received a long-delayed letter that he was too ill to travel to Russia as once planned, and now she wanted to see him.

"Igor, I assure you she is intent on going."

"All her remaining family are here." He begins to fidget with a chunk of malachite just shipped to him.

"Only you, and now me. Your mother died well over thirty years ago, your father twenty years ago, and Uncle Giuseppe is only recently buried in Moscow. She stayed in Russia because she felt obligated to her sister's son, and then to help you as an adult."

"Are you attempting to make me feel guilty?" he asked, squinting suspiciously at me.

"Of course not."

"Perhaps she would want to stay if we had children . . ."

"True, a great-nephew or great-niece would be someone for her to spoil and perhaps make her feel more needed. That, however, does not appear to be happening."

Sensing we are on thin ice, I am nonetheless unprepared for his retort: "It might *be* happening if you did not visit the apothecary's shop so often for those little packets."

My mouth drops.

"For your information," I enunciate slowly and distinctly. "I have not used *any* herbs in several *months*."

That stops him—both in his malachite fiddling and in his speech. His face seems to freeze.

"So," I continue, feeling my anger grow. "If you must, you may blame it on me that we do not have children. Or perhaps on yourself! Or blame it on God! The point is that Aunt Gina is old and ill, and she wants to go to her beloved homeland to die! How can you be so insensitive to her—let alone me?"

When he does not respond immediately, I toss my apron in a chair, stomp out of the workshop, and slam the door behind me. He yells something, but I cannot hear what it is. At this moment I do not care.

With no idea where I'm going, I find myself wandering up the canal toward Nevsky Prospekt.

Today I look at the thoroughfare differently. After nearly two decades in the past, I still can recall the far-off future with this same avenue filled with traffic, bustling sidewalks, pastel architecture, crowded underground passageways, designer stores, and screeching megaphones hawking excursions to palaces and places I now take for granted.

That was my world. A world where you could let off steam going to the movies, as Aunt Roberta used to do, or a shopping mall, as I did. A world where flush toilets replaced the need to seek a privy or pull out a chamber pot every few hours. A world where trying to get pregnant in your mid-thirties for the first time did not make you a freak.

Having left home without coins, I cannot stop for a cup of chocolate, let alone a Big Mac. The concept of a hamburger, of course, doesn't yet exist. At the series of archways that divide shops in the Gostiny Dvor market, I whirl back and stride toward the Winter Palace. I would rather visit Tanya or Anya than return to Igor's frozen face.

Take that, husband, I think angrily. You could have been more patient. Whether he is right or I am—whether I waited too long to try or not—isn't the point. The point is that after all these years of pretending he understood why I did not want to give birth in the eighteenth century, the truth has emerged: he does not understand and perhaps never did. He resents me for it.

I walk briskly, despite the heat, passing the usual summer floral displays and vines trailing down wicker baskets. Past emaciated dancing bears and talented jugglers. Past holy fools everyone reveres and reviles at the same time. Past my favorite glove maker and competing jewelry shops and metalsmiths.

The area that someday will be called Palace Square is spacious and partially wooded without all the future's massive buildings and the central column of Tsar Alexander II that will eventually stand in the center. I have the same disconcerted sensation that I often do strolling past the relatively small wooden church, knowing it will be replaced by the massive St. Isaac's Cathedral. Who will construct it and when, I do not know. I just wish it were there today so I could enter its cool depths. Best of all, it would not mean dodging five dozen camera-toting tourists shuffling from corner to corner.

At the palace I'm admitted to the atelier, where Anya issues orders in between sorting fabric samples and checking the work of her seamstresses.

"Maria! I'm so glad you are here. I want to show you the fabric for the dress."

There is no need to ask which dress. Here and now, there is only one that matters: the coronation gown.

She reaches her wooden table and picks up a swatch of silver silk. "We will use this, and embroider it all over with the Romanov double-headed eagle—in gold thread!"

I clasp my hands together. "Perfect!" I'd like to tell her that this gown will go down in history, preserved in the Kremlin's Armoury in Moscow where I recall seeing it the first time Aunt Roberta brought me to Russia as a child. It is one of the few things I remember about the future Moscow besides the same golden cupolas that have already crowned Cathedral Square for at least two centuries. The same ones that will oversee the coronation.

There is a portrait, too, in those guidebooks, that depicts a majestic Catherine II glittering in the gown and wearing an elaborate diamond-encrusted crown.

"And what about Igor?" Anya asks. "Has he received imperial commissions?"

"Sadly, no." It suddenly occurs to me that there may be more than my childless state that is bothering my husband. Resolved to mend things with him when I return home, I force myself to concentrate on Anya.

"He will get the commissions," she assures me. "There is much to accomplish, and too few talented workers to do all of it in just over a month. Her Majesty must have forgotten."

"I shouldn't wonder, with all that is happening."

"And I have news!"

"Good news, I presume?"

"Yes! My father took the liberty of sending a case of one of his flavored beers to Grigory Orlov, who enjoyed it so much he has ordered more!"

"That *is* marvelous news."

"It is all because of you, Maria Sergeievna. You were the

one who secured this position for me. How can I ever thank you properly?"

"By stitching this fantastic gown that undoubtedly will be immortalized someday. As will Her Imperial Majesty."

Anya's face shines. "I do not doubt that. Even in this short time they say she has accomplished more than all her predecessors who followed Emperor Peter the Great combined."

"Undoubtedly."

"Oh, Maria! It is as if Russia has come alive again! I must find time to attend chapel and thank God for all his blessings."

Her mood shifts then. "Will you attend the late emperor's funeral?"

"If I must."

"Maria, you must be visible now. It is the best thing for your and Igor's business."

How unexpectedly pragmatic of her, I note. She is no longer the timid girl I met so many years ago. "Then I am certain we will go."

She leans closer and says softly but urgently, "When you pay your respects, show no surprise at his appearance. He looks worse than he did in life."

"He would, would he not?"

"There is something not proper about it all," she continues to whisper. "God knows I detested him, but now . . . well, tell me when you return what you think!"

Anya's voice adopts a louder and more matter-of-fact tone. "I do have much work ahead of me if my team and I are to play our small role in making this coronation as splendid as possible."

We embrace, and before I've left, she has turned back to her tasks and her staff.

Igor and I are barely speaking despite my earlier intention to apologize for our quarrel. We stand wordlessly in a short line at Nevsky Monastery to view Peter III's body. Thankfully there is little need in this grim atmosphere for conversation.

The mourners are significantly fewer than the endless crowd who filed in and out for weeks on end to pay their respects to Peter I's daughter, the Empress Elizabeth. The corpse rests atop a bier illuminated at the head and feet by candles. Soldiers urge viewers to move quickly, and no one seems to mind. A clerk stands at the exit, scribbling on a sheet of paper the names of those who have attended. I am not certain whether it is a good or bad thing to be named on this list.

Ahead of us two of Peter III's former supporters shuffle past, barely looking. They pause mere seconds to cross themselves before moving away. I recognize the first as Michael Vorontsov, Peter's chancellor, and the second as Prince Alexander Golitsyn, his vice chancellor. Surprisingly, both men have retained their posts, and I'm certain Catherine must have ordered them to be here today.

Word has it that she will not attend the funeral due to illness. My dear friend Tatiana told me that she believes the senate advised the empress against it.

Perhaps recognizing me, the guards do not force us to move too fast, and I am able to get a decent view of Peter in the time it takes to cross myself several times.

He is dressed in a powdery blue Prussian uniform, with a Prussian ribbon around his neck. That same neck also is wrapped with a broad cravat, his head half concealed by a large hat. Mindful of Anya's advice, I observe that the visible part of his face seems dark, almost black.

The only other surprising thing I note are his hands, which, according to Orthodox custom, should be bare and crossed. His are thickly gloved, appearing damp from a fluid that might or might not be blood. I shudder, preferring not to know if that is the case. As we exit, I close my black lace funeral fan with a snap.

"You will accompany us to Moscow, of course," Catherine informs—or commands—me later that week.

"I would be honored, Your Imperial Majesty." In truth, I am elated.

"Then it is settled. And I must apologize to your husband Igor, of course."

"Apologize, Your Imperial Majesty?" I have no idea what she is talking about, as I have been expecting an apology from him to me rather than to him from the empress. Things at home remain chilly.

"Of course. While we've no doubt Monsieur Blukhov *could* design the perfect crown, Monsieur Jérémie Pauzié has an entire workshop at his disposal. He and Monsieur Betskoy assure us it will be a massive job. Recalling the weight of our bridal crown, we can hardly imagine that our poor head will not be squashed like a turnip."

I smile weakly, both at her more frequent use of second person to refer to herself and at the memory of her small sixteen-year-old head of brown curls pressed under a huge weight of diamonds so many years ago when she married the grand duke.

Then, even though Catherine is still speaking, I realize with horror what a blow this must be to my husband. He is not the official imperial jeweler. Nonetheless, designing the crown or at least being consulted may have been one of his dreams. Was this, then, the true source of his frustration, his recent temper flares?

"However, I hope to compensate for this," Catherine continues, "by asking you, Maria, to assist me in selecting the jewels for what I hope will be an auspicious occasion for our citizenry."

She rushes on before I can react: "You will need to coordinate with Anya who, incidentally, is more than competent, as you promised. I believe the two of you already work well together. As for Igor, I would be interested in his thoughts or perhaps would consider his assistance in this matter."

I curtsy on my way out, overwhelmed on the one hand with the honor of selecting the coronation jewels, on the other hand eager to get home to my husband.

There are many ways to end an argument. Igor, it seems, prefers the intimate.

After Aunt Gina has taken the carriage to church, he ushers me up to our bedroom with his own sense of the spiritual.

"I want *you*," he whispers, nibbling my earlobe. "Not babies. Just you."

And then he proves it.

We have not made love in weeks, primarily due to all the stress and then excitement of current events. Followed by our quarrel. This sexual drought obviously has inspired my husband to devote hours to my body.

He starts with gentle kisses while his warm hands explore every inch of my skin, gradually adding pressure as if polishing amber. I can almost sense my body turning gold, then bronze, then copper. When heated, amber also becomes much more transparent, and I must be aglow with all the shimmering orange light of the Amber Room.

Then he begins all over, this time with his tongue.

Regardless of all my arching and pleading, he refuses to enter me. "Please!" I pant over and over, clenching and unclenching my fingers to stop from tearing him to pieces.

When he does give in to my demands, we change positions several times. I do not question how Igor can keep going, know only that I am slippery with desire and mindless with need. When our orgasms arrive simultaneously, I am heedless of our noise, of our mingled sweat, of anything and anyplace.

I am a *very* happy woman.

CHAPTER 6

(CATHERINE) MID AUGUST 1762

"It was a death she had not planned, but it suited her purposes. She was free of her husband, but . . . the shadow over her character and over Russia [was to remain] for the rest of her life."
—Robert Massie

Imbecile!" Catherine cried, tossing aside the European newspaper she had just read, which compared her to Ivan IV, the former tsar commonly referred to as Ivan the Terrible. "As if I don't have enough to do and to worry about." Other papers called her a usurper, or bluntly accused her of murder. One journalist referred to her as "a barbarian in charge of a barbarous realm." These criticisms from abroad remained deeply hurtful to someone who viewed herself as a monarch in the mold of Peter the Great and sometimes England's Elizabeth I.

"Europe be damned!" Panin would commiserate when this happened. They both knew she had inherited a disaster and needed time to prove her detractors wrong.

It *was* true the laws of hereditary succession mandated that Peter III's heir should have been their seven-year-old son Paul Petrovich if he had named no other. Technically and perhaps legally she had no right to the throne she'd seized. And although no one dared mention Elizabeth's cousin—the baby from whom the former empress had usurped the throne before imprisoning him for life—she thought of young Ivan VI often. No doubt her enemies did, too, referring to him in whispers as little "Ivanushka" despite Empress Elizabeth's having forbidden all mention of him and ordering all likenesses of him destroyed when she exiled his entire family.

Just as Elizabeth had triumphed in her successful coup, most of Catherine's subjects seemed to accept her accession as a positive development for the Russian Empire. Nor had Peter's death, regardless of her fears, imperiled her throne in the eyes of the Russian people. She vowed never to take their faith in her for granted.

Already it had been a summer of calamities, initiated in part by natural disasters such as floods and droughts that had led to famine and that was exacerbated by pirating on the Volga and bandits roaming the roads. Simultaneously, Turks and Tatars decided to test the new leadership by making periodic raids on the edges of Ukrainian borderlands, where they seized and then enslaved the local peasants.

By mid-August, Catherine was forced to move quickly to

foil two attempted revolts by groups of guards. Most of the perpetrators were arrested and exiled to unknown destinations.

It also became rapidly apparent that an antiquated system of government had fostered unreliable local and provincial management and hence an imminent collapse of many of those bodies. The deterioration of local governments was compounded by the lethargy and corruption of her inherited senate—long accustomed to doing little and pocketing much, which frequently tried the empress's patience. Senate members had sought early on to set up a system by which a council of ministers would make decisions jointly with Her Majesty; Catherine simply ignored them until they gave up. She would rule as an autocrat—and in her mind a benevolent and enlightened one.

"I feel as if I were a hare hounded by hunters," she confided to the French ambassador. "I am forced to dart in a dozen directions at once, always alert to danger and always striving to prove my detractors wrong!"

However, Catherine was far from unprepared, and within days, let alone weeks, it became apparent to every official from the lowliest to the highest that things would be quite different under the new empress compared to her predecessors. Only the elderly who could recall all the way back to the reign of Peter the Great were unconfused and somewhat prepared.

Each day she arose before dawn, tossed another log on the fire if it hadn't been done already, scratched the ears of whichever of her dogs had slept beside her, and rubbed her face with pieces of ice. She ate a modest breakfast of rusks, cucumbers with honey, and fruit. At her insistence, her coffee was prepared from one pound of coffee per five cups of water.

Immediately after breakfast, she arranged herself at her desk, where for hours she read and replied to dispatches, made appointments, and reviewed the detailed reports she required from almost everyone in the civil and military structures. Nothing escaped her attention, including the grain speculators she thwarted by ordering the creation of imperial granaries to regulate prices. She initiated something similar with the College of Foreign Affairs, demanding regular reports on various societal conditions. She also concerned herself with how to institute the best European models for housing and how to handle the insane.

As for the antiquated justice system, she dealt with it initially by, with one stroke of the pen, emptying all the penal colonies and prisons in the realm. Only murderers were excluded from her amnesty.

Laudatory comments comparing her to Peter the First were already frequent. Like her much earlier predecessor, she missed nothing as she strove to emulate and enhance his far-reaching reforms. She addressed disputed fishing rights, road conditions, the consecration of religious shrines, and distribution of back pay for the military. The latter was necessitated by the massive fiscal crisis she had inherited. With a seriously depleted treasury exacerbated by mounting debts, Russia's credit was deemed worthless in foreign markets. Most observers assumed a woman alone incapable of dealing with all these insurmountable problems.

Yet Catherine II was determined to rebuild her realm.

Grigory, impatient almost from the beginning with Catherine's fourteen-hour workdays, continued to attempt to slow his lover down. "Katinka, you will have plenty of time for all these minute details. A lifetime, hopefully."

"I've wasted eighteen years already, most of them waiting to govern in some form. And I have not begun to initiate the most major projects, which cannot be accomplished until this dastardly government is reshaped into something fundamental!"

"I've been speaking with Lord Buckingham—"

"Don't! The new English ambassador is a naysayer. He is convinced, I know, that we cannot succeed. He's completely wrong."

"His primary concern is that you cannot possibly continue to rule alone."

Catherine did not respond at first. She knew Grigory Grigorevich Orlov wanted to marry her, and that many in the court and the empire agreed. Rumors abounded that just such a thing would happen. Sometimes these were accompanied by an undercurrent of discontent. Secretly she agreed with the opponents to such an idea. She preferred to do what previous empresses had done, albeit not always capably: to be mistress of her own—and her empire's—destiny.

She never gave Grigory an outright negative response. "I believe," she replied slowly, "that that is exactly what I have been doing: ruling alone." Her voice sharpened. "Does Lord Buckingham find fault with my decisions?"

"Of course not. I just want you to know that he is no friend to the throne."

"Noted. Now, my dear lover, I must return to my reports."

She did not say she also must write back to her former lover Stanislaus Poniatowski, who had not ceased his pleas to be welcomed back to Russia. Once again, she must discourage him, urging that he remain in Poland where the two of them, with the collaboration of the late British Ambassador Sir Charles, had decided long ago that Stanislaus would make a good king.

This time her letter also gave Stanislaus details about the June coup, adding, "All minds now are still in a state of ferment. I beg you not to come here now, for fear of increasing it."

"Do not write at all, I beg you," she finished in a later correspondence. "I must walk straight ahead; I must not be under suspicion."

Even with the hundreds of ukases, proclamations, and orders Catherine wrote, signed, and issued, a great deal of time had to be devoted to planning the coronation. She must be anointed by the Holy Orthodox Church in Moscow, a solemn event that would be witnessed by her subjects, before she could feel the crown securely on her brow. As for that crown and the other regalia, she appointed her chamberlain Ivan Betskoy—who already served a variety of roles including head of Siberian gem mining—to oversee that project. "All of the diamond-cutters in my realm are at your disposal and under your supervision," she informed him.

Prince Nikita Trubetskoy traveled to Moscow with a sum of fifty thousand rubles to prepare for what she demanded be a spectacular event. Grigory also went ahead to ensure her

wishes were carried out and to orchestrate the entire occasion. Out of her own funds she ordered 600,000 rubles worth
of silver loaded onto one hundred oak barrels and delivered
to Moscow. During the festivities, the coins would be tossed
to the crowds overflowing the streets. She ordered circuses
and games for the people, as well as masquerades and pro-
cessions.

No detail would be left to chance. Catherine personally
selected all the fireworks and special illuminations that so
delighted her and her subjects. Everyone and everything
involved must be given the same attention, from the number
of chamberlains who would carry her train (six or perhaps
seven) to the names of the nine senior officials who would
carry the silken canopy under which she would move from
place to place. It was also necessary that each component,
from carriages and livery to saddles and attire, be gilded or
encrusted with gems.

For clothing and uniforms, she ordered Anya's staff to
plunder storerooms that contained thousands of pieces from
Empress Elizabeth's old wardrobe—once consisting of fifteen
thousand gowns. Seamstresses worked around the clock to
cut, stitch, and re-hem gowns. They wasted nothing, extricating the tiniest jewels from shoes, buckles, and buttons;
transforming perfectly good velvet gowns into fine new liv-
eries, and stripping pearls from headdresses and bodices for
reuse elsewhere.

"I heard that Queen Caroline of England had to borrow all
her own coronation jewels from her friends and ladies. This is
not acceptable for Russia!" she declared to Countess Praskovia Bruce. Her childhood friend agreed, and willingly and

briskly devoted her days to striding back and forth between the sewing rooms, furriers, and the jewelers' workshops.

It was to be an extravaganza the likes of which had never been witnessed.

CHAPTER 7

(MARIA) LATE AUGUST 1762

Aunt Gina has decided to stay. "I may as well," she tells me over breakfast. "I've endured decades of this cold while yearning for the Venetian sun."

"It must be difficult for you."

As I watch helplessly, she coughs for several minutes.

When she recovers after a few sips of coffee, she continues. "It is losing my church that has been the biggest challenge. It would not have been right when I arrived here to search out a Catholic one, not when my daughter had already devoted so much effort to adopting the faith of her new country. She needed to fit in, so I joined her in the Russian faith. And when she met Igor's father, who was not particularly religious, they still had to be wed in the Orthodox Church."

After all these years, I still feel as if I know little about Igor's mother, who died within days of childbirth. That, I still suspect, is why Igor initially had seemed fine with my decision not to have children.

"Tell me about the wedding."

We've had this conversation before. Today, though, Aunt Gina seems much more philosophical than her usual loving albeit pragmatic self. In that way she often reminds me of my own aunt. Today I merely smile rather than wince at how I have missed my Aunt Roberta.

Then Aunt Gina turns to the real rationale for her decision to stay in Russia. "I do not believe an old woman like me could make it back to Italy alive. Most likely I would die somewhere in Austria or Prussia, and then what would be the point? Better to plant these old bones in Igor's and my daughter's beloved Russian soil. At least here I have a chance to see my nephew whenever he can tear himself away from his jewels."

"Is that the only reason?"

"There are others, dear child. First and foremost, I suppose, is that I feared the former emperor's intentions. How would I adapt to yet another religion? I was raised to consider the Protestants heretics, and he wanted us all to become one. I dreaded what would happen, and when Her Gracious Sovereign became our *matushka*, I did not know what to think. I do believe now that all will be well. Already *matushka* has undone what her horrid husband did as quickly as one would unravel silk." Her fingers shake as she lifts the coffee to her parched lips once again.

"You said there are other reasons?"

"Perhaps only one."

"Are you going to tell me or do I have to bribe you with some of that Italian liqueur you fancy so much?"

"Of course I will tell you, child. It is because of my nephew. And you. I realize you don't believe you need me . . ." She shakes her head at me as I start to object. "I believe that you do. Or that you will."

I'm silent with gratitude for a moment, then eye her more suspiciously. "Why, Aunt Gina, I do believe you are waiting to become a great aunt."

Her brown eyes twinkle. "It could happen, my sweet Maria Sergeievna. If God wills it."

I shake my head again, not with disagreement.

"Maybe," I concede. "Now I must return to the palace and meet with Her Imperial Majesty."

Before summoning the carriage, I carefully wrap my arms about my frail aunt. She has seemed like mine almost as much as Igor's. I yearn to tell her she has helped fill the gap in my new life here left by the loss of my previous aunt and adoptive mother.

"I love you, Aunt Gina," I murmur.

"I love you, too."

My life is so full. This evening Igor and I have been invited to join Catherine and Grigory, as well as numerous similarly honored guests, at a small banquet. The only problem I have now is deciding what to wear.

Dressed in a pistachio silk gown embroidered with dragon-flies on the skirt, I stare at my reflection in our new mirror. Rather than a necklace, I'm wearing a dark green silk ribbon tied as a fichu around my neck. A brooch shaped like a dragonfly fashioned from peridot and blue opal accentuates the gown's bodice. It is certainly the most intricate piece of jewelry I've owned, not to mention the first design Igor and I have collaborated on in equal parts. With my hair swept up, the matching dragonfly earrings sparkle in green and blue with each turn of my head.

"I'm almost afraid Her Imperial Majesty will resent that we didn't design this for *her*," I muse, as Igor comes up behind me and kisses the nape of my neck.

"She will not be jealous, at least not the way Empress Elizabeth was when someone upstaged her. Our new Imperial Majesty is undoubtedly a handsome woman, yet no one could wear our jewels the way my wife does."

"Flattery will get you everything you desire, my sweet husband."

"Truly?" He pauses and holds up the pocket watch he now carries. "Perhaps there is time for you to prove this statement?"

I laugh. "There is not. We are due at the palace soon. *This* is not a court that begins meals at midnight."

"Thankfully!" We both recall Empress Elizabeth's late-night habits, as well as Peter's midnight parties. Our empress rises before dawn to start work and tends to retire early unless she returns to her papers and writings. It seems to me as if she must work roughly fifteen hours per day.

"And Igor, we do want to be there in plenty of time for the whole court and all the visiting diplomats to have an opportunity to lust for our designs."

"Right, my lady." He kisses me again, his tongue seeking mine.

I pause before we leave to adjust the matching dragonfly pin glittering from his lace jabot. The buttons on his cutaway coat and velvet vest are made of alternating peridot and opal.

We are a handsome couple, I daresay. As we enter the reception area for the banquet hall, I sense a few heads turn, and am so proud to be with Igor. I've lived long enough to see the fracturing of so many relationships that I had expected to be happy ones, and know we are fortunate to still be madly in love. We chose one another out of passion rather than submitting to the more common arranged marriages, including the one Empress Elizabeth once attempted to foist on me.

Catherine arrives shortly thereafter on Grigory Orlov's arm, and most of the courtiers seem accepting of the relationship. Rumors have swirled all summer that the two might marry, yet I cannot imagine the empress ever permitting herself to be in any way subject to control by a man again. She may not be the Virgin Queen that Queen Elizabeth of England purported to be and she may thrive when in a love relationship; however, I remain convinced that never again will she permit herself to be in the secondary social position of a married woman. I smile, having heard so much gossip around court and in the city about when she might remarry.

Now her distinctive melodious voice drifts over the din around me. Igor and I are to be presented to her shortly. When we are, she acknowledges our curtsy and bow, then lifts me to my feet and hugs me.

"My dear Maria Sergeievna. It is always so wonderful to see you."

She moves on to the next guest, leaving me suffused with pleasure—realizing that not only did I see her earlier today, I am just one of dozens wanting to be recognized, orbiting her like planets circling the sun.

After Catherine and Grigory leave the banquet, the merry-making is permitted to continue. My husband appears tired, though, and I suggest we return home.

"I will do so, on one condition. That my lovely and talented and intelligent wife remains. Flash those dragonflies if you must, just above all have some fun." He nods in the direction of a not-yet-visibly pregnant Tatiana and her husband. "Be with your friends. You have undoubtedly earned some relaxation."

"I would rather stay with you, Igor."

He kisses me hard. "Here you could catch up on court gossip and perhaps initiate some business. Not that I have time to fulfill any more orders, with the entire aristocracy commissioning jewelry for the big spectacle. Still, I would just like to go home and sip some brandy. And check on Aunt Gina."

We part then, and I watch his proud, handsome form until he is out of sight.

Tatiana—her friends call her Tanya--suggests we walk

some halls of the new palace, a delight after an hour of watching dancers. Without Igor, I have little desire to join them.

When we encounter the fabulous white marble staircase recently completed according to Rastrelli's design, I recall that it will be called the Jordan Staircase in my own time. It looks similar to its future version even without hordes of tourists posing on both flights of steps with cameras. "It's all made of white Carrara marble," Tanya mentions as she notes my look of awe at the carved balustrade, sculptures, molding, and gilding.

"Come," she urges, after we examine one of the palace's glassed-in roof gardens. "I will show you the new sculptures for the coronation. They have all been commissioned in honor of Her Imperial Majesty's new reign and the artists are fighting for space in their workshops."

We carefully descend a staircase that seems somewhat familiar before emerging into an unrecognized section. Sometimes the palace's twists and turns remind me of a rabbit warren.

If the unexpected reference to sculptures made me slightly nervous, it is nothing compared to the way my stomach flip flops when we enter the second of a series of rooms converted into artisans' workshops. There must be at least a half dozen marble statues. No artists are in sight.

And one of those statues is mine.

I am almost certain of it.

"Who is this?" I stammer, pointing at the one with a helmeted head and mysterious eyes. The hand is grasping a spear, which I do not recall.

"Ah, that is our Catherine. Or rather, the Goddess Minerva."

"Who?"

"I'm not as versed in my gods and goddesses as I should be, though I think that in ancient Rome she was considered the Goddess of wisdom. Much like Athena."

"She does not resemble Catherine." My mouth is dry, and I keep attempting to swallow.

"No, it is the idea that matters. Minerva was also the patroness of literature and art, as well as medicine and virtue. There has been much talk that the coronation will have a theme: Minerva Triumphant. Already the people speak of her as if she is a goddess. There is to be an entire festival after the coronation that will be built around this idea, lasting all the way into the winter and spring. Poets are composing odes. Actors are rehearsing performances."

I sink onto a bench in front of Minerva. Can it be? Thoughts swirl and crash into one another. Am I in the same spot in the Hermitage where I was transported back through time? Does it matter? Is this, in fact, the same statue that I foolishly touched so long ago? And what, if anything, will happen if I touch it again? Or what if my companion Tanya does? And what of the artisans who have worked on it? Wouldn't it have affected them and catapulted them to the future the way it did me to the past?

"What's wrong?" Tatiana interrupts my thoughts. "You look positively ill. Should you have gone home with Igor?"

I shake my head. "I'm fine. I just want to sit for a while."

"We should return to dancing. Come." She reaches for my hands. I pull them back.

"No! I must stay here."

Puzzled, Tatiana settles beside me. "What is wrong with you? Are you certain you are not feeling poorly? Because you are unusually pale."

"I am fine," I repeat. "Would you mind going to get me some wine, Tanya? Or perhaps go back to the hall and dance, and I will join you there later."

"I cannot do that. The latter, I mean. I would rather send a servant to get you wine than leave you alone."

"I *want* to be alone, Tanya."

"Very well," she says briskly, rising and smoothing her scarlet dress. "I shall meet you upstairs. And in the meantime, I will seek out a servant to deliver a drink for you."

Relieved at her departure, I return to my thoughts. It is not as if I haven't had plenty of time to explore the possibilities for eighteen years. The "what ifs" never had a sense of urgency since no such statue had ever materialized. Now I know why: *it hadn't been created yet.* This makes no sense in that it brought me back to a time when Catherine was a teenage Sophia, not a grown and now reigning empress. Somehow it connected me to her.

Am I prepared to lose that connection? And I have more than a full life now, one that includes Igor, Aunt Gina, Anya, Tatiana . . . and of course, Catherine. If I *could*, would I leave them all forever?

A servant arrives with an entire open bottle of wine. He pours the first glass and then backs out bowing, paying me the respect afforded one of the empress's ladies.

Perhaps I should get drunk. That might dull the pain of

making a decision. Because that, in fact, is what I am doing. Deciding.

To touch or not to touch. And surely Shakespeare would agree this constitutes a clear case of "To be or not to be." The question is to be *where*. To be *when*.

Enormous unknowns continue looming behind that question. Where and when might I end up? Back in modern St. Petersburg or even the USA? If so, how many years have gone by since I left? Is it the same number?

Above all, I wonder whether Aunt Roberta will be alive. Has some alternative version of me—the real Maria Sergeievna—been living my life and would she come back? Would that mean she is wedded to Igor—or will be when she returns? It's not as if I haven't pondered these same questions for nearly two decades. But in all this time, I have never been able to locate the *right* statue.

I pour a second glass of cabernet.

There are risks no matter what I do. If I give up this opportunity, the statue might be hauled off to Moscow, cutting off access to it—and the future.

I thought that long ago I'd resigned myself to living out my life in the eighteenth century. Now I realize that is not necessarily true.

By the third glass of wine, I'm worrying about what might happen if the statue *does* work. Would I be able to return here if it does? Could I return to my beloved husband and my life here in imperial Russia?

And if this statue is definitely a conduit to the future—or an alternate past—what if I end up in another time? I could find myself amid the Napoleonic wars. Or World War II. Or further backward to Peter the Great's time. Or ancient Russia. I could not adapt again to another historical period; of that I feel certain.

The candles in the sconces are waning, and all the statues slip into shadow. I should leave. Should retreat upstairs and take the carriage home.

I nearly empty the bottle and, clutching the glass, stand.

It doesn't matter how many *what if's* I posit. The fact remains that I must know.

Perhaps if I only graze it with my fingertip. I set the empty glass beside the empty bottle on the floor. Most likely nothing will happen.

Eye to eye with Minerva, I clasp and unclasp my hands.

Just a touch.

I do it. Reach one fingertip toward her face. I do not recall exactly where I put my hand on the sculpture all those years ago, and this seems safe.

Nothing happens.

I take a huge gulp of air in relief. *I think.*

This statue is new, after all, whereas when I touched it—or its twin—in 1999, it had been in existence for well over two hundred years. That had to make a difference.

Feeling slightly braver, I stroke Minerva's (or Catherine's) shoulder.

My stomach flutters in an odd way.

The candles flicker and then brighten.

I know my eyes are wide open, though for an instant everything is black.

Then suddenly it is as if the sun has pierced the walls.

A loud staccato clatter of high heels echoes on the wood

floor. Someone yells at me, and I struggle to understand the words. Is it Russian or some other language? For a moment I think the sculptor has shown up and is furious at me for touching the statue, from which I cannot seem to detach my hand.

"*Devushka!*" What does that mean?

I realize I'm huddled inside a roped off area in a room lined with windows. Or at least the statue and I stand inside the ropes. I still wear my pistachio dragonfly gown, reassuring because when I "entered" the past years ago I had done so in entirely different clothes.

A woman races toward me, waving one arm and clutching something small and rectangular in the other.

A noise like a security buzzer is going off loudly, and the sun unexpectedly pouring through the windows hurts my eyes.

Exactly where or when I have arrived, I may not know. But even to my wine-muddled mind there's no mistaking the angry woman's motions as her fingers rapidly key in some numbers: she is using a cell phone!

I remove my hand from the smooth marble statue, tears filling my eyes as I sink to the polished parquet floor.

CHAPTER 8

(CATHERINE) SEPTEMBER 1762

On the first of September, 19,000 horses and 63 carriages commenced the long migration from St. Petersburg to Moscow. Countless other conveyances transported nobles and supplies, requiring hundreds of replacement horses at posting and relay stations. Count Panin, escorting the young tsarevich and his retinue, had left days earlier with another 257 horses and 27 carriages. Thousands of peasants, beggars, tradesmen, servants, and lackeys trailed behind them on foot.

Catherine was ready, albeit resentful of time wasted on the road.

Halfway to the ancient city, they received a message that the earlier retinue had stopped because little Paul was ill. "Could you please travel more slowly?" the note ended.

This was difficult for Catherine to do, and eventually they caught up with Count Nikita Panin and Paul at a relay post. "The heir is much worse, Your Imperial Majesty," Paul's tutor pronounced gravely. "I do not believe we can continue."

"We have already delayed four days, as we were consumed with work."

"Please see the boy and advise what is to be done," Panin begged.

Little Paul shivered in bed and maintained a high fever. His mother stroked his face and fretted. She admitted to herself that she harbored few of the maternal feelings she was supposed to have, as this was a boy she'd seldom seen since he was torn from her body and her presence almost eight years ago. Still, he was her heir, not to mention the tenuous connection to the legitimacy of her claim to the Romanov throne. There were still many—including Panin—who believed the intention of the coup had been to elevate the boy to tsar and appoint her as regent; those same people were convinced her position as sole ruler had occurred almost accidentally. Although some still questioned the validity of her rule, she prayed such perceptions and doubts would eventually be dispelled.

Paul's health had been problematic for some time. Now Dr. Kruse proclaimed him plagued by treatable digestive problems. Already the boy was forced to endure a special diet intended to "correct the stomach juices," as well as a variety of remedies ranging from soapy and alkaline substances to Peruvian bark and goats' and asses' milk. Dr. Kruse was blunt in his assessment. "The former empress may have loved the boy. However, she was misguided," he grumbled. "She insisted his servants fill him with ridiculous special oils and syrups from his infancy, and now see where we are!"

Catherine could only shake her head. She'd realized that Elizabeth knew virtually nothing about babies, but had assumed that the late empress at least was well-meaning in her pampering. Now she had little faith in Dr. Kruse's remedies.

Worrying not just about Paul but about the impact of his absence if she were forced to march into Moscow without him at her side, she slept restlessly.

Mercifully, in the morning the boy's fever had broken.

"You cannot leave us!" Count Panin complained as she prepared to do just that.

Torn, Catherine lingered, deep in consultation over other matters with her advisers and ministers until the inevitable decision had to be made.

"The coronation details cannot be disrupted or rearranged," she told Panin firmly.

Panin continued to protest that she should wait for Paul to make a complete recovery before entering Moscow.

"This is too critical. For us to postpone the coronation would be neither good nor safe for the kingdom. You will catch up when you believe the tsarevich sufficiently well to travel."

Panin almost immediately declared the boy recovered well enough to rejoin the migration.

On Friday, September 13, Catherine II, Empress of all the Russias, was greeted and feted by a city wild with joy.

Led by squadrons of the Horse Guards and a grandly attired cavalcade of aristocrats, the golden carriage drawn by eight white horses proceeded along cobblestone streets slick with ice crystals. A plethora of viewing stands filled with jubilant Muscovites, as well as peasants and nobles from the countryside and nearby towns, oversaw her entrance.

Beside his mother in the carriage sat an ashen Paul, at times appearing more confused than proud. If he had doubts about the outcome of his father's death and his mother's sudden accession to the throne, he did not express them to this elegant and powerful woman he knew was his mother but did not know as a person. His father had virtually ignored him, and his death was sad and left Paul with few options. He would do what he was told, at least at this time in his young life.

The triumphal entry stretched four miles from the city gate to the Kremlin, the entire route heavily decorated with greenery, some formed into trellises and arches. Chinese silks and Persian carpets hung out windows and draped balconies, lending splashes of color to the buoyant atmosphere. The cheers were nearly as deafening as the full-throated pealing of church bells.

Inside the crenelated red- and white-brick Kremlin, Catherine attended a celebratory service at the Cathedral of the Dormition before taking up residence in the Great Palace. For over a week she would seclude herself here to fast, cleanse her soul in preparation for the holy rituals, continue her studies of previous coronation ceremonies, and review every detail of the upcoming event with Prince Trubetskoy. Their goal was not only to outshine any previous coronation. It was to stage a quasi-religious event befitting a monarch assuming the mantle of both church and state. Not one sentence could be skipped, not one word mispronounced.

Russians viewed Moscow as God's holy city: the Third Rome after the Vatican and Constantinople. Catherine had traveled here to be anointed as God's representative on earth.

It was during this time she again noticed the absence of her lady, Maria Sergeievna Blukhova. Maria's husband Igor also seemed uncharacteristically absent. With so many people surrounding her and so many details to manage, however, she resolved not to worry anymore about this one.

At precisely five a.m. on Sunday, September 22, a twenty-one-cannon salute served as the harbinger of this glorious day. Three hours later, all the bells of the "forty times forty" churches in Moscow rang, backed up by the pronounced sound of trumpets and kettledrums. Soldiers surrounded the cathedrals that formed a square in the Kremlin, where a long red carpet extended down the famous Red Staircase used only for coronations. With six chamberlains supporting her train, Catherine walked sedately down the carpeted stone stairs, preceded by her confessor who sprinkled her path with holy water as she crossed to the Assumption (Dormition) Cathedral. The end of her train was born by Count Sheremetyev, the same man who had failed miserably at performing this task for a disrespectful Peter at the late empress's funeral. This procession, by contrast, was carried out with supreme decorum.

Viewers did not know which was the most magnificent: the setting with dozens of gold and silver cupolas reaching like bubbles from the square to the sky, the breathtaking interior of the cathedral, or the slight regal woman who glittered as the focus of the spectacle. Her dress alone shimmered, its silk brocade material thickly embroidered with shiny gold and silver threads in the form of double-headed Romanov eagles. A larger eagle adorned the gown's front, emphasizing Catherine's slender waist. The dress also bore lace sleeves and a lace neckline, accented by a mantle train lined and trimmed with over four thousand ermine skins. In her heavy regalia, Catherine entered slowly, maintaining a majestic expression and holding her head high.

Within the five-domed cathedral, one could hardly take in the profusion of gem-encrusted icons, gold and silver crosses, and massive pillars painted with frescoes gleaming on a gold background rising from floor to ceiling. Everything was illuminated by candlelit shrines and thousands of additional candles, overshone only by the gigantic silver chandelier weighing more than a ton that swung from the central dome. It was the same cathedral where Catherine and Peter had become betrothed so long ago, though she pushed such thoughts far from her mind.

On a scarlet-draped dais in the cathedral's center, the new empress seated herself on the ruby- and diamond-studded throne once commissioned for Tsar Alexis. Around her in a semi-circle stood fifty-five ecclesiastical dignitaries. After reading aloud the Holy Creed, she draped herself with a purple imperial mantle decorated with the Romanov eagle, encrusted with gemstones, and fastened by a wide jeweled clasp.

The ceremony lasted for hours, highlighted first by a replica of the fur-trimmed crown worn by Prince Vladimir Monomakh in the twelfth century, and then the Grand Imperial Crown. Jérémie Pauzié and his partner Monsieur Ekart had outdone themselves on the latter, using nearly five thousand diamonds plus an array of other precious stones hand-picked from the Imperial Treasury. All these, along with an arc of seventy-five lustrous perfectly matched pearls, were fashioned into an ancient Byzantine-like design: two half-spheres, one silver and one gold, symbolizing the eastern and western empires of Christianity and resembling an Orthodox bishop's tall miter.

The most stunning feature was an enormous 389-carat ruby spinel glistening at the top, surmounted by a diamond cross, framed with diamonds, and sending out more darts of light from the glittering empress. Catherine carefully picked up and lifted the crown, weighing nearly nine pounds, and placed it herself atop her chestnut hair.

The regalia also included the golden state scepter, grasped in her right hand. In her left hand she held a gleaming gold imperial orb, encircled with two bands of diamonds and topped by a forty-seven-carat sapphire.

Cannons once again fired salvo after salvo, followed by high mass in the Old Slavonic language.

It was then that Empress Catherine did something no female ruler before her had dared: passed through the doors of the male-only iconostasis reserved for priests. As she knelt, the archbishop anointed her on the breast, brow, and both hands. She rose and approached the altar. In another unprecedented act, she lifted the heavy bejeweled chalice and partook of consecrated leavened bread soaked in consecrated wine, giving herself the Holy Sacrament of Communion. If viewers were shocked, they hid it gracefully.

As the ceremony ended, she moved regally across Cathedral Square to two other ancient cathedrals—those of the Archangel Michael and the Annunciation. Here she knelt before the tombs of Peter the Great's predecessors before proceeding to the opulent Palace of Facets. In the center of more floor-to-ceiling paintings and frescoes, she handed out awards: honors, titles, jeweled swords, and decorations. All five Orlov brothers officially became counts. Princess Dashkova (Little Catherine) was appointed as one of Catherine's ladies-in-waiting as part of her compensation for her role in the coup.

Remounting the Red Staircase outside, the new empress bowed three times to the crowd. She could barely hear over the thundering cannon amplified by clanging Moscow bell towers. For just a moment she recalled a Berlin monk who, when she was a child, had turned to her mother Johanna and insisted that someday little Sophie would wear three crowns. Now her titles ran to nearly ten lines of text. She was the sole ruler of an empire already dwarfing Rome at the height of that empire's glory.

She returned to the palace in a sumptuous golden and scarlet carriage with six-feet-tall wheels. Outstretched hands tossed pieces of silver. They passed hundreds of long tables sagging with meats, cakes, and wine casks for the people. She had little time to think about all those who saw her as their light at the end of a long tunnel of hedonism and ineffectuality.

If anyone missed the little Grand Duke Paul, prevented from attending once again due to illness, there were no shouts for him in the crowds that lined the streets.

This was Catherine's day. Hers alone. The festivities marking her accession, however, would extend for weeks and then months.

That night she stood atop the Red Staircase, savoring the moment and enjoying the fireworks splashing the sky.

There were memories that had come to her recently, not the least of which were her own childhood observations about the role of women and those who had had the largest influence on her, including her childhood governess Babet. Nor could she forget the comet that had streaked the sky eighteen years ago as her carriage had crossed the Russian border, terrorizing her escorts and thrilling her with wonder as its celestial sparkle illuminated black velvet sky. Today she, too, felt every inch a star from the heavens—or perhaps the sun emerging from the shadow of an eclipse.

CHAPTER 9

(MARIA)

I cannot stop weeping. A woman in uniform has yanked the rope surrounding the statue of Minerva. I know this is the exact spot where moments ago I examined the artist's *new* work: in the just completed Winter Palace during a celebratory banquet for the recently anointed empress.

Except it's not. At least it's not the same period. This is the *modern* Hermitage Museum built well over two centuries ago in St. Petersburg. The same one I stood in when I was nearly seventeen and just before inexplicably ending up in the older version that existed in the early 1700s.

A persistent loud buzzer has attracted a cadre of guards.

I'm on my knees until two strong women yank me up and back to the other side of where the rope was. My hands hold nothing.

I am no longer connected to the past. To my home in 1762. To Igor, my husband.

This is why I'm crying. I cannot answer when a man in a suit coat shows up speaking English to me.

"Who are you?" he keeps repeating. "Why are you damaging a priceless sculpture? Are you stealing it?"

"No," I manage at last. "No. No. No."

The cacophony of whistles, loud alarm buzzers, flashing lights, and raised voices assuring me I've done something terribly wrong begin to subside.

Like a wild animal frozen in headlights, I'm too startled to react beyond "No" and then "*Nyet*" before attempting to explain, "I did not try to damage it. I don't want to steal it."

"You will come with us!" the man insists, and the same two women who removed me from my place at the statue each take an arm and half drag me through the museum past a crowd of curious tourists. Futilely I attempt to extricate myself, desperate to get back to Minerva, because touching her is undoubtedly the only way I will be able to travel back in time. Back to the place I spent over half of my life.

Hands grasp my wrists harder, and I end up shuffled farther and farther from the place and time that had become my new reality.

Clusters of tourists aim phones and cameras, often blinding me with forbidden flashes as they apparently find my "crime" of more interest than the antiquities. We follow endless hallways decorated with tapestries, more statues, and gilded furniture before I am shoved into a small room and then less forcefully into a chair.

The door closes and no one re-enters for several minutes. I stand, immediately realizing two things: that I must look terribly strange dressed in an elegant pistachio silk gown with plenty of visible cleavage, *and* that the door is locked from the outside.

Of course. I was at a ball. Igor left early at my insistence and my dear friend Lady Tatiana sent a servant to me with a bottle of cabernet. She, too, departed, only because I begged her to leave me alone in the room full of statues that contained the one I had searched for since arriving in 1744 Russia. After that, I consumed an entire bottle of wine. Does that make me now drunk and passed out? Or am I truly back on the brink of the twenty-first century again?

I know the answer, really. Electric lights are everywhere. Everyone wears modern clothing. And in the time in which I've been living, I am accustomed to drinking a *lot* of wine with no real impact on me.

Is it still 1999 when I inexplicably touched the statue of the goddess that whisked me back into the past? Could Aunt Roberta be waiting for me? Or is it some later year?

When the door opens, a uniformed woman strides in accompanied by the man who was translating.

"What is the date?" I demand.

They look at one another meaningfully. Neither replies.

Instead, they begin nothing short of an interrogation, initially in Russian. After years of language fluency in the eighteenth century, I suddenly and inexplicably can no longer understand more than a few Russian words.

Forcing myself to concentrate, I attempt to answer their questions with as many protective lies as I can think up. "I'm so sorry," I stammer repeatedly in English. "I won't touch anything again. It was an accident."

"I think not. You clung to the sculpture. To the precious marble. Simply touching it deposits traces of your finger oils." The man addresses me sharply in English, leaning slightly forward as if examining my pupils for signs of drug use.

"I must have gotten dizzy and leaned against it for support." The man translates this into Russian for his companion.

"And why are you dressed in such a way?"

"I was . . . I was going to a costume party tonight."

"Where is this costume party? Do you mean masquerade?"

I stop answering questions for a while, and someone enters to place a glass of water in front of me.

The questions continue to swirl around me, alternating with a lecture on the importance of protecting the museum's treasures. I can only nod or shake my head.

"Who are you?" the man translating says for the fifth or sixth time.

How am I supposed to answer that? "Maria Sergeievna Blukhova."

No, I realize at once. I must give them my maiden name. "No, it is Maria Meekhof," I correct myself.

"Why do you not know your name? And do not pretend to be Russian. Only Russians use patronymics as middle names."

"Where *are* you from?" the woman interrupts, switching to English.

"Peters—no, I'm American."

"This does not surprise me," she responds, frowning.

The man matches her frown. "And in America you are permitted to touch priceless works of art in your museums? To deface them?"

"No. I *told* you, it was an accident."

"Who are you?"

"My name is Maria—"

"I mean what do you do, for a living? Or are you an art thief?"

What do I do? I attend the Empress of all the Russias and I assist in designing and making her jewelry. I take care of and work with my wonderful husband Igor and his gentle Aunt Gina.

I cannot say any of that. Best to stick close to the truth, however.

"I don't know exactly. I lost my memory—and I design jewelry." I point to the dragonfly brooch on my bodice then touch both ears to indicate the matching earrings.

"And this is why you are here? To spy on our jewels?"

"I just enjoy them!" Both study my precious gemstones suspiciously.

The woman taps furiously into her cellphone and then asks, "Why are you dressed like that? Who are you?"

"Please, please, just tell me the date!"

"Where is your shop?"

"I don't have one. I work at home."

"Address?"

I'm trapped, of course—and it's not new for me to feel like an insect mired in amber with no conceivable way out.

As they continue firing questions at me, I attempt a different approach.

"I was staying with my aunt," I stammer.

"Her address?"

"We are at a hotel. Or we were. I lost her."

"Which hotel?"

"I don't know! I can't remember."

"How did this come to be? You lost her in the museum?"

"Yes. No, I mean, I'm not certain." I have only one choice, and so I say firmly: "I believe I've lost my memory. Have amnesia, I mean."

Both of my interrogators seem to know that word, and for a few minutes they engage in rapid-fire Russian chatter.

"One moment, please," the man says, and they both leave the room and lock me in again.

My glass of water is empty.

At least an hour later, a new woman arrives. "Vash passport!" she demands.

"I don't have it. I did have it at the hotel. That," I add, "was a long time ago."

"How long ago?" Her English is perfect, and I stare down at her red fingernail polish in search of an answer. Or a stall tactic.

"Please, can you tell me the date?" I plead.

"Do you belong to a terrorist group?"

"Of course not!"

"Are you working as a prostitute in our museum?"

"Of course not!"

"Why are you dressed like that?"

"I don't know."

"You seem to know very little," the woman says in a nasty voice that for a moment reminds me of the late Empress Elizabeth's.

"Could you please tell me the date? Today's date?"

"The thirtieth."

"Of what? When?"

"August."

"And the year?"

Eventually she responds. "Two thousand seventeen, of course."

Two thousand seventeen. I think I have a hangover. Or maybe this is a nervous breakdown. "Are you certain?"

"Madame, where is your visa? And your passport?"

"I think that you might want to call someone from the American Embassy or Consulate or wherever I can try to obtain a new passport."

As if the idea had already occurred to her, the new woman with henna hair and a faded uniform leaves the room.

What can they do to me? I didn't actually damage anything. Surely fingerprints do not really damage marble, do they? And when or *if* they let me go free, where will I go?

Two hours later they release me with a stern warning. "We would not look kindly to seeing you again in the Hermitage," the henna-haired lady says firmly.

"But—" I am already trying to figure out if on the way out

I can get free, find that room again, touch the statue, and get *home*!

This plan is shattered moments later when a woman in a navy business suit arrives, and she and three museum security staff escort me to the exit after a quick pat down and scan. She introduces herself as Penelope Shanner from the American Consulate, and the two of us end up in a courtyard garden facing the main gate leading to what I remember as Palace Square. Or, more recently in my life, a patch of forest and construction debris.

As Penelope and I settle on a bench at the edge of a fountain, people pouring into the garden from the direction of Alexander II's statue pause to admire or take photos of me in what they undoubtedly presume is my period costume.

"So, let us try to clear this up," Penelope begins in a friendly voice.

Relieved that this woman is not restraining me, I quickly assess my chances of running into the busy square ahead of us. I wonder if she has a gun.

As quickly as I discard that idea and realize I am here without money, permission to re-enter the Hermitage, transportation, or a place to stay, I fight the urge to cry again.

Penelope, as if sensing my feelings of hopelessness, pats my arm. "May I get you a coffee or an ice cream?"

Ice cream. I've missed it in a life without refrigeration when ice desserts bear little resemblance to creamy modern ice cream. She pauses at a vendor's stand and waits while I select a nut-covered cone.

"Now," she continues as we return to the bench. "Is it your contention that you have amnesia?"

"I believe so, Ms. Shanner, since I cannot remember anything."

"What is the last thing you recall?"

"Going to the museum with my Aunt Roberta. To the Hermitage." She eats ice cream daintily. Mine, on the other hand, is finished.

"And how many hours or days ago was that?"

"It was eighteen years ago, I believe."

Penelope drops the bottom of her cone.

With a sigh, she offers me her hand. "Let us go to the Consulate, shall we?"

I obviously have serious problems. And we both know it.

A brief walk across Palace Square—excruciating in brocade slippers on cobblestones—and then our short drive along Nevsky Prospekt both shock me with ultra-modern shops, women in high fashion clothing, and thickened traffic. Much seems to have changed since 1999, let alone since 1762. Between noting all the American and European touches, signs, restaurants, and boutiques, I cannot help staring at Ms. Penelope Shanner's dashboard. The vehicle looks like cars I recall; however, the dashboard resembles an airline cockpit with computers. One screen even seems to indicate where accidents are and how to avoid the heaviest traffic, and a second one maps out our route. Somehow not once during my life in the eighteenth century did it ever occur to me to wonder how much things might've changed technologically in the present while I was gone.

The heavily armed security guards and man in a booth protest only slightly when Penelope waves me inside without identification. After she writes down the spelling of my full name, she leaves me in a much more comfortable office than the one in which I was sequestered at the museum.

At least an hour passes.

The time enables me to examine my predicament. Without a passport (unattainable immediately), I cannot go anywhere. Without money, I've no place to stay. Without "normal" clothes, I cannot wander the city. Without a cell phone, I cannot make any calls.

My only hope is Aunt Roberta. That presumes that she is still alive and can obtain a visa and a flight over here at a moment's notice to vouch for me. I feel tears filling my eyes again, and thick eye makeup running down my face. I've never stopped missing the woman who adopted me when, as a child, I lost both parents in an accident. She is—or was—my father's sister, who raised me until the day she insisted my resistant sixteen-year-old self accompany her to an historical conference in Russia.

I've always wondered what she thought. What she did when I didn't meet her at the prearranged place in the Hermitage. How she must have searched for me and for how long and where. How she must have grieved. How she must have agonized over whether and when to declare me legally dead. Did they have funerals for "permanently" missing people? Was something "buried" somewhere with my name on a tombstone?

If she *is* alive and still teaching at Michigan State University, how will this news affect her? Perhaps she retired, though I cannot figure out exactly how old she must be. In her fifties or sixties, for sure. No, she must be about fifty-two. What kind of shock will this be? Suddenly I want nothing more than to see her.

Someone offers me tea and biscuits. That someone turns out to be diplomat Kyle Perkin, who cordially greets me and sits on the opposite side of the desk. Penelope enters moments later and pulls a third chair to the corner of the desk between us.

As Kyle asks questions and scribbles on a notepad, Penelope pulls out a laptop and starts what appears to be a search on me. Occasionally she seems startled at what she reads.

"Age?" Kyle asks for the second time.

I'm stymied. Yes, I left 1999 in early summer (just before my seventeenth birthday) and arrived in the past during the winter. Now it appears to be the end of summer—just as it was when Igor and I attended the party. I've never been exactly certain, just assumed when I left the past this morning that I was in my early thirties. Catherine is or was thirty-three. If the date I've been given is accurate, it's obvious that I am, for certain, thirty-five.

"Are you the same Maria Ann Meekhof, who went missing in 1999?" Penelope interrupts abruptly. "The one we spent *years* searching for?"

"Yes." I hesitate before saying what I must: "That is, maybe. I'm not certain. I seem to have recalled my name and all I can tell you is that my last memory is of being with my Aunt Roberta—Dr. Roberta Meekhof—-in the Hermitage almost twenty years ago."

Penelope turns the screen to show me, and I am shocked to see my teenage self dominating the computer. I know from museum mirrors that I am physically my thirty-five-year-old self. I had wondered if I would come back young again. No, if time runs parallel in the past and present—although I am not certain it does—I could *not* have jumped eighteen years into the future as my old self.

A barrage of questioning continues.

"What is your address?"

"Can you tell us what happened that day so many years ago? Did you run away?"

"Where have you been—and with whom?"

"Where did you stay? Did you ever leave the Russian Federation?"

"Is there anyone who could identify you or attest to your story of being Maria?"

"No," I say slowly. "I didn't know anyone else while I was here."

Penelope gazes sharply at me. "Neither Kyle nor I, you understand, were with the consulate then. We have called in some diplomats who were. We have arranged a Skype interview with a former consulate general."

That sounds scary. "Who is Skype?"

"Not who. What. We do the interview over the computer. You will see." Penelope's words sound a bit ominous.

"What happens to me now?"

"We are trying to reach Dr. Meekhof."

"Is she okay? May I talk to her?" I demand eagerly.

"You may, but not until we do. However, you must realize," Kyle emphasizes, "what a shock this will be for her if you are who you claim to be. For nearly two decades she has assumed you were dead!"

I had imagined us engaging in a happy reunion, though I know my aunt probably will have a difficult time adjusting to being reunited with a high school girl who has evolved into an almost middle-aged woman. I guess I've not sufficiently thought through what staggering news this will be to a woman who all these years has been alone. Presumably.

The two depart, leaving me in the room for at least another hour. Perhaps they are taking a dinner break. My own stomach rumbles beneath my tight gown. A young woman enters with another cup of tea and no other refreshment. She refuses to respond to me except to point to the sugar bowl when I ask.

I've barely finished my tea when two uniformed women enter for the purpose of doing a more thorough pat-down and waving a metal-detecting wand similar to the one they waved over my body before I left the museum. Only the brooch causes an unwelcome beeping. It seems as if this more significant search should've taken place before I left the Hermitage, but perhaps the Russian officials surmised I couldn't have stolen something as large as a statue.

When Penelope and Kyle return, their questions seem less friendly. "While we are relieved to find you alive after all this time, both the U.S. authorities and all those Russian officials who searched for you and investigated your disappearance will want answers. We need to know where you have been living, working, and with whom," Kyle reiterates.

"I told you—"

"Why in secret?" Penelope asks. "Why didn't you come forward earlier?"

"I told you—"

"Yes, you claim you suddenly developed amnesia in the middle of the Hermitage and then wandered off on your own for nearly two decades. And now suddenly you remember that part—just not all those years that followed it?"

"I told you—"

Kyle stands and slams his notebook shut.

Penelope logs out of her laptop.

"We do have," Kyle says after a long silence, "someone here you can talk to. Someone who might be able to assist you in recovering some of those memories you claim to have lost—or at least give us a clue as to what has happened."

I swallow the rest of my cold tea. "Do you mean a psychologist?"

"Let's say more of a friend," Penelope responds.

"What happens next?" I ask, stifling a yawn. After hours and hours of fear and worry, I have lapsed into weariness.

Kyle seems to notice and amazingly relents a little. "I imagine you would like to get some rest, and as you claim you have no place to go, or no place you remember right now, we can arrange to put you in a guest room. Then we will wait a couple days for your aunt and for her to bring your old passport so we can arrange a new temporary one."

"I'm sure you can understand," Penelope adds. "We really have no alternative since you are or claim to be an American citizen with no papers."

"Can't I just stay in a nearby hotel?"

"No papers, no hotel," Penelope says firmly.

Kyle adds, "And you have no wallet and supposedly no money. Is that not correct?"

"Yes." I sigh. "Then of course I'd be happy to stay here until my aunt arrives. Is there any chance . . ." I hesitate. "Any chance of getting some different clothing?"

"I'll see to it," Penelope promises before leading me up some flights of stairs to an elegantly furnished bedroom. Neither of us mentions food.

So here I am. The last place I expected to be after Catherine's celebration ball. Still in Peter the Great's city on the Neva . . . over two hundred fifty years later.

There is a robe in the closet, and I slowly remove all my hairpins, undo the fichu around my neck, unfasten my stays, and try to maneuver out of the rest of my bulky eighteenth-century gown. I'm stunned and grateful for a real bathtub and running water. I jump when the toilet flushes: a sound I'm not certain I have missed. Right now, though, I'm too exhausted to argue with myself over the merits of one century or another.

Surprisingly, within minutes I fall asleep.

The psychologist (or whoever she is supposed to be), Dr. Marina Pakov, is kind but persistent. She strongly suggests hypnosis, which I cannot permit.

"Don't you want to have the opportunity to account for nearly two decades of your life?" she asks incredulously when I refuse.

"Of course," I lie. *I know exactly where I've been and what I've been doing. And you, lady, do not need to hear it.* Nor would she believe it anyway.

I've never been hypnotized. I fear I might be *too good* a subject. After all, I seem to have the ability to migrate between centuries and magically learn and unlearn foreign languages. Who knows what might happen? And right now I have to hang on to who I am. Where I am. When I am.

Our session turns out to be non-productive. I do insist, however, that I haven't been harmed in any way—or committed any crimes, let alone espionage.

I'm unsurprised when Dr. Pakov does not mention a second session.

Two days after I arrive, Kyle announces, "Your aunt is on her way to Russia."

A great weight lifts. "And she has been able to get a visa that fast?"

"She has one, as she travels here frequently." This seems odd, as I recall how many months it took for us to obtain one to come here in 1999.

So many little changes. Maybe big ones.

"She is bringing your old passport and other paperwork, so we should be able to confirm your identity and verify some things," he adds briskly.

In the meantime, I'm given access to the Consulate library, albeit without permission to use its computers. At last I discover a bookcase crammed with *TIME* magazines and copies of *The Moscow Times*, all in English.

And so I begin my re-education

I'm flabbergasted, pouring myself more and more tea from the pot in the corner. If I've ever yearned to take up smoking, this would be the time. I start with the oldest editions, deciding to work my way up to the present in world news.

The dreaded Y2K problem seems to have gone off without a hitch. I don't regret missing that.

Then the shocks come one after the other.

I cry after reading how three planes piloted by terrorists wiped out the World Trade Center and part of the Pentagon in September 2001—a mere two years after I left the modern world. How would I have handled that? Then two wars ensued in the Middle East, and it appears as I continue to scan much later issues that the wars go on and on, along with a scattering of incursions in other places.

Surprises continue as I skim headlines and cover stories. George Bush Jr. elected twice. The collapse of the stock market and economy. An African-American U.S. president? For two terms! Hillary Clinton running as the Democratic candidate and losing to a billionaire reality show host?

I opt to take a long nap.

CHAPTER 10

CATHERINE II (LATE 1762)

"Few observers, in Russia or outside it, believed Catherine's government would last long. A young woman ruling alone, lacking the protection and authority of a husband and largely without experience in rulership, would surely be devoured by a palace revolution, or a governmental crisis, or a revolt of the guards."
—Carolly Erickson

Catherine stared intently through her reading glasses, unable to take her deep violet eyes off the scrap of parchment. She had sifted through stacks of documents from the State Archives before accidentally discovering it.

The note, tucked inside Elizabeth's papers, was indisputably in the late empress's writing:

"My nephew is a monster. The Devil take him!"

It obviously referred to her own successor: Catherine's predecessor and husband, Peter III.

She tapped bejeweled fingers restlessly on the marble table. Now she knew for certain: The woman who'd summoned her fourteen-year-old self to marry Peter truly *had* detested him. For most of those years, Catherine, too, had tried to hide the fact that she loathed him.

So why, if Elizabeth felt so much revulsion toward the boy she'd brought here to be her heir and Catherine's groom, had she never bothered to change the succession and bypass Peter? Catherine must have asked herself that question a thousand times.

Nor was it her fault that he'd died so quickly after his wife's coup. There would always be those who suspected her of being complicit in what most considered his murder. She tried her best to ignore them, firmly believing it had been her fate—and that of Russia—that she seize the throne before her husband destroyed the nation. Peter also had been on the verge of having her arrested and locked in a convent so he could marry his mistress. In turn she had imprisoned her husband, yes, but the fatal altercation that Alexis Orlov and his guards had had with the weak and petulant deposed emperor days later was not of her making.

Even amidst a whirlwind of policymaking and formal activities, she never ceased regretting that he was gone. That she couldn't have left him in a comfortable prison where he could play with his toy soldiers and create music on his collection of rare violins. She feared that such a massive cloud would hover over her reign forever.

Catherine did not fool herself that she had ever (at least not since the earliest years of their teenage courtship and marriage) felt anything romantic for Peter. Nor could she deny that his death had freed her from what surely would've been years and perhaps decades of attempts by her enemies to release him and mount a countercoup.

She also believed that if Elizabeth had seen the future, she'd have been pleased to see Catherine seize the throne from Peter.

If nothing else, the note Catherine now held confirmed this.

Pushing aside the small hill of parchment in the mountains of papers she dealt with daily, she rose and stretched. Still wearing a loose, trapezoidal sarafan in the old Russian style, she knew she must dress for dinner.

First, though, she would check on Grand Duke Paul, the son she never really had known. Admittedly, though, his existence lent credence to her claim to the throne of this vast, unwieldy country over which she'd ruled for a mere six months.

Paul was recovering from another bout of illness, having suffered a relapse during and then again after her coronation. The frequency of his inexplicable sicknesses baffled the court physicians as much as they had when his father—or alleged father —was a sickly young man himself.

The boy appeared as a small face surrounded by pillows, looking wan and not responding to her entrance to his chambers with any interest. Having grown up horribly spoiled by

Empress Elizabeth, recently he had shown almost a hero wor-
ship of the man he called father: a man who ignored him
and spent most of his own adolescence and young manhood
awaiting the crown he'd worn for a scant six months. Little
Paul, too, considered himself heir to the throne of Russia,
and occasionally he now questioned—albeit only in private—
why it was his once estranged mother who ruled.

"How do you feel, Paul Petrovich?" she asked worriedly,
bending over the canopied bed at the same time she looked
up at his physician for confirmation.

"Tell your mother—Her Imperial Majesty the Empress of
all the Russias—what you told me," the doctor urged.

Paul muttered something she had to lean closer to hear.
All she got was a resentful "I'm improving, Your Royal Majesty" from the stiff little boy who now kept himself apart from
his mother. Physically isolated when possible. Always aloof in
her presence.

"That's good to hear," she murmured back before adding
brightly, "Have you heard what we are going to do?"

Silence from the bed.

"We are going to decree that we establish a new public
hospital right here in Moscow in your name. Children like
you will be cared for regardless of whether they don't have
access to all these wonderful doctors you do. We will see that
they are helped in a manner befitting a grand duke."

Paul had fallen asleep, however. After conferring for a few
minutes with his physician, Catherine moved quietly and resolutely from the room.

Would anything ever reconcile the two of them, she wondered idly as she had so many times, especially since he had

recently turned eight. Before this, they'd spent virtually no time together during his childhood by order of Empress Elizabeth, who literally had stolen the infant away moments after Catherine gave birth. Now that she worked nearly round the clock to organize the chaos that was this nation, things had not changed. She wondered if she could ever be a real mother to her biological son. By the time her maids had arrived to dress her, she had pushed the thought aside.

Every evening since her coronation, her presence was demanded at a banquet, play, opera, private dinner, wedding, or reception. Usually she made a cursory appearance, enough to satisfy the local aristocracy and the entire court, before returning to her rooms to work or sleep. Grigory often accompanied her to the festivities, his chest glittering with medals and orders, his gold-embroidered coat and breeches a handsome decoration on her arm. With his six-foot-plus figure and broad shoulders, he towered over nearly everyone and awed most. No one questioned the presence of her lover.

Sometimes Grigory lingered at the receptions after she had left, expertly playing his role without ever upstaging his empress. If someone attempted to engage him in politics, he managed to sidestep the question or respond with a joke or a story about an old battle against the Prussians. He was everyone's war hero, though never overplayed his position.

Before the evening activities ended, he would often come to her room, untie his cravat, and stretch on the couch until the empress finished her paperwork. Then, with a sigh of weariness, she'd carefully shuffle the papers into piles on the desk before sinking down onto the couch or loveseat with

Grigory—a man whose appearance often struck her as what she imagined the Archangel Gabriel to look like.

What no one realized was the major role he served as Catherine's rock. It was on him she leaned when she wanted just to be herself, or to rage, or to worry.

Grigory was also the only one she still trusted implicitly. Princess Dashkova, despite aiding them in the coup, continued to demand more credit than was warranted and hence was no longer welcome at court. This was a huge loss, as she and Little Catherine, as Dashkova was known, had spent countless hours together before the coup. In some ways they were an intellectual match; they devoted their spirited meetings to discourse on everything from literature and philosophy to the need for the emancipation of both women and serfs. They agreed, too, on the need for improved education, libraries, and museums. Yet with her hot temper and impatience for immediate change—not to mention an overly pompous view of herself and her role in the empress's accession—the younger princess no longer served as an asset and barely a friend, let alone a lady-in-waiting.

Without Little Catherine to bounce ideas off and minus two of her closest ladies left behind in Petersburg, she had no one dependable to keep her informed.

To make matters worse, her favorite maid of honor, Maria, was still missing. "Any news of Masha?" she asked Grigory tonight, deciding not to reveal the former empress's note about Peter right away.

"No, my darling, I told you I sent additional officers to Petersburg. They have located her husband Igor Blukhov, who remains in his shop. He has locked the doors and seems unable to speak. We await a letter from him. The poor man appears to have had some type of breakdown."

"Truly? That does not sound like the strong, confident jeweler I know. We must send for him."

"We will, we will. However, you well know that many maids and ladies fled after the late emperor's arrest and then death. It is difficult to believe that they preferred that louse—"

"This is a conversation I refuse to have again, Grigory. Maria Sergeievna Blukhova and I have known each other since we were fifteen. I was only fourteen when I arrived and she became one of my maids. For nearly twenty years she has been loyal. She even spied for us. For me and *you* and all our supporters. As did Igor Igorevich. And she served me for months after the event and almost until the coronation. The idea that she left me because of the coup is preposterous! I'm not going to say it again."

"Hush, hush. I am sorry, Your Majesty." Grigory recognized the flare of anger and the look in her eyes that could turn them from deep to ice blue. "I was merely speculating about all the possibilities, and I prefer to believe Maria left of her own will than that something awful happened to her."

Catherine shuddered. She simply would have to wait for Igor's letter or presence to discover what had happened. She could not believe that Maria would have left her service without an explanation, let alone permission.

"Enough unpleasantries, my darling," Grigory murmured. "I want to massage your feet. To sip brandy with you and eat sweets and gaze into those magnificent eyes. To ensure that you stop overdoing things."

"I must, Grisha. You know I must toil from morning

through evening. Especially after what just happened . . ." She pressed fingers against her temples, fraught with worry over this latest challenge.

He waved his massive hands dismissively. "It was all a mistake, my love. A few drunken guards who made some ridiculous statements they didn't recall in the morning."

"It could have succeeded!" Her voice rose again and then dropped cautiously. "The Izmailovsky Guards wanted that idiot Ivan on the throne!"

"Only a handful, who had no illusions that they would get away with a coup—nor that a child caged up with no human contact could rule this nation. It was a matter of jealousy, you know that. The guard Semyon Guryev thought he himself should have been given a higher post after standing watch for us at Peterhof during the coup."

"And now I am cornered. Forced to act as the Empress Elizabeth did. Have I told you how vengeful and paranoid she was? How she had a guard sleep at the foot of her bed each night and kept everyone guessing until three in the morning which chamber she would sleep in? That she actually ordered a lady's tongue cut out simply because she wore the empress's favorite color, pink?"

Grigory held her close, stroking her chestnut curls. "I know, you have told me many times. You are not her. *You* will not sanction the awful punishments she ordered nor the deaths that her predecessors, including her larger-than-life father Peter the First, sanctioned. Everyone knows that!"

"Perhaps they should not know that. I dare not show fear. I must *be* feared." She reached for a glass of brandy on a tray and sipped, her eyes watery.

"What did you say, my Katya?"

"I said," she repeated softly, "I want my people to love me. The way I love them."

"They do love you. Yet you are correct to be stern if you want to hold the crown."

"Absolute power, I know," she half-moaned.

Guryev had not acted alone. It turned out that he and a fellow disgruntled guard, Peter Khrushchev, had started a rumor that the imprisoned Ivan VI—once a baby dethroned by Empress Elizabeth and held in solitude until adulthood— secretly had been released from the Fortress of Schlüsselburg. It was conjectured that they were mounting their own coup to topple the new empress in favor of Ivan VI. Fortunately, word of the rumor had reached Catherine, who ordered Colonel Kiril Razumovsky to conduct a secret investigation.

Two days later, fifteen arrests had been made, with the two chief offenders beaten with sticks and the rest threatened with transfer to other garrisons. The investigation concluded that nothing more than drunken, empty boasts had occurred. Catherine disagreed, seeing even talk of a coup as a threat and demanding harsher sentences. The investigators dutifully did what their empress commanded by proposing that five of the offenders be tried by the senate.

Just this week the senate had handed down the sentences for three, demanding that Guryev and Khrushchev be beheaded. Catherine, while having no problems with the idea of exile, had made her point, and graciously commuted the sentences to having their swords broken over their heads before they were stripped of rank, surname, and noble status. They would be shipped to Yakutsk in Siberia and the island of Kamchatka in the Far East for life. These orders were to be carried out the following day.

Unlike her predecessor Elizabeth, who condoned horrible punishments yet forbade capital punishment, Catherine envisioned somewhat of a reverse, milder policy. She had spent enough time in Moscow to realize punishments meted out by the nobility to their servants stretched beyond vulgarity and cruelty to outright torture. Her maids whispered to her that nearly every aristocratic home had its own Chamber of Horrors, a situation that reminded her all too much of Elizabeth's personal room for observing the hideous, innocent souls and deformed "freaks" she'd captured. In Moscow even a tiny infraction as perceived by the aristocracy could get you a trip to a special berth underground filled with whips, chains, and brutal instruments of tyranny.

What vexed her most was that almost immediately upon ascending the throne, she had recalled all Russian soldiers home, ceased hostilities with Prussia, withdrawn from the war that Peter III had just begun with Denmark, and attempted to remedy the fact that soldiers had not been paid in months. In short, she had brought peace to her country for the first time in seven years. Perhaps, she speculated idly, the military leadership is happier when they have a war to fight than they realize.

"I am executing another decree soon," she told her lover now. "From henceforth torture will be used only sparingly—and in accordance with the severity of the crime committed—in order to protect the innocent."

"Excellent idea, my love. Now, let us get you into bed."

She started to bolt the door when he stopped her. "No,

Katinka, let your ladies enter and prepare you for bed. I will stay here on the couch if you like, though we must sacrifice the pleasures of the flesh tonight."

As she started to protest and reach for the laces on his breeches, he gently removed her hand and laughed. "You know you need your rest. You do too much. And you know our baby needs his rest, too."

In the hectic months of assuming control of an empire that resembled nothing so much as a giant puzzle with all its pieces knocked out of the box, she had almost forgotten the pregnancy she tried so hard to hide. It was not the first time she had been forced to bind her stomach beneath flowing gowns or to disguise morning sickness. The people must not know.

Ironically, it was pregnancy that had prevented her from acting when Peter took the throne upon Elizabeth's death, and she and Grigory had been forced to hide her condition and send their illegitimate baby boy to be raised elsewhere lest she be accused of treason. Although things were different now, she feared the idea of a marriage to a common soldier she'd only recently proclaimed a count would not be a popular decision. Paul would remain heir. Only a few people knew, however, that she and her late husband Peter had shared very little during their married life, including sex.

Sadly, Grigory was correct: she apparently *had* overdone it.

As a crowd gathered in Red Square the following morning to witness the formal proclamation of the accused traitors' sentences, Catherine lay listlessly while a couple trusted attendants cleaned up the blood on her sheets and her personal physician examined her.

This time the baby had died rather than been sent away. Either way she had miscarried her second child by the man she loved.

After several sips of watered-down wine, she rolled over and turned toward the tapestry so that no one would ever know if she wept.

She must not demonstrate grief or terror, must show that the conspiracies mushrooming around her almost weekly were not to be disregarded—at the same time not taken too seriously. Reluctantly she reinstated the Secret Branch Elizabeth had utilized to ferret out plots, treasonous voices and actions, and betrayals. When she traveled to and from the senate, she allowed herself to be accompanied by only two lackeys. In this balancing act, she must exhibit neither fear nor recklessness.

She did intersperse work and social obligations with merriment, taking advantage of the blanket of snow minimizing the city's dirt so she could watch ice skaters, sledge races, orchestras, and bands that transformed the deeply frozen Moskva River into a months-long winter carnival. She would outlast it all, she vowed, meanwhile yearning to return to her beloved Petersburg. To her collection of sleighs each large enough to accommodate a dozen riders. To the pastel buildings that softened the night even in the dead of winter. To the White Nights that transformed the city into various opal shades for twenty-four hours on early summer nights.

For the present she must remain steadfast in the capital, working harder and longer than any monarch before her. If she sometimes felt like Sisyphus, condemned to roll the same rock up the hill, she also resolved that unlike the beleaguered Greek hero, she would succeed in ruling this great and powerful empire.

CHAPTER 11

(MARIA) 2017

M y reunion with Aunt Roberta is tearful. And amazing. Neither of us expected to see one another again, and we stand in the embassy entryway hugging wordlessly for a long, long time.

New lines frame her eyes and strands of silver-gray streak her now short brown hair, although she looks almost the same as before—except for wearing a casual Native American dress rather than her traditional business suit. I know I look different. I sense she retained her memory of me as a teenager, and "getting back" a mature thirty-five-year-old woman must be disconcerting.

We remain at the embassy for several more days, with official questioning sessions attempting to verify our stories gradually supplemented by a few media interviews. By unspoken consent, we refuse to allow television cameras. "No photos," Aunt Roberta insists before every interview.

After our official release, we must spend three nights at a hotel near Pulkovo Airport. Here we continue to dodge journalists while trying to renew our relationship. It seems like my new documents will never arrive.

In between more interviews with authorities from both countries, Aunt Roberta entertains me by doing humorous imitations of the reporters, bureaucrats, and police investigators. We also watch Russian reality shows and CNN while enjoying some awful room service and an occasional food delivery.

"This is nothing," she comments after my tenth complaint about a journalist calling on the phone or pounding on the door. "The first couple weeks after you disappeared, some brilliant officials decided to replace interview tactics with interrogations. You know, in case I killed you and stashed the body in one of the tsars' carriages or behind a wall-size Dutch canvas."

My jaw drops. This has never occurred to me. "Oh my God! I am so, so sorry you had to go through that!"

"Well, I won't deny it was upsetting," she admits while extricating herself from about the nineteenth hug I've given her. "There were some humorous theories and headlines about a murderous history professor. You can look them up when we get back if you want a good laugh."

Horrified, I try to imagine my aunt tagged as a murder suspect. "They didn't arrest you, did they?"

"No. Eventually I stopped being a 'person of interest' due to 'a preponderance of lack of evidence' or some such thing. Then the Russians *and* the Americans let me go home. That just left the reporters and the bloggers."

"The what's?"

"Bloggers. I'll explain later. All I know is that after all these years, I have you back. And I get to find out where you've been and what happened!"

"The truth is probably crazier than the idea that you murdered me," I force a light tone, knowing my aunt is giving me the perfect opportunity to segue into my experiences. It is futile, however, as I am not ready to tell her where I have been. Or when. I don't want to be locked up somewhere in an institution, which would seem my likely fate if she does not believe me. I want to get safely back to the United States, where I suspect the prisons are more palatable than Russian ones.

"Are you married?" I ask at one point, trying to deflect her curiosity.

"No." Silent for a moment, she looks at me oddly. "Are you?"

It's too soon to answer truthfully, especially since I cannot account for my husband's current whereabouts. "There is much to tell," I sigh. "Please, Aunt Roberta, not today."

Confined to the room, I find the silence often unbearable. Even uncomfortable, especially when my aunt sits across from me and gazes at me with her open, curious stare. "Was it drugs, Maria? Honestly, you can tell me."

"Because I don't remember anything?"

"That and because you were caught defacing a priceless statue."

"I did not deface it. It was my conduit!" I press my lips together and let the tears I've tried to suppress roll down my cheeks.

Aunt Roberta apologizes then, disregarding the mention of a conduit. I feel guilty at the lies and at the same time regretful of the deception. It is too soon to "confess." To risk it all, including my freedom.

We board a predawn Finnair flight. My aunt is anxious for me to come home, and as for me, I have little interest in seeing any more of St. Petersburg. The eighteenth-century memories, albeit of a much less populated city with fewer buildings and monuments, I must put behind me. And there is no way that so soon after they detained me in the Hermitage they will let me back inside or anywhere near *my* statue.

Nonetheless, my thoughts consistently drift back to my life in the past. Mostly I try to figure out how Igor and Aunt Gina are handling my disappearance. I also think about Catherine a lot. I hate that I missed the coronation. I am curious about so many things that must be going on in her life, as well as her reaction to my sudden absence from her court. Is—or was—she still with Grigory Orlov? Now that they are free to demonstrate their love openly, I wonder if they remained a couple after he and his brothers so ably rallied the military to back the coup. He is a dashing, capable soldier who obviously loves her, albeit no match for her intellectually. And will little

Paul someday attempt to mount his own coup and replace his mother on the throne? I don't think so, given that history apparently still calls her "The Great."

Catherine's relationship with Orlov circles my thoughts back to Igor, and I am in tears by the time we land in Helsinki.

Aunt Roberta, who cannot help notice my apparent grief, squeezes my hand. *If she only knew.*

After making a tight connection for our transatlantic flight to Chicago—further delayed by my failure to know I was supposed to remove my shoes and display my toiletries—things are strained between us at first. I resolve to try living in the moment, and to compensate for my frequent silences, I encourage my aunt to fill in more details on the spectacular and tragic medley of news events I've missed. There is so much to discuss, and so many questions.

By the time we fasten our seatbelts for the landing at O'Hare, we still have not truly caught up to *this* year—which seems to be the oddest period of all in recent American history.

To prevent questions on the ride in the car from the airport, I comment on all the changes in Lansing: new or renamed restaurants, businesses, roads, street names, housing developments, and university buildings. Unlike in Russia, where things have modernized since the eighteenth century but still seemed familiar to me on my return, I feel overwhelmed at all the fast-food restaurants, billboards for types of businesses I don't understand, and stores the size of football stadiums. It is all too much.

We are unloading luggage at the exact same apartment complex she—and I—lived in for so long when Aunt Roberta pauses, sets down our suitcases, and asks *the* question.

"You are going to tell me what *really* happened, aren't you? Eventually?"

I bump my head on the trunk's hood. "When you are ready, I think. Yes, yes I will."

"Don't you mean when *you* are ready?"

"No, Aunt Roberta. *You* will be the one who must be prepared enough to hear it."

"Very well," she sighs, unlocking the once familiar door.

I enter slowly, wondering belatedly if there is even a room for me here anymore.

Aunt Roberta, however, has transformed my room into sort of a combination tearoom and den. My old bed is still there, now covered with a rose-patterned quilt and floral pillows. My former dresser and nightstand have been replaced by an antique matching set with nineteenth-century burgundy lamps.

I have few possessions in the suitcase we purchased in the hotel gift shop in St. Petersburg. I did keep my silk gown and brocade slippers, and of course the dragonfly jewels—wrapped up and hidden from my aunt, not to mention customs officials. Now I slip the package into an empty bureau drawer.

I'm baffled as to what to do with myself in this new life. One thing I know I *will* do soon is sit down at my aunt's computer and start researching. Learning what happened to my loved ones and friends from centuries ago is a priority. Still, I am terrified of what I might find.

For right now, however, I do not need or want to know some of these things. If I can find a way back—an idea that has not left me since I arrived in the present—it might not be such a great idea to know what happens to everyone and when.

It is not a matter of *if* I can get back, it's *when*. I vow to discover a way, no matter how long it takes. I cannot face life here if I cannot believe I can return there.

CHAPTER 12

CATHERINE (1762-1763)

"It was as if she derived her legitimacy from the very obstacles she surmounted. Day by day she sank her roots deeper into Russian soil. Already she had chosen her style of government: a mixture of charm and hardness, generosity, and mistrust . . . She fired off drafts at a speed that surprised and even vexed the copyists."
—Henri Troyat

Have you located him yet?" the empress demanded of the two officials in her office.

"No, Your Majesty," Chancellor Nikita Panin replied. The other, the former Chancellor Bestuzhev—recalled by her from the exile to which he had been sent by her predecessors— stared uneasily at his diamond shoe buckles.

I don't believe Panin, Catherine thought, noting the way

his eyes shifted slightly. She knew him well, and he'd been loyal to her throughout months and then years of planning for this day. Except for the Orlovs (and the unseen jeweler Igor), these were the only men to whom she remained grateful. Still, she trusted neither completely. Of the two, she believed that Bestuzhev did not lie to her, meaning Grigory's absence must not be attributed to some severe reason.

Grigory remained missing while Catherine grew more angry than worried. A few days ago he'd mentioned he planned to gamble with his brothers the following evening. She suspected he might have stretched that game into the morning hours, which also meant he undoubtedly quaffed beers and gulped vodka with his often raucous, boisterous brothers. Could he have stayed *another* day and evening?

It wasn't that she needed her lover, who participated little in the day-to-day running of the empire. He did manage the various estates she'd awarded him, along with a string of honors that required little effort. Yesterday, however, he couldn't find the time to show up for the French lessons she'd arranged for him. His new tutor had left, reportedly muttering a string of French curse words on his way out. It was a little thing she asked of him. Still, Grigory preferred to content himself with *oui, non, merci,* and *c'est la vie*—the latter sometimes seemingly his motto. In a court where French served as the common diplomatic language, this was a weakness in a man on whom she depended: he could speak no language other than Russian.

At times like this she compared him to her senate, whose members seemed totally unaware of their own ignorance. She still smarted from the day early in her reign when she had listened as the senators could not agree on how to handle a problem in a particular province.

"So exactly where is this territory?" she interrupted. "Might its geographical location matter?"

The senators had grumbled under their breath and stumbled over their words, and it took little time to establish that they had no clue where the place about which they were making decisions was situated.

"Very well," she said irritably. "Check the map."

"Your Imperial Majesty," someone broke the silence that had followed her idea. "We have no map of Russia."

Catherine slammed her fist on the wooden conference table. "I don't believe it!" she said. Then, after fumbling in the little reticule she carried, she produced five rubles and firmly placed them one by one on the table.

"The Academy of Sciences! Bring back an atlas of our empire," she ordered a servant. "Quickly!"

She was still fuming when the messenger dutifully returned. Carefully she opened and spread out the atlas on the long table, barely keeping her fists in check. "There you go, gentlemen. My gift to you! Now find me the damned missing territory."

Her problems with the senate went well beyond their indolence. Since the era of Peter the Great, this body's function had been to administer laws and ensure that decrees issued by the monarch were carried out. It would take them awhile to realize, like the rest of the court, that everything was changing. Catherine kept her head and hands in each aspect of the empire, from grain prices and a temporary ban on certain imports to busting the private monopolies families such as the Shuvalovs held on salt and tobacco. When one of the chief senators suggested that, like her predecessors, she might be spared the inconvenience of reading so many reports and dispatches, she reiterated her desire to read every piece of paper that passed through the senate's hands and those of all her ministers.

"Full reports from *everyone* must be delivered to me each morning," she insisted. "And I will not sign anything I have not read. Do you understand me?"

The latter put them on alert. For two decades many of these same men had served under the late Empress Elizabeth Petrovna, a ruler notorious for refusing to sign documents if for any trivial reason it was not deemed a precipitous day by the seers. When she did agree, she usually scrawled her name with barely a glance at the contents. If the senate supposed, as it had hoped, that business (and corruption) would go on as usual, they were sorely disappointed. Catherine intended to have her finger on the pulse of every aspect of the empire, and she would have her way. In the meantime, she rapaciously bent over letters, memorandums, translations, diplomatic reports, and all aspects of kingdom business.

By autumn she had established or reestablished relationships with all the ambassadors and diplomats from other countries, and devoted hours to writing ten- to fifteen-page letters to each European monarch. She even made peace with Peter's former favorite, Baron Bernhard von Goltz, the Prussian ambassador. Although at first she terrified him, she won him over so quickly that within months they were playing cards together.

She was always wary. One of her informants had reported

to her what Lord Buckingham, the British ambassador, had conveyed to his ruler, George II: "Right now Russia is one great mass of combustibles with incendiaries placed in every corner." This wasn't the first time she'd heard a similar statement from her spies, and regardless of how long ago during her reign he might have said it, she did not confront him with her royal displeasure. Instead, she singled him out by grilling him pleasantly about England over card games. If she were forced to win over each diplomat nation by nation, one hand of cards after another, she would do so.

When Grigory Orlov did show up, she didn't scold about his disappearance. "You missed your French lesson," she observed somewhat tartly. "Let me arrange with the tutor to give you another."

Grigory shrugged. "I prefer to imitate the French in cuisine and lovemaking. It's their speech that is too challenging for me."

In fact, the tutor reported that the first couple of lessons had been abysmal failures, as it appeared Grigory had no aptitude for languages.

"Enough!" She turned toward the window and gazed at the square of cathedrals and palaces in her view.

They both knew this had little to do with French and everything to do with his "debauchery," as she now termed it. On his knees, Grigory begged forgiveness. Yes, he had embarked on a bout of gambling and drinking, he confessed. "Only with my brothers. I meant no disrespect, Your Imperial Majesty," he pleaded.

Infuriated, she called him "an irresponsible cad" before dismissing him.

Days would pass before she attempted to forgive his actions. She did file away the incident in her memories, not to mention the list of reasons she kept to herself for not marrying Orlov. A hefty percentage of her subjects believed theirs was a romantic love affair that culminated only *after* her coronation, and that before that time he had worshipped her from afar. It was a falsehood good for the empire, and only a handful of those she trusted knew that they'd been clandestine lovers—even producing a secret child—long before her husband died. If anything, the people were happy to see their empress happy, especially since she did not flaunt the affair, only appearing on Orlov's arm at court festivities.

She forgot her anger one day when he ushered in the jeweler Igor Blukhov for an audience.

For a moment she barely recognized the jewelry designer. His handsome waistcoat and breeches could not make up for such a haggard face and soulful eyes. His wigless hair appeared streaked with strands of gray.

She allowed him to kiss her ring and bow astutely before she tapped him on the shoulder indicating he should rise. "My dear Igor Blukhov," she murmured. "We have worried excessively over you. Not to mention my dear friend, your lovely wife."

At these words, he nearly stumbled, and Grigory quickly eased Igor onto a divan and presented him with a tumbler of vodka. Igor refused neither offer.

"In your letter," the empress said gently, "you indicated you have no clear idea where Masha is, only that she intended to travel to Italy to be with your relatives."

Both of Catherine's Italian Greyhounds took this as an

invitation to leave their place beside their mistress and jump up on either side of Igor for some attention, which he absent-mindedly gave them.

"Did you two have an argument?" Grigory asked, although his men had ascertained long ago from Igor that this was not the case.

"No. No sir. We just . . ." He seemed unable to go on. Then, making a valiant attempt to pull himself together, he added, "We were ecstatically happy, my Maria and I. Always."

"This is why we are so concerned," the empress chided gently. "Happily married women do not simply flee to Italy."

"Especially women who are property of . . ." Grigory, as if suddenly realizing what he'd been about to blurt out, interrupted himself and poured another glass of vodka for Igor.

"I asked her to go," Igor said weakly, and as if gaining confidence, said firmly, "My aunt wanted someone to check on her ill brother and her vineyard interests, and she herself was—and is—too ill and frail to make such a journey."

Catherine reached for the elaborate ruby snuffbox she favored. "Then why all this mystery? Why didn't you confide this in your letter?

"Do you not realize how worried we have been?" her voice rose. "And right before my coronation, when she had promised to assist me with the jewels? I cannot understand why she did not tell me that she wouldn't be there!"

"It was last minute," he stuttered, and then apologized profusely for keeping his empress in the dark. He also apologized for not being able to stop his wife from her journey. He even apologized for keeping his shop closed for months and for taking so long to travel to Moscow.

"I did bring this gift," he said awkwardly, reaching into his pouch and pulling out a package wrapped in velvet and holding it away from the dogs.

"It's from us. Maria and me," he explained. "She conceived of it long before I began to craft it, and we were looking forward to presenting it to you in honor of your coronation. I decided to await her return to give it to you. Now so many months have passed that I believe it is best that I do so."

Catherine opened the velvet gently. She stared for a long time at the brilliant emerald cameo engraved with her own likeness as empress.

"It is breath-taking," she said simply, and showed it to Grigory, who could not keep his eyes away from it either.

"Is everything satisfactory?" Igor finally filled the silence. He tightened his grip on the dog now attempting to join the other on his lap.

Catherine gave him one of her dazzling smiles before turning serious. "Igor, tell me. How is it that such a glorious piece of jewelry, which I surmise required months and months—if not years—to carve and create, was done in time for my coronation?"

Igor blushed, then said bravely. "Two years, Your Imperial Majesty. It required over two years."

"How could you know?" she persisted. "No one, least of all me, knew I would succeed to the throne that long ago."

"Maria knew. She had a premonition—a dream. She envisioned Your Imperial Majesty upon the throne and when this piece of emerald arrived in my possession, she and I discussed the idea."

Overcome, the empress did not argue. She was too rational

to believe in dreams and forecasts. Unexpectedly she recalled the memory she'd had during her coronation: the wily priest her mother had hauled her to see as a teenager, a man who had declared that someday she would wear "three crowns on her head." At the time, the vision had seemed laughable. Russians, however, put much faith in dreams and prophecies, and she had become enough of one that she couldn't entirely dismiss this possibility.

"It is undoubtedly a masterpiece!" Grigory declared, leaning over to examine the two layers—one of emerald and one of agate—surrounded by onyx and diamonds. The entire setting of the intricately carved cameo resembled an eight-petaled flower. "Only a gemstone carver with highly refined artistic skills could have created such an object," he added.

In the center, Catherine's portrait appeared in a silhouette only slightly older than she was now. The empress seemed delighted with that aspect. "Now it will be ageless," she declared, "and I will treasure it forever."

In a rare gesture, she reached out to embrace the man who'd been a faithful friend, a spy for her, the husband of her dear maid of honor, and a master craftsman. She had an inborn respect for the talents of others, including those of the merchant or serf classes.

Embarrassed, Igor took this as his cue to depart, and backed out with tears in his eyes.

"Maria must return at once," Catherine declared, telling Grigory to summon her back to Russia "at all costs." Staring closely at the emerald cameo, she knew she would treasure this piece above all others. "And see to it that Igor Blukhov gets several new commissions. Not only have I always admired his work, I believe the man must keep himself occupied from morning until evening right now."

"I still do not understand why he could not have sent us word immediately of her departure rather than secluding himself in silence."

"One never knows exactly what goes on in a marriage," Catherine said softly, motioning for her two dogs to cuddle up on the divan with her. She resolved to get the truth from Maria when—and if—she returned.

CHAPTER 13

(MARIA) 2017

I've been in the modern world for well over a month: pacing floors, taking long walks on a greatly changed campus, napping endlessly, and eventually signing up for a night class on jewelry-making and an audit of an MSU geology class. Both begin this coming January.

All that free time only occurs after sacrificing my first couple weeks of liberty to the reporters and bloggers camped out in our parking lot. Although the outside entrance of the building has locks, they prove little deterrent to the tricky press devils. Only after their interest in my "mysterious reappearance" dwindles do I dare leave the apartment—and then usually at night wearing a hooded parka.

No wonder they were so enamored of the story. A Google search of my name turns up dozens of news sites between mid 1999 and late 2001: *American Tourist Missing in Russia. Teen Vanishes from Hermitage. Foul Play Suspected on High School Student's Vacation. Runaway or Kidnappee? American Woman Had Close Ties to Russia. Teenager May have Sought Asylum in Former Soviet Union. Teen Allegedly Involved in Art Heist Vanishes.*

After September 11, 2001, the press understandably lost interest, except for a few anniversary features after I'd been gone for five and then ten years. Luckily, all the media outlets reprinted my eleventh-grade yearbook photo. My features and hair have altered just enough that I no longer resemble the "old" and youthful me too much.

The only security camera that captured my teenage likeness in the Hermitage that day reveals me in profile, standing in a contemplative pose wearing shorts and a t-shirt in front of Gainsborough's *Portrait of a Lady in Blue*. It strikes me now, looking at the reflection of the Rococo oil painting, how much the subject resembles the ladies of my eighteenth-century world in apparel, hat, hair, pose, and tone. She could have been someone just like me. Or Anya or Tatiana or even Catherine. What an odd foreshadowing of what would happen less than an hour later.

It turns out Aunt Roberta was and has remained a staunch defender of my privacy—and hers. She granted few interviews in all this time, particularly not in the United States. Nothing has changed as she heads for campus, sweeping past reporters with a haughty "No comment" that I can hear through the partially open window. We did release the amnesia story via an MSU press release, which seems to be discouraging all except the conspiracy theorists.

The remaining stories have gotten crazier, with blogs speculating on my spy status (for one side or the other), my life as a "sex slave," my secret affair with a Russian official who hid me for nearly twenty years, my art thief career. . . the list goes on.

One afternoon I'm sitting on the loveseat daydreaming about Igor, as usual, when I hear Aunt Roberta's key in the lock. I heave a sigh, knowing the truth cannot be postponed forever. Not only do I owe it to my aunt, who's been incredibly kind and patient, but I already made one mistake: keeping the truth from Igor for so long that I nearly lost him. At least now he knows enough to suspect I've returned to the future or somewhere else in the realm of time. Hopefully he is not agonizing over my possible death.

If—and when—I ever make it back to the past, I owe the aunt who adopted me and loves me nothing less than the truth. I cannot vanish again without explaining why I would leave her and where I've gone, regardless of whether she accepts my unlikely tale.

"What do you think? Pizza for dinner?" Aunt Roberta breezes in, dropping twin briefcases on the floor.

"Sure. I've missed it."

"They do have pizza in Russia, do they not?" I catch the hint behind her words.

"Not where I was, and I think it's time we talk about that."

"About whether or not you still want mushrooms on yours?"

"I do. If you don't have papers to grade tonight, we could . . . well, talk about my life for the past eighteen years."

"I'm all yours. No papers, no exams. And thank God for that!"

I cannot help laughing, having met few professors who enjoy the grading process.

After we finish pizza and breadsticks, Aunt Roberta emerges from the kitchen with a second glass of chianti for each of us.

"You might as well bring the entire bottle. Or two," I say wryly.

"Oh, dear. And just when I was getting used to you being old enough to drink, you admit to having turned into a lush." She settles in the facing armchair, looking expectant. I cannot imagine how curious she's been—not just these past weeks but for almost two decades.

"I'm not certain how—or where—to begin."

"At the beginning," she grins. "And we don't have to do this all at once."

"No, and we couldn't possibly. Maybe one bottle per night per year of my absence?"

"I'll order a case tomorrow," she says lightly.

"Aunt Bobbi." I haven't called her that since I was a child. She sets her glass down as if the seriousness of my situation might be more than she wants to handle.

"I don't know if you will believe me."

"You've never lied to me." She reaches across the coffee table and touches my arm. "I've known you all of your life—

well, maybe only half now—and I've never once known you to be untruthful."

"What happened to me is beyond belief. Probably beyond science."

She leans forward, stands, and then retreats into the kitchen for a full bottle and a wine opener.

"I'm ready," she announces nervously, stretching her legs out on the ottoman.

So I go for it.

"It started at the new Winter Palace." When my aunt raises a puzzled eyebrow, I add, "What we now know as the Hermitage. Well, I mean that it started there. *This* palace wasn't built when I touched a statue in the classical section in the basement. I mean after I did that, I couldn't get back because the Hermitage hadn't been constructed yet."

More eyebrow raising. This is not going well. It's all convoluted.

"You touched a treasure in the Hermitage? *Before* the one they just caught you touching this summer?"

"Yes. Way back in nineteen hundred ninety-nine."

She is silent at first, then asks, "So did they arrest you?"

I try again by just jumping in: "No, I've been living in the past. During Empress Elizabeth's reign, in fact. Somehow the statue took me there. I have no clue how that could have happened. One minute I was in our time exploring the basement of the museum, and the next I was outside with a bunch of people living in the seventeen hundred forties." I shrug helplessly.

Silence dominates again. Nonetheless, my aunt grasps the idea immediately. "You are trying to tell me you traveled back in time? Like in the movies? In novels?"

"Yes, Ma'am. That is what I am saying, though again, I cannot expect you—or anyone else—to believe me."

Her expression seems grimmer than I'm accustomed to, though not necessarily skeptical. She closes her eyes and then stares into mine. I wonder if she is checking to see if my pupils are dilated. "So let me get this straight. You've been living in the middle of eighteenth-century imperial Russia?"

Encouraged by her failure to simply dismiss what I'd said, I plunge into the tale that even I would never believe if not for living it. "Do you remember when we split up after lunch at the Hermitage that day?"

"Nearly every day." She looks sad now, and I launch into an account of that afternoon, which has played over and over in my thoughts for nearly two decades.

"I still had my hand on the statue when it disappeared. I found myself standing outside wearing a formal gown and a cloak in the middle of a freezing Petersburg night."

I continue hesitantly at first, and then more confidently as I describe fourteen-year-old Catherine's and her mother's arrival and their meeting with Empress Elizabeth.

Expecting my aunt to wave a hand of dismissal or start to laugh, I am gratified and surprised when she asks, "Tell me what she was like—Peter the Great's daughter."

Does her question mean she just *might* believe me—or is she testing my knowledge of the period she knows so well? I offer my initial impressions of Elizabeth.

"Go on," she urges, pouring us another glass of chianti when I finish with my abbreviated version of Elizabeth's temper tantrums and eccentricities. Of her cruelty to Catherine.

Of her ultra-suspicious nature. Of her tolerance of a slow-witted nephew and heir so obviously unfit for the throne.

"For days after I arrived, I assumed I was in a coma. That I'd fallen in the Hermitage and hit my head on the floor or the statue. Everyone accepted me as someone else also named Maria, and I have no clue what became of *her*. Do you?"

"No," she answers thoughtfully. "No one showed up in my life to take your place, if that's what you mean."

"It is. The idea has tortured me." I slow down on my wine. "Interestingly, I was an orphan in the past, as well."

"Really?"

"I—or whoever I was—had parents who died a few years before I arrived. They were both sculptors in Empress Elizabeth's court."

"Does that seem odd to you?"

"Why?"

"Well, you supposedly were transported to the past via a sculpture. How did you get back?"

I *want* to stick to the story chronologically. Instead, I describe the last few minutes of the trip I took back to the present two months ago and how I touched another statue—or presumably the same one.

Aunt Roberta catches on immediately. "Who carved the statue?"

"I don't know. It was of the goddess Minerva. How anyone could have sculpted it so fast for Catherine's coronation, I have no idea. And the 'other' Maria's parents would have been dead long before then."

I can see Aunt Roberta's speculative look, the one she wears when immersed in her Petrine research. "Minerva Triumphant," she says. At my puzzled look, she adds, "That's what they called Catherine the Second almost from the beginning of her reign. It was the theme of her coronation."

I don't know what to think. I excuse myself and retreat to my bedroom, returning with the gown and accessories I was wearing when I reentered the present.

To an historian, the gown must be a shock, not to mention somewhat of a holy experience. My aunt fingers the gown, examines the stitching, and admires the jewels.

She is speechless—and particularly fascinated with the flimsy bejeweled brocade slippers, which resemble nothing you would find in a shoe store now and do not distinguish left from right the way modern shoes do.

I replace the apparel in my closet, careful to slip into my robe and to give Aunt Roberta a little time to absorb what must sound like science fiction or something paranormal.

When I return, she is crying, and I sit beside her and wrap my arms around her. I must ask: "Aunt Bobbi, are you upset because you think I've had a mental breakdown? Because you cannot possibly believe such a thing? I mean, I didn't expect you to accept it. I just hope and pray you won't lock me up." I am half teasing when I add, "Or turn me over to the government."

Regaining control of herself, she forces a smile that resembles a full moon suddenly brightening a dark landscape. "It's not that. I'm just relieved, I guess, that you weren't kidnapped or sold to black market slavers or murdered or locked in a secret prison or the gulag."

Again, I feel anew the pain she must have felt, struggling to go on with her life without knowing absolutely anything.

We talk—mostly I do, with some of her questions inserted into the conversation. "I was placed in the young Prussian princess's service, and later in Elizabeth's. When she became ill, I went back to Grand Duchess Catherine's court."

My stories go on until after midnight, by which time we are both drowsy from the wine.

"To be continued tomorrow?" she asks.

"Absolutely. Good night," I hug her again and go into my room to crawl emotionally exhausted into bed.

Almost immediately I fall asleep, relieved above all that my aunt has not given any indication that she disbelieves me. It is more than I could have hoped for, and I feel as if the albatross around my neck has been released.

CHAPTER 14

(CATHERINE) 1763

"Her whole life was a theater, and she was the director."
—Prof. Mikhail Piotrovski

Late in January, the nonstop celebrations that had transformed Moscow into a giant carnival culminated in a spectacle that nearly eclipsed the lavish coronation of a few months previously. The festival, dubbed "Minerva Triumphant" in keeping with the name of the goddess Catherine likened herself to, lasted three days. It required fabulous street decorations that stretched for two kilometers.

Months of planning had gone into the massive public masquerade, boasting over four thousand actors and musicians in costumes and masks who reenacted a total of forty scenes that "lampooned the preoccupations of narrow minds," as

Catherine put it. Some scenes depicted drunkenness, deceit, bribery, and ignorance; others demonstrated the vices of pride, arguments, deceit, and mockery.

Catherine herself assumed the leading role, riding in the final scenes as Minerva surrounded by actors portraying a golden age of peace and a goddess of virtue.

All the celebrations, however, could not mitigate the constant threats. As Paul regained his health, there were new worries and terrors. Recently a plot to murder Grigory and one of his four brothers, Alexis, had been uncovered. Amazingly, several of the conspirators were those who had assisted her and the Orlovs in the coup.

Most suspected that it occurred because the subject of her potential marriage to Grigory recently had stirred up half the empire. Even some of her former allies believed that the four Orlov brothers were a threat to Catherine herself.

Simultaneously, the church began to make noises of displeasure, although Catherine had attempted to undo the damage, threats, and land thefts from the Orthodox church committed by Peter III. She'd since felt the need to rescind some of her protections. The most controversial decision she made was to reinstate an agency in charge of administering church properties with the goal of budgeting and staffing all Russia's religious institutions and ecclesiastical properties. The reason was simple: she had no intention of destroying the church, as her husband had attempted; she envisioned a much greater function for it.

Few could dispute that the church gathered riches and properties for its own benefit, and the rich, lavish religious trappings barely disguised a great deal of greed. Catherine had a quite different vision of the church's role: it should not merely gather riches and keep the people "in line." It should minister to the poor and the sick.

"They won't do it," Panin declared in late winter. "They value their serfs and their riches, so will not share."

"Maybe they will at least agree to the teaching duties if not to the secularization," another government minister added hopefully.

"One would presume that they would be only too grateful for the chance to educate our Russian people properly, in everything from philosophy and theology to astronomy and mathematics. Imagine: I am giving them the opportunity to start their own schools! To properly educate our young people, most of whom cannot read!" For a moment her eyes and face glowed as if contemplating taking on this responsibility personally.

"If they will not dedicate some of their coffers to ministering to the uneducated, the ill, and the poor, then they shall find themselves enriching the coffers of the kingdom," Catherine threatened.

Money. It was the supreme problem from which so many others stemmed. One of her first tasks had been to find a way to replenish the state coffers. She already had abolished some of the monopolies held by the highest members of the nobility; created or increased taxes, and ensured that military personnel received the eight months in back pay they were owed thanks to Elizabeth's and Peter's neglect. She consulted the senate, though that body seemed incapable of coming up with any ideas of value.

"A bank," she announced one day to Panin and Bestushev,

reaching for grapes from an engraved silver bowl that always overflowed in her chamber with cherries, strawberries, and melon slices.

"We have too many of them already—and mainly corrupt ones," they both argued.

"*Nyet*. I will establish a new bank. One that issues promissory notes as required by the imperial Treasury."

Panin, still harboring a secret resentment that she had taken the throne to rule as an autocrat rather than regent for Paul, nodded and looked thoughtful. "It could work here," he said slowly. "Only here."

"I realize that," Catherine nodded. In other countries, most notably Britain and France, her idea of manufacturing large quantities of paper rubles would have resulted in the chaos of inflation and bankruptcy. Russia did not rely on gold, copper, or silver backing. Instead, public confidence in its currency depended on an almost moral authority: respect for their sovereign. As one philosopher had phrased it, "The material that coin is made of is of small importance. Were it the will of the sovereign to attribute the same value as a coin to a piece of leather, or to a sheet of paper, that would suffice and it would be so."

With the value of the new currency guaranteed in this unorthodox fashion, the seventeen-million-ruble deficit she had inherited could be handled.

Up by five each morning, she demanded other officials begin their days earlier than they were accustomed to and work later than they desired. She herself continued to tackle reports, memorandums, accounts, and diplomatic correspondence at an indefatigable rate; her workdays consistently approached seventeen hours. Her servants, maids, ladies, groomsmen, etc. also remained busy, though in their case she made allowances. In the pre-dawn, she usually did not awaken any servant, content to light the stove herself. Nor did she keep them up until all hours the way Empress Elizabeth had done.

In this atmosphere and at such a high energy level, Catherine literally glowed; however, she was not infallible. Only Grigory seemed to realize that, as well as convinced her of the importance of exercise. That which she normally got in the bedroom had dwindled as she fell exhausted into bed each evening after a post-dinner event.

He urged her to begin riding again, and while permitting him to choose their horses, she always galloped far ahead of him on the banks of the Moskva River. Still slim, even if some observers had noticed she was beginning to grow a little "stout" as her reign continued, she ate modestly. She took it for granted that innumerable hours sitting at tables and desks would plump her up a little. On the other hand, countless church holidays demanded a corresponding number of fast days, so she worried little.

Catherine dutifully fasted and followed all the rules and holidays of the church. No one could question her piety. The problems she *did* have with the church might've been resolved much sooner were it not for one powerful and outspoken member of the Holy Synod: the Metropolitan of Rostov, Arseniy Matseyevich. This metropolitan—the fieriest, wealthiest, and most vocal critic of the recently reorganized and revised institution—had emerged as a formidable opponent to total reform of all ecclesiastical bodies and properties.

Arseniy rallied his fellow Holy Synod members (each responsible for thousands of serfs) to garner support for the old policies that permitted the church to own everything itself.

Meanwhile, her key advisers could not agree how to handle the rumbling clerical anxiety. Most priests had no real desire to fight—and the near destruction the church had faced during Peter III's brief reign had left them a haunting vision of what might have been if he had lived. The metropolitan would not be silenced. "The church has been given its property by God for spiritual purposes only!" was his favorite refrain.

And to whom does he believe God gave the church? Catherine often muttered back to herself. Unlike the British, who'd broken from Rome over two hundred years ago, the Russian Orthodox remained firmly attached to their Eastern roots and their monarch—unquestionably anointed by God and the church to do what He saw fit. Now an even more enlightened empress had come along, determined to take over the administration of what the church considered its own serfs, lands, and buildings.

"Monsieur Voltaire has written of all this extensively," Panin mentioned one afternoon early in the year right before Catherine was scheduled to go on pilgrimage to Rostov for the consecration of a newly canonized saint.

"Voltaire! Humph. The esteemed Frenchman can hardly be called a man of God," Bestushev protested.

"You may disagree with the philosopher all you like . . ." Panin said, his voice drifting off meaningfully.

Perhaps recalling that Catherine was a long-time admirer who emulated the man, Bestushev lowered his voice and growled at Panin. "How can you hand over church affairs to intellectuals and atheists like that? A man like Voltaire who freely admitted, when asked why he took Holy Communion if he were an atheist, responded, 'Because I breakfast according to the custom of the country'"?

"Gentlemen," the empress interrupted smoothly, and both men blushed at her embarrassingly keen hearing. "I am considering postponing our small trip to Rostov."

"Your Imperial Majesty," Panin protested, shocked at this affront to Metropolitan Arseniy Matseyevich.during such an inflammatory time.

"Saint Dimitri the Miracle Worker's bones can await their silver shrine awhile longer, I believe."

Against the advice of her main advisers, she did not change her mind. She seldom did after she had thought everything through, and in this case suspected that the metropolitan was anxious for her visit so that he might confront her afterward. Each believed in his or her correctness on this massive issue, and only one would get his or her way.

Rather than going to Rostov, Catherine devoted some of her rare free time to Grigory.

"You will win in the end," Grigory assured her as they sat in her massive, canopied bed feeding one another sweet cherries.

"I shall win at many things," she smiled confidently. "And I suppose I shall lose at others. To which battle do you refer?"

"Never mind." He moved the fruit platter to the floor and bent to suck her nipples. "Much tastier than cherries, I believe."

She pressed his mouth more firmly to her breasts, already

yearning for him to enter her. Her sexual appetite had only increased since Grigory had become her lover, and she had to admit the satisfaction of the act often tempered her anger about daily affairs.

Sometimes Catherine suspected her body needed to make up for all those years as a virginal young bride and then a not-so-young bride still untouched by her own husband. She also wondered what might have happened had she not taken matters into her own hands. She could have remained a virgin her entire life, left with no heir and undoubtedly sent back to Prussia or into a convent, replaced by a second wife.

Besides fulfilling her principal duty of producing an heir, she had always yearned for love. Having imagined herself in love twice, she now realized that what she had mistaken for it was perhaps not the genuine emotion. Sergei Saltykov had taught her lust before betraying her after Paul was born, and she felt nothing for him. Similarly, she'd maintained an intellectual and physical relationship with Stanislaus, yet easily had adjusted to life without him. Only Grigory, despite the vast chasm between their intellectual capabilities, made her feel secure and content. Perhaps this then was true love—a handsome escort to whom she could turn for confidences, reassurance, and sexual pleasure.

Could she survive life without him the way she had with the other two?

As he entered her, however, such thoughts ceased, and she arched her back to savor these moments.

There were immediate consequences to the canceled pilgrimage. Metropolitan Arseniy perceived it as an insult and a stall tactic on the empress's part. In a vicious denunciation of secularization, he distributed to the entire Holy Synod a lengthy condemnation of not only secularization, but of his fellow clergymen who, he insisted, just "sat like dumb dogs without barking."

Perhaps they did. Certainly very few wanted to underestimate, let alone challenge, the new empress. In fact, some read Arseniy's document and heard his inflammatory statements at a minimum as insulting to the empress and at a maximum as treason. Undeniably it could be seen as downright heresy against the imperial head of the church.

Nor did everyone disagree with all of Catherine's ideas; the aristocrats were already overtly secular and often viewed the church as little more than a body of wealth hoarders. They saw no conflict with requiring the church to assume additional responsibilities such as teaching and aiding the poor. Government officials viewed this reform as a better use of the wealth of the church in a nation with a struggling financial condition. The wealthiest landowners were eager to get their hands on church-owned lands.

Arseniy persisted: "This travesty of secularization would make bishops and priests no longer shepherds of the people. They would be little more than hired servants, accountable for every crust of bread!"

The day Catherine read Arseniy's petition herself, she paced angrily up and down parquet floors while her advisers awaited the storm that would surely break when she realized how much of it was aimed at her.

"These are perverse, inflammatory distortions of what we are trying to accomplish!" she insisted to all around her. "I want this liar and humbug punished!"

Just ten days after Arseniy had denounced the empress in writing, he was put on trial at Catherine's order. In a series of nocturnal sessions, the metropolitan sat across from her night after night as the synod in Moscow interrogated him in the empress's presence. Even seated in his sovereign's presence, he would not stop. He questioned Catherine's right to the throne, accused her of Peter III's murder, denied her faith in God.

"Enough!" she cried, and the synod declared their verdict: guilty.

In a punitive public ceremony in Red Square, Arseniy underwent a ritual disgrace that included stripping him one by one of his ecclesiastical robes and garments. Throughout the ceremony he continued to rail against the empress, to yell insults at his fellow churchmen, and to predict a violent death for everyone.

"I thought they would never shut him up," Grigory complained as they strode back into the palace apartments.

"He can make all the vile noises he wants," she said calmly. "Now he will make them for the poor gulls on the White Sea." Arseniy had been banished to a remote monastery, condemned to hard labor cleaning cells and chopping wood.

As a final insult, Catherine ordered that he should be denied pen, ink, and paper.

Arseniy had no idea that she made a speech shortly thereafter telling the Synod, "You are the successors to the apostles who were commanded by God to teach mankind to despise riches, and who were themselves poor men . . . If you wish to be my most faithful subjects, you will not hesitate to return to the state which you unjustly possess."

It would require nearly a year before her imperial manifesto declared all ecclesiastical properties now those of the government, and before the church itself was transformed into a state institution. Church serfs were converted to state peasants, clergy and priests became salaried employees, and roughly half of the churches and monasteries were forced to close. And this short, energetic former Prussian teenage arrival to Russia had accomplished such massive societal and cultural upheaval without any other serious opposition.

To further complicate matters, amid her heavy workload, Catherine found herself betrayed by Bestuzhev, the very man who so many years ago had urged her to seek the throne. It was his widely circulated petition insisting that she wed that caused headaches. Rumors swirled through Moscow that she'd secretly married Grigory Orlov while on her nonexistent trip to Rostov. Plots were uncovered to murder the Orlov brothers. An infuriated Catherine could not understand why this beloved elderly counselor, whom she always personally rose to greet in the council chamber, would stir up so much trouble.

Not surprisingly, perhaps, everyone at this point still assumed that she needed a husband, be it Grigory or a Russian prince or some prince or king from another monarchy. Various factions sprung up, each orbiting around one royal circle or another. Yes, she knew that perhaps she needed to have more children who would be deemed legitimate heirs. But she had spent too many years in the shadows of others— starting with her mother, then Empress Elizabeth, then her husband, and these days her male advisers and so-called supporters.

I don't want to be married, she realized, keeping this a secret. Although in love with Grigory, she had no intention of having him or anyone else as a consort. For the first time she wielded her own power, and on countless occasions drew strength from the long-ago reign of Queen Elizabeth of England. She, too, had faced a coalition of senior statesmen pressuring her to marry. And if Elizabeth was, as she claimed, married to her country, Catherine felt herself no less married to Russia.

She knew some saw her as "weak and feeble," firmly believing this was because of her being female. Her predecessors had at first faced the same challenges, and she drew on their later strength for her own. Having no idea how long this pressure would last, she argued with herself daily lest the pressure for her to decide intensified and interfered with the business of her reign.

In early June Catherine issued a proclamation. The Manifesto of Silence was read aloud in every square to warn her subjects that they should go about their own business and "refrain from all unseemly gossip and criticism of the government."

She was surprised that the manifesto had the desired effect. However, the issue of whether she should marry Orlov—or had in fact done so secretly—would persist for years unless she put a stop to it. To test the waters and potentially break the impasse, she made a great show of formally requesting permission to remarry lest her son and only heir, Paul, pre-decease her.

Her subjects might continue to push for a wedding, but surprisingly, the senate denied the suggestion. It turned out that most government officials and most factions actually disapproved. "So that's that," she told Grigory. "The matter is now dropped—at least for the time being."

Grigory could barely assuage his bitterness, forcing him to face the fact that the wedding he craved so much would not come to pass.

His proposals ceased. He did increase attempts to please her—even taking a stab at becoming more scholarly. His main efforts involved astronomy; he patronized the scientist Mikhail Lomonosov and asked permission to have an observatory built atop the Summer Palace.

"Remember, though," he assured her as they cuddled together the day he told her of his plan. "You will always be the most brilliant star in my universe."

She made love to him then, wondering to herself why she could not detach herself from this handsome man who could never equal Stanislaus in so many ways, yet made her tingle and filled her with desire and love. For now, though, he and his love were all she had time and passion for outside of her almost maniacal drive to rebuild her country. As Count Panin had once so aptly observed, "A Madame Orlov could never be empress of Russia." Sadly, she realized how right he was.

Meanwhile, work proceeded in all aspects of the empire, and often smoothly. When not writing or reading, Catherine strode the grounds, dictating notes and letters and bending to sniff or press a kiss on one of the newly budding plants she loved so much.

"I will walk," she insisted, waving a dismissal to the carriers of her sedan chair when she visited the senate or a church. Like Moses parting the Red Sea, she lifted bejeweled hands just enough to get the flood of petitioners to make way. One day, nearly submerged by a deluge of people, she witnessed her own police wielding knouts in preparation for beating the petitioners. Throwing out her arms, she nearly knocked two people over. "Stop! These are my people!" she declared to her troops, who obediently resisted their urge to beat her loyal subjects.

Whether the incident happened once or a dozen times, it grew in its retelling. "Have you not noticed?" Panin mentioned a few weeks later. "Now the crowds weep when their new Little Mother appears in public."

Catherine flushed with pleasure at this evidence of her people's love—something she'd craved since arriving in Russia as a fourteen-year-old princess with little knowledge of what the future held. At long last she was living that future, and thus far succeeding beyond her wildest dreams. If some of the other stories of her benevolence threaded through the empire—each embroidered a little more—she accepted her new role with relief. And with a generous portion of satisfaction.

She loved Muscovites as her subjects, albeit detested the city nearly as much as the man she emulated, Peter the Great, had hated it. From a distance, Moscow's over five thousand splendid gleaming domes, each gilded gold or silver or enameled in checkerboard patterns or painted with gold stars, could not fail to bedazzle those who passed by the hundreds of white churches and six monasteries resembling fortresses. Most of these surrounded the city's white and red brick circumference. But for Catherine the sixteen hundred huge and sonorous bell towers clanged incessantly. They pealed out their cacophony for festivals, saints' days, Sundays, funerals, fires, and even to mark workday hours. Sometimes she felt she could not think straight, and in her rooms would wear a muff over her ears. Nothing helped.

"I think they ring more now than ever before," she complained to her head seamstress, Anya, who was designing another gown for a mistress who intensely disliked standing still for fittings she considered a necessary waste of time. "It's overwhelming. They remind me of the great throats of dragons roaring so loudly one could go insane. Yesterday I canceled a meeting because I couldn't hear half of what my ministers said."

"Last month a priest told me they rang them to frighten away the demons that day, Your Imperial Majesty."

"And that is another thing I dislike, Anya. This is a city full of symbols of fanaticism, alleged miracles and icons, not to mention priests and convents. And the devil take this ceaseless clanging of bells!"

Anya, who had turned out to be the best recommendation for the job that the missing Maria Blukhova could have made, tried to calm her. "It is rather humorous, though, when newcomers first arrive and start rushing around covering their ears. Sometimes I see them run and hide in a building."

"They are probably hiding from the city's giant flies. If they were smart, they would just keep running. All the way to Petersburg."

Nor could anyone who spent time in labyrinthian Moscow avoid noticing the endless towers of decay and trash—thankfully snow-covered part of the year. The city was the antithesis of St. Petersburg. Since Peter the First had severed its role as capital, medieval Moscow had declined precipitously, its infrastructure ignored and its populace dominated by greedy nobles lording it over poverty-stricken citizenry. Since spring, the clanging and pounding of unremitted construction signaled the replacement of countless wooden buildings that had burned over the winter. The noise only made the relentless bellringing more intolerable.

Between the dust, the construction, the flies, the bells, the fact that the haughty Moscow aristocracy had fled to their country estates, and constant murmurs of the citizenry about her marital status, the new empress grew frustrated.

As she and Grigory wrapped around one another in her bedchamber after one particularly trying day, he asked, "Is it time to return home, my love?"

Catherine thought back, as she had dozens of times over the past months, to the evening she and her mother had arrived at the old palace in Petersburg where she'd been greeted by her new ladies and a host of dignitaries. Where she had toured the city of pastel baroque buildings dripping with snow diamonds beneath a faded citrine sky. Where she had sensed almost instantly she was at home and fell in love with it. Where she had ladies like Tatiana and Irina and Maria who were to become close friends.

"It's time," she murmured back.

Preparations ensued quickly, with Catherine undertaking those duties she officially felt necessary to leave behind a lasting impression. Most of these involved reviewing troops. She also cemented relationships with an obligatory whirlwind tour of her most favored courtiers' estates. She sought to flatter them into abandoning what they considered the more traditional Moscow to follow the court to the frosty marshland of Peter I's newer capital.

Catherine and her courtiers also made time for sailing, hawking, card playing until past midnight, and viewing the fireworks that welcomed her everywhere.

In a reverse migration of the one that had brought her so jubilantly to ancient Moscow the previous summer, she halted to examine the progress made at Oranienbaum, her favorite palace. Clapping in delight, she issued more orders for renovations of the place she and her husband had shared so unhappily.

On June 28, 1763—the one-year anniversary of her succession—she joyfully re-entered Petersburg as a crowned monarch. Seated in a gilded coach beside Paul and preceded by twenty-six horsemen and a carriage procession of courtiers, she was followed by Count Grigory Orlov and his detachment of horse guards. Huge crowds filled the streets. Foreign ministers lined the palace's staircase like a contingent of smartly uniformed nutcrackers.

Catherine spent the next hours offering prayers in the chapel, receiving hand kisses from well-wishers in the throne room, and thrilling to the fantastic fireworks bursting over the Neva River. Watching them glitter the sky, she squeezed Grigory's hand, inwardly vowing only to return to Moscow when she absolutely must. She was back where she belonged: in her own city.

CHAPTER 15

(MARIA)

As much as I savor rifling through Aunt Roberta's substantial library on Peter the Great and Petrine Russia, I avoid reading beyond Elizabeth and Peter III's life. No books chronicling later reigns. No Catherinian biographies. Many evenings Aunt Roberta and I curl up in front of the fireplace well past midnight, having long conversations about the larger-than-life Peter the First's influence, not to mention his female successors up through Elizabeth.

Occasionally my aunt jots notes on what I recount. "I know your experiences will never constitute a legitimate source for my work. I just don't want to forget anything," she smiles. "That reminds me, did *you* write all this down? Keep some sort of journal?"

"I started to. I believed, though, that it was too dangerous. What if someone had read it? And now," I throw up my hands helplessly, "I can't seem to get far."

"Not far with me either," she says quietly.

"I'm sorry. Truly I am. I enjoy being able to have someone to talk to who knows so much about the past I lived. I just can't."

I've related much about my life, clothing, social activities, court life, meals, and especially Igor. My computer searches for Anya, Tatiana, and of course Igor Blukhov yielded nothing; I suspect a trip to the Russian State archives might. We've paged through books depicting period costumes. I've had my aunt in stitches describing the flotilla of gentlemen forced to humor Empress Elizabeth by squeezing into wide-berth female gowns amplified by bustles and hoops. "They crash into one another so much they resemble off keel cargo ships sinking in a too-narrow river. Catherine loves reverse gender parties, too, since the slimmer and younger women aren't the least bit embarrassed about dressing as gallant noblemen."

We also laugh about my struggles with the lack of menstrual products, not to mention underwear. "Honestly, I think the best thing about being in *our* time is the lack of stays, laces, corsets, wigs, thick stockings, shoes without left or right, starchy cosmetics, and all manner of other constraints." I describe Elizabeth's and then Catherine's fondness for loose-fitting traditional garments, pointing them out in a book.

I find it surprising now to look back on some of the things I missed then—and the risks I took. "If I can get back," I tell her, "I'm going to find a way to smuggle painkillers, tampons, and antibiotics. And I need a dentist—and soon!"

"Peter the First famously yanked teeth from his soldiers' mouths with no regard for their health or pain. Was it the same with dentists then?"

"Oh, yes. I'm surprised that most of the older people—and I'm including my own age in that category—seemed unconcerned about their chipped or cracked teeth. Some have at least one totally black tooth."

"Still, I cannot help envying your chance to go back and live that history," she says wryly.

"I suppose you *might* like it, but there's still so much more to tell that I'm afraid it will take years."

"You don't want to discuss anything else about *her*, though, do you?" my aunt asks gently.

"No. I mean yes, I do, but . . ."

"Too many memories?"

"It's not that. I savor the memories. It's just that I don't want to know. What happens—or what happened—after I left."

"I would think that unnatural if I didn't suspect the reason."

I feel myself blush. "You know?"

"That your fondest dream is to return to the past?"

Silently sipping tea, I realize I might be crushing my aunt's feelings. "It is. I'm sorry, Aunt Bobbi. *If* I do . . . well, I don't want to arrive back knowing all about the bad or even the good things still to come."

It is Aunt Roberta's turn for silence as she clears the tray of half-eaten scones and cherry crumble. Her eyes fill with sympathy.

"You're still assuming there is a way to get back?"

"Right now I could not survive—emotionally, I mean—if I didn't believe that."

I make my way slowly to my room, and fruitlessly attempt sleep as my thoughts keep me examining and re-examining possible ways to return. And keep me worrying that after my disappearance Igor might find another woman, or that he might go to his grave bewildered and resentful of my leaving.

Tucking a second pillow against my back, I pretend Igor is lying with me. That I can smell his scent on my own pillow.

I know all too well, though, that he is gone. Lost in the past. Dead whichever way you look at it. How many more nights and months and years here in the present will I mourn him?

It is the conversation about the lack of underwear, sanitary pads, tampons, and ibuprofen for cramps that bothers me much later that evening. I realize something odd: I've not had a flux, as we called it back then, since I arrived. I've read that international travel can interfere with menstrual periods, but *time travel*?

I have only one night to ponder the possibility before I start vomiting the next morning. Counting back, I cannot remember having a period since quite a few weeks before I "left."

Is it possible? Could I be carrying Igor's baby?

Thankfully, Aunt Roberta has no morning classes, and I find her pounding the computer keys with two cups of cold coffee precariously close to the keyboard.

Sensing me there, she stops typing. I must look as strange as I feel, wrapped in a robe, hair standing in sleep spikes, face registering a conglomeration of feelings: terror, surprise, fear, joy.

"What is it?" she asks quietly.

Immediately I start crying, and she wraps her arms around me. "Maria, what is it? What happened? Did you have a bad dream? Are you okay?"

She settles me onto a chair and kneels beside me, producing a tissue.

I cannot answer, my throat filled with something scratchy. And large as a peach pit.

"Should I call someone?"

"No. no. It's just that . . ." At last I manage to get the words out: "I believe I'm pregnant. I'm having Igor's child!"

Stunned for only a moment, Aunt Roberta then wraps me in her arms. "Congratulations, my child."

Congratulations. Of course. This is a happy event. Or it would be if I weren't alone without the man who wanted this child so badly. The husband I most likely will never see again.

If the sound of a heart breaking is audible, I hear it: a rugged snap, and then brittle shards piercing me with a hurt more excruciating than the physical pain that will undoubtedly accompany childbirth.

I cry the entire day.

CHAPTER 16

(CATHERINE) 1763

"Like an actress who finally manages to get the leading part she has always dreamed of, she developed almost overnight a dazzling authority, wit and eloquence, and a graciousness at once smiling and distant— for she was still at the stage of playing at being empress."
—Zoe Oldenburg

The messenger stumbled over the wording of the letter, quaking at the woman dressed in heavy brocade seated at her writing desk. "It is certain," he began reading, "that the reign of the Empress Catherine the Second, like that of the emperor her husband, will make only a brief appearance in the history of the world."

Rather than react to these sentiments with a litany of swear words, Catherine waved her hand, as if dismissing both him and the entire idea. She bent back over her correspondence. The comments had been intercepted by her spies. She would not deign to confront the author, Prussian Envoy Solms.

It was a year of reorganization. No one was unaware of his or her schedules and responsibilities. She'd assigned each member of her personal cabinet certain times and days of the week and established a workday schedule she would try to adhere to for her entire reign. "I rise regularly at five or six," she wrote to Stanislaus. "I read and write all alone until eight, at which time I listen to business and meet with anyone awaiting an audience until eleven in the morning."

She continued to be frustrated that not everyone worked as hard as she, or at least not hard enough to deal with all the administrative duties that must be accomplished. Neither oral nor written orders were followed on schedule, and her frustration led her to compile a list of one hundred forty-eight personal instructions. She followed that up by dictating that henceforth the Russian Senate's workday should be extended until they had cleared up the backlog.

Her own routine she followed steadfastly, varying it only to attend Mass on Sundays and feast days. All afternoon she listened to petitioners and then took early dinner.

Ivan Betskoy usually arrived in her chambers shortly thereafter to read to her until nearly six p.m., when she might attend a play or theatrical performance before an occasional late supper.

In addition to overseeing the regalia and ceremonial aspects of her coronation, Betskoy now served as an unofficial minister of education, overseer of the Diamond Workshop and gem mining, and founding president of the Imperial

Academy of Arts. Years ago he had been her own mother's paramour, and years after that played an instrumental role in Catherine's coup. She felt comfortable enough with him that he was welcome on a daily basis.

When Grigory complained that her routine required retiring by ten—eleven at the latest—she informed him, "I am ruled like manuscript paper now. You must understand, my love, that the kingdom must come before our dalliances."

"I consider making love to you to be more important than the kingdom," he said petulantly.

"Then you never should have helped to put me on the throne," she replied, half jesting.

Grigory left then, often to play cards in his own chambers situated directly overhead and linked by a hidden staircase. Other times she welcomed him into her bed, making it clear their lovemaking must be brief if she were to get up before dawn.

Alas for her, he knew all the special places to touch her and ways to satisfy her that left her yearning for more of him. She would sacrifice some sleep for lust. Nonetheless, she would not permit her desires to keep her asleep even one minute past six a.m.

"You are never idle, Your Most Gracious Majesty," Count Panin observed while updating her on the latest situation with Denmark. In addition to maintaining his title of Grand Master of Grand Duke Paul's Court, he had been appointed senior member of the College of Foreign Affairs. For all intents and purposes, she'd given him the responsibilities of a chancellor without the title.

In fact, she saw herself as both empress and chancellor,

allowing the existing Chancellor Mikhail Vorontsov's responsibilities to dwindle until they were non-existent. She resolved no one would ever hold that title again.

In addition to serving as her own minister of war and foreign affairs, she functioned as Russia's minister of finance and of the homeland. Her other ministers carried out her orders faithfully and, if asked, offered advice. In short, she legislated alone.

She and Panin, like she and Betskoy, had an unusual, co-dependent relationship. It was still early in her reign, and she knew Panin's support was paramount—especially since he had insisted right up to the coup that it was Paul who should rule with his mother as regent. His power and contacts easily could have led him into a role centered around her opposition, thus making him a formidable enemy.

Instead, he frequently took advantage of their close working relationship by attempting to best her. "Kings, kings," he hemmed and hawed on more than one occasion. "They are a necessary evil which one can do without."

When she strode up and down the room railing about this or that minister or agency, he cut in, "What are you complaining about? If everyone were perfect or capable of being perfect, we would not need you kings."

"*Touché*," Catherine laughed, all the time keeping him at her right hand where she knew they would work well together.

Bestuzhev retired that year due to old age and weariness. Her former mentor and conspirator could no longer finish sentences or thoughts, any more than he could prevent most of the liquor aimed at his mouth from dribbling down his clothing.

As far as she was concerned, with one mentor rewarded and one gone, her major debts had been paid.

Now she could concentrate on plans to establish a Medical College, not to mention overhaul the health care and education systems. When her son Paul had been so ill in Moscow, she'd vowed to build a hospital in his name. She met this commitment when Paul's Hospital opened in Moscow's outskirts.

She had plenty of other plans for health reform. By her thirty-fifth birthday, she planned to officially open a foundling home that would double as a place for unwed, destitute mothers to receive prenatal care and safely deliver their babies. She also persisted with plans for a boarding school where young ladies could get a solid education.

Weeks and months whirled by, with Catherine having her hands in every pie.

When news arrived that King Augustus III of Poland had died, she leaped from her chair.

"Your Imperial Majesty," Panin said dryly, after hearing of her reaction. "Such exuberance would seem hardly appropriate, even for Herself."

"Don't blame me for jumping out of my chair. I hear that King Frederick of Prussia jumped from his table!"

"With all due respect, Your Gracious Sovereign, he whom they already refer to as 'the Great' can escape notice. Perhaps in part due to his gender."

"Nonsense! This is my opportunity to keep another promise: to put Stanislaus Poniatowski on the Polish throne."

It was a calculated response to the succession of the Polish principality, and Panin knew it well. He often vexed her intentionally, and here, Catherine recognized, was his opportunity to express his own dissatisfaction for losing the chance to crown her son Paul.

Anticipating this reaction, she was nonetheless angry at the open challenge to her right to rule. She spoke loudly enough so all in the immediate area could hear: "Our own Great, Peter the First and emperor of all the Russias, was also foresighted and wise enough a half century ago to permit the current sovereign to appoint his—or her—successor. The fact that this resulted in some poor statesmanship on the part of a few of his heirs has absolutely nothing to do with whether they wore breeches! In fact, I've decided to commission a statue befitting our great predecessor and to assign such a critical task to someone highly recommended by our friend Monsieur Denis Diderot. That will be all," she added abruptly.

She did not summon Panin for nearly a week lest he ever again think it appropriate to insult her gender.

Fearing that she might resume her former relationship with Stanislaus, a number of advisors approached her more warily thereafter.

She had no intention of recalling Stanislaus to court, let alone to her bed. Grigory, her current (and third) lover, continued to fulfill the thirst for affection that she needed quenched.

Yet the two argued.

One night after a longer than usual billiards game, they retired to her chambers. Catherine, overtired and a bit cranky at losing, expressed a touch of impatience with their lovemaking.

Grigory playfully bit too hard on one of her nipples.

"That hurts!" she chided. "Do it more gently or such inflicted pain might be a hanging offense—regardless of you being the most handsome man in Russia."

She'd uttered and meant the words lightly, though Grigory ceased his ministrations and stared at her motionlessly. He might have transformed into one of the palace's marble statues. However, his beautiful eyes flashed anger. Then—simultaneously fire and ice—he came to life and abruptly began pacing the room.

It took her a moment before she recalled an incident just before her coronation. It had occurred at an intimate dinner party before she departed for Moscow.

Minutes after dessert, conversation inevitably had turned to the recent coup. Beside her, Grigory had reached over and placed his hand on hers. "The guard regiments follow me as easily as baby ducklings follow their mother," he'd boasted. "Our dearest Little Mother knows that it was because of me that she took the throne so easily."

Catherine had frowned. She must admit the coup had turned out less dangerous or challenging than she herself had predicted, and yes, Grigory and his brothers had been paid handsomely for their essential role. Others had served her equally well, and it was a contingent of allies and the people's love for her that had facilitated her accession. She did not think it prudent for her lover to brag about his role.

Rather than leave it at that, Orlov continued: "Not only did I raise her atop that glorious throne with so little trouble, I surmise that I could lift her down just as easily. Let's say in no more than a month."

Catherine froze. Everyone at the table did.

Before she could rise from her chair and shower him with verbal abuse and warnings, Kyril Razumovsky boldly interrupted her with a raised hand.

"Monsieur Orlov, perhaps you are correct in your assessment of your own powers." He forced his lips into an icy smile before his equally cold voice rang out louder. "What you don't seem to realize is that before the month ended, your neck would be in a noose."

Every guest, including Catherine, remained silent. Yet her blue eyes flashed and her lips hinted at the glimpse of an almost triumphant smile.

Too shocked to respond, Grigory begged leave of their company and retreated to lick his wounds. This had been more than a chastisement; it was a threat that served to remind those present that the woman who sat on the throne was a force with whom to be reckoned now. She'd attained a powerful following on her own, and the part that Grigory and others had played in this drama was essentially over outside of the bedroom.

In that same bedroom so many months later, she recalled that particular rebuke and the reference she'd just made to hanging. "I didn't mean it!" she assured him.

Grigory, however, retrieved his boots and stomped out of her chambers.

Although they reconciled the next day, she made a mental note never to mention the gallows in his presence again.

After such arguments she would feel a strand of loneliness, though her life had become more than she could have dreamed of—with or without a circle of people she could trust.

Occasionally she still experienced a passing regret at the absence of her former lady Maria Blukhova, who, in addition to her other duties overseeing the royal jewels, used to read to her when she was busy with something else or her overworked eyes needed a rest. If only her loyal friend would return from Italy.

Meanwhile, she had Grigory, who, if not capable of carrying on the kind of witty debate and philosophies she could with her pen pals abroad, at least loved her unconditionally.

CHAPTER 17

(MARIA) 2018

My obstetrician tells me the pregnancy is going well. My body resembles a water-filled balloon, though, and I don't think I can stand one more day of this.

It occurs to me now that the flutter I imagined in my belly while returning to the present might have had more to do with my baby than time travel. As near as my doctor can estimate, the baby (a boy, the ultrasound reveals), is due in the spring.

Since I remain unemployed, my aunt has been stuck with all the medical bills. This month, however, I have been able to buy a policy through something called the Affordable Health Care Act that will cover me and my child.

I am paying for it by taking on research, typing, and other miscellaneous duties ranging from pet-sitting to plant tending for my aunt's colleagues. I feel guilty about not getting a full-time job, yet Aunt Roberta has encouraged me to "stay off the radar."

"Too many questions could come up, and so far you have no current identity papers."

"I have a passport."

"True, but no driver's license, not to mention no legitimate job experience to list as a reference."

Thus, in between dealing with the frustratingly uncomfortable swelling of my body and all its extremities, Aunt Roberta and I also stay busy trying to re-establish my identity and that of my unborn son. At the same time, I desire to get rid of the Meekhof name that could draw unwanted attention.

My requests for a name change without record of a marriage have made this a challenge, and we end up in front of a series of judges. Only the last one buys my flimsy story about getting married overseas to a husband who abandoned me and absconded with all the paperwork.

"So now you are officially Maria Blukhova, minus the patronymic of Sergeievna you would've had in Russia," Aunt Roberta says proudly. "I never expected to have a Russian niece."

"Well, for eighteen years I never expected to have an American aunt again!"

"We still have the social security problem," she reminds me. Using my old number for most purposes would not be a problem except for one thing: I intend to apply for a new passport and then a Russian visa to re-enter that country.

Our hope is that my visa application with the new name will get processed carelessly amidst thousands of others, and that no one from the Russian Consulate in the U.S. will connect me with Maria Meekhof. Yes, I will have to tell a few lies when the time comes, such as changing my parents' last names, omitting my marital status, and altering information on my baby's father so that I can "pass" the lengthy and stringent visa application process. We decide that from now on I should indicate that I'm single rather than divorced or widowed to avoid having to produce a marriage license, divorce decree, or death certificate.

"There is good and bad news," Aunt Roberta announces right around the time the baby is due. "The U.S. Embassy in St. Petersburg has been ordered shut down effective the end of this month."

I'm relieved, and don't worry that our two countries are now in what my aunt calls "another inevitable phase" of poor relations. At least if anything happens to get me in trouble when I go there, I won't be hauled in front of the same embassy people who questioned me after I appeared in the Hermitage hugging a priceless sculpture.

It's also exciting that the Russian Federation's consulate now issues entrance visas good for three years rather than one visit, like the one my aunt has stamped in her passport. My plan is initially to visit on my own, confirm the location of the statue, and develop a solid strategy for bringing my son with me when I attempt to return at a future date. There is absolutely no way to predict whether holding a baby in my arms will ensure we both go back. Right now I confess to being more fixated on Igor than the unknown child in my womb.

Gradually I open up to my aunt about not only my own life, but Catherine's. And despite Aunt Roberta's studies and an academic specialty that guarantees she knows much more than I do about the empress's reign, she promises not to reveal anything that might influence me "if you succeed in your venture back."

One winter afternoon I am shivering on the living room couch despite being wrapped in a fluffy robe and blanket. As my aunt stirs the fire and then checks the temperature, I observe, "Her Imperial Highness ordered a thermometer hung in every room and one outside each window. The servants were constantly breaking the glass, so there were always replacements. Once she told me that if she were in charge, she would buy up the entire factory in Tula and order improvements in how they were made."

"She probably did do so," my aunt said, carrying teacups to the table. "She also was—or will be," she corrected herself for my sake, "a great proponent of something unknown back then: free trade."

"Meaning?"

"Meaning one of the first decrees she issued—or will issue—in her reign is that anyone will be free to establish his own manufactory. She also will break up most of the big monopolies. Under Catherine the Second there will be an explosion in everything: agriculture, furs, shipbuilding, textiles, linens, foreign exports, you name it."

"I'm not surprised. She spent a lot of time writing down

her plans, especially when she'd been reading Montesquieu."

"I think I recall she even gave instructions for sheep- and horse-breeding, crop rotation, potato planting, and beekeeping, of all things."

"Good. The Russian diet back then needs potatoes."

Stirring my tea reminds me of something else. "Catherine always insisted Russian tea was superior to Chinese tea. She told me that when it's imported, the long sea journey weakens the flavor."

"You shall not tell her about this then," Aunt Roberta smiles.

"It wouldn't matter much. She is—was—an inveterate coffee drinker. She put so many spoons of ground coffee in her cup each morning that the servants would reuse them after clearing her cups away."

"Perhaps that's where she got so much of her energy—a perpetual caffeine high."

"Speaking of Catherine, I miss keeping my hands constantly busy the way she and all her ladies did before she had an empire to run."

"So how did you occupy your hands?"

"Mainly by knotting." I explain the process of utilizing silk or linen thread and a small instrument called a shuttle. "We knotted the thread into shapes to decorate everything from our gowns to reticules. Purses, I mean. It was a favorite pastime that even I liked, and you might remember my aversion to sewing."

That reminded me of the months I'd spent banished to the sewing atelier by Empress Elizabeth, which seemed to interest my aunt.

"Why were you demoted?"

"Because Her Imperial Majesty Elizabeth Petrovna didn't like my choice of husband. She had selected someone else for me, which was how it was usually done. Catherine interceded on my behalf, although it didn't sway the empress. Eventually I lied and claimed I was pregnant and already secretly married to Igor, which I was."

"And how did you get away with that?" I see her suppress a laugh. Of course, there was nothing funny about my situation at the time.

"Pillows," I confess in response to her question, patting my now genuinely sizable belly. "Then I faked a miscarriage. Igor stole me away one New Year's Eve, and by then the empress was too ill to notice or care."

"From what you've told me, it sounds as if it was Elizabeth and not Catherine who was the least likable."

"Absolutely. They could both be soft-hearted. Catherine, though, was not the one who was cruel."

"One of my mentors used to claim Catherine the Second had a heart of iron."

"Not when I knew her. If she became so, it would be because she was forced to forge a strong heart. She certainly had it trampled enough times up to her early thirties." Gradually I have started to relate some of the horrible wrongs done to Catherine by Elizabeth and Peter.

"You've led a much more interesting life in the past than you might have in the present," Aunt Roberta observes.

"I've thought a lot about how my life would've turned out staying here—if all of this hadn't happened. I just cannot fathom it."

"College, of course, though as I recall you had no idea what your major would be."

"I still don't know. Certainly nothing in the sciences."

"And I'm guessing not history or business."

"Nope. And maybe I'd already have a few kids. Marry someone else, though? I don't see how I could've loved anyone more than I love Igor." I shift uncomfortably, my belly always in the way.

Aunt Roberta pours more tea. "I envy you that kind of love. It's never happened for me."

"It still could," I assure her. She only looks distant and then gazes down at me affectionately.

"At least I have a daughter. And soon a grandson!" *At least for now*, I can almost hear her thinking.

"Enough of the cookies or you'll give birth to a thirteen-pound boy," she jokes, whisking the tray away. "Now, let's hoist you off that couch so you can take your nap."

"Wow! I thought the court ladies had a lot of rules and regulations," I laugh.

"Such as?"

"Oh, lots of silly stuff. Everyone had an opinion about what might harm the unborn child. Not funny, really. I watched Catherine suffer through all the nonsense during two pregnancies. She wasn't permitted to wear a necklace, for example, because people believed it would strangle the baby while it grew inside her."

"I suppose those were what we call old wives' tales."

"Definitely. She wasn't permitted salt on her food lest it lead to a child born without fingernails. She couldn't cry, because her baby might be permanently sad. For some odd reason they claimed all her reading would affect the child's well-being. Speaking of books, Aunt Bobbi," I say as she helps me to bed, "could you bring the one I left in the living room? I'm afraid I may never get myself back up."

As the pregnancy grows more uncomfortable, I decide the absolute best thing about the present besides flush toilets is that I'm free of those corsets and stays that should more appropriately be called torture devices. I cannot forget how all the layers of garments itched and stung. I am also released from the silk stockings that felt so hot and miserable in Russian summers.

So now I lounge around in maternity sweatpants and billowing blouses. I laugh imagining what Anya, Tatiana, Catherine, and all the ladies of the court would think if they could see me now.

And Igor? I'd like to believe he won't care how I dress if I return. This is when I must shove aside my deepest fears. Will he still want me? Will he be furious? And worst of all, will he have found someone else to take my place in his heart and in his bed?

On Saturdays I carefully walk the two blocks to a community center for my jewelry-making class. The instructor, Mr. Haaksma, believes I am a genius, and suggests I find a position in his field after the baby is born. He may be right about the job. I do not want to continue living off my aunt.

I love the class, though we work with rhinestones rather than real gemstones. And here no one seems to recognize or recall Maria Meekhof, so I blend in inconspicuously. Right now we are making a pair of earrings, and I wonder what Mr. Haaksma would think if I dared show him the peridot dragonfly pair in which I arrived, now secreted in my bedroom.

My university enrollment also is under Meekhof. Aunt Roberta has found a way to get me free tuition as part of her faculty benefits despite my non-traditional age. Geology 101 has not been a huge challenge, although I dislike the unfamiliar concept of hybrid courses. I don't really mind the online portion, since sometimes during face-to-face sessions I imagine my professor looking at me oddly. Of course, my aunt's colleagues know something about my disappearance, so I'm grateful for blending in amidst nearly forty thousand students plus faculty.

I soak up the fascinating material thirstily, struggling to memorize everything so that I can share it all with Igor– assuming he and I are ever together again.

No, *when* we are together. It must happen. I refuse to remain in the present if there is any chance in this universe for me to return to the past.

CHAPTER 18

(CATHERINE) 1764

In Riga, the city where she and her mother had overnighted enroute to Russia over twenty years ago, Catherine found herself much more welcome as an empress than she'd been as a Prussian princess. Thousands of flower petals littered Latvian roads, and to ensure she had the best of everything, the Baltic aristocracy bent over backwards—in some cases literally. At one point she was aghast when volunteer runners harnessed themselves to her six-seater carriage, keeping up a valiant human pace.

She spent her early days in the Baltic provinces inspecting

fleets and dockyards, making avid trade plans, and meeting with foreign ambassadors. Brimming with enthusiasm, she was in her element.

And then it all crashed.

A series of urgent messages arrived from Panin, on whom she depended to oversee those responsible for guarding Prisoner Number One. The first letter astounded her.

"Dead? Are you certain?" she pressed the messenger in disbelief.

Perhaps because no one was supposed to acknowledge the prisoner's existence or because he had no knowledge of the letter's content, the man who delivered the stunning news hung his head, unable or unwilling to answer.

Ivan VI, or Ivan Ivanovich, was no more. She'd tried to make him slightly more comfortable in the one-room prison where he had remained at the Schlüsselburg Fortress since his imprisonment by Elizabeth over two decades ago when he was an infant tsar. Apparently, however, he'd been assassinated by his own guards. It happened when they'd been confronted by a fellow guard attempting to liberate the potential heir to the throne.

Both she and her predecessor Elizabeth had made it plain to the two men in charge that, should any attempt ever be made to free Prisoner Number One, they should dispose of him immediately rather than let him be taken. The instructions could not have been clearer: "The prisoner shall not be allowed to fall alive into the hands of any rescuers."

The two men literally forced to give up their own freedom and prevented from leaving their post for a full six years had taken their instructions seriously. They'd thrust their swords eight times through the twenty-four-year-old man who had never seen daylight, could barely communicate, and may or may not have been insane rather than simply uneducated and unsocialized.

Indisputably, the young man had created a shadow on her reign: a dark and formidable one, whose continued existence had terrified the former Empress Elizabeth who'd overthrown the toddler and his mother.

Catherine, too, suffered worry mingled with guilt over his long-term solitary existence. Two conspiracies to put him on her own throne had been thwarted earlier in her reign, preventing her from more than idly considering easing the restrictions on him. Yet she had maintained kindhearted intentions.

At first Catherine dismissed Panin's account of the confession of a somewhat odd second lieutenant from the Smolensky regiment. His name was Mirovich, and he swore he'd acted alone in a one-man conspiracy to free Ivan and replace her.

The issue would not, of course, go away, and after a week she told her secretary, "I am hastening to Petersburg to terminate this affair and to put an end to all foolish rumors."

Upon her return, she ordered a full investigation and the arrest of fifty guardsmen at the garrison; however, as the detailed trial dragged on, no new evidence of more than one plotter surfaced.

Her reluctance to sanction torture manifested itself at Mirovich's trial, as it had in the past and would continue in the future. "This is not to be tolerated," she wrote in one memorandum claiming torture was unavoidable in special cases. She then scribbled, "When humanity suffers, there are no special cases!"

In the end, the lengthy trial in which she refused to intervene concluded with the inevitable: she reluctantly signed Mirovich's death warrant.

Now she must find a way to live with herself regardless of her innocence. Just as when her husband had been murdered, plenty of discontents—particularly in Europe—believed her to have been Mirovich's accomplice in some manner, and the moral respect she had worked so hard to earn faltered. Even her friend and correspondent, the great Voltaire, wrote, "I think in this Catherine has provided the playwrights with a subject for a great tragedy."

Torn between angst at the brutal death of the innocent Ivan VI and relief that his potential legitimate claim to her throne had been removed, she tried her best to ignore Voltaire's words and not to ponder what had happened.

Her practical mind simply would not let her dwell on the past when she faced so much work in the kingdom. She had put in a great deal of thought before appointing Prince Alexander Vyazemsky as the new procurator general of the senate. The prince had proved his mettle in many ways, including quelling an outbreak of labor unrest amongst miners in the Ural Mountains. To him she astutely summed up the current state of the senate's situation: "Each of two bodies will now try to get you on their side . . . You will find honest people of limited intelligence, as well as those who harbor much more long-range plans. It has often taken it upon itself to issue laws, grant ranks, honors, money, and lands, and having exceeded its limits for so long, this senate now finds it difficult to adapt itself to the new order within which it must confine itself."

She also wrote him a letter early in his tenure: "If I see that you are loyal, hard-working, open, and sincere, you can be assured of my unbounded confidence. Above all I love the truth, and you must feel free to say it, without fear; you can argue with me without danger . . . you will find that an honest man thrives in court. Furthermore, I do not require flattery from you, only sincerity and a firm attitude toward business."

Prince Vyazemsky understood exactly what she wanted. He not only served faithfully as her go-between, he would remain Catherine's eyes and ears in this split body that had become all too accustomed during previous reigns to doing little to nothing.

She also made time to pay a personal visit to the man she most admired in Russia: Mikhail Lomonosov, patronized during both Peter I's and Elizabeth's reigns for his brilliance.

Lomonosov, cofounder of Moscow State University at Elizabeth's behest, excelled in and advocated strongly for the Enlightenment ideas Catherine also promoted. Both believed that a wise and benevolent ruler could ensure the well-being of his or her subjects by following the dictates of reason.

Dressed in a white gown and all white furs, she arranged herself eagerly in his rooms brimming with bookcases, globes, and telescopes. In the next chamber, beakers and scientific equipment crowded the shelves and tables. She peered in with interest. If Lomonosov, known for being somewhat narcissistic and condescending, was aware of what an honor and a rarity such a visit was, he did not acknowledge it when she arrived.

Catherine, justly as proud of her own accomplishments, dismissed his vanity as rightfully earned. "You are a true polymath!" she pronounced, leaning forward. Her eyes sparkled with excitement.

Rather than blush at such praise of his multifaceted genius, he replied in a rare moment of modesty, "to label me as such, Your Gracious Imperial Majesty, would equate me with our great Renaissance predecessors. Men like da Vinci and Newton. I merely do what I must."

If he suspected he sat across the table from a woman who might deserve such an appellation in her own right, he did not mention it. Catherine would never know whether the great man considered his new empress in his own league. He *had* written glowing elegies and panegyrics to both Peter the Great and his daughter Elizabeth.

They spent the entire afternoon immersed in topics that included chemistry, which he taught at the Academy of Science, and mineralogy, a subject in which she took an avid interest.

"One of my ambitions," she said enthusiastically, "includes founding a School of Mines."

"Did you know, Your Gracious Majesty, that there is already a plan in place to open such an academy in Freiburg?"

She drummed her fingers on his table. "Frederick outpaces us once again. Well, then we must hasten our own plans."

Lomonosov, eager to show off his inventions, found a willing audience in his monarch, who listened avidly as the conversation then roamed to poetry. "Despite all my scientific accomplishments," he admitted, "it is my poetic work for which I expect to be known forever."

From there they spoke of philology, the arts of mosaics and glassblowing, ground-breaking theories about the formation of icebergs, and the freezing properties of mercury.

"And I have made substantial progress in my observatory," Lomonosov said proudly. "Only three years ago, with the aid of the new reflecting telescope I designed, I observed the transit of Venus and recorded its likely atmosphere. I tried to bring this discovery to Her Imperial Majesty Elizabeth Petrovna. Alas, she was ill and totally uninterested." He unsuccessfully attempted to hide the bitterness in his voice.

"Rest assured, Mikhail Vasilyevich Lomonosov, that this will not be an impediment during my reign. In fact, we insist you send us regular reports on whatever discoveries and experiments you believe are worthy."

"I am pleased to hear this, especially since another transit of Venus—the last for perhaps two centuries—shall occur in a few more years."

Standing now, conscious of the small contingent of courtiers who accompanied her, Lomonosov bowed. "Your Gracious Sovereign is most welcome to my knowledge, such as might interest you."

Before she took her leave, she promised, "We shall send Count Grigory Orlov to call upon you, if he has not already done so. As an avid amateur astronomer, he will be most interested in your observatory."

Only after she had left did she recall she'd meant to ask him about the marvelous comet that had appeared during her girlhood journey to Russia. Each night she'd watched in fascination as it brightened the sky, eventually sending six tails fanning upward until it resembled a massive peacock of light.

Had it been an anomaly of astronomy or a portent of her future, as she so often surmised? She shrugged, convinced it was the latter. Nevertheless, she resolved to obtain a scientific explanation.

CHAPTER 19

(MARIA) LATE 2018-2019

Alexander Igorevich Blukhov took his first steps last week. Already he delights in reaching for the couch and pulling himself up, then stumbling into my waiting arms.

Everyone in jewelry-making class seems amazed when I relate that he's succeeded in walking on his own at eight months. Secretly I believe he's inherited his father's persistence.

Part of my joy—and more than a little relief—stems from the presumption that the sooner my son walks, the sooner we can attempt to travel to the past without me carrying him conspicuously through the Hermitage.

We call him Sasha—a nickname for Alexander. I've shortened his middle name to Igor rather than Igorevich to avoid raised eyebrows at the Russian consulate when we apply for our visas.

"Where's my darling?" Aunt Roberta hurries into the room where his playpen resides beside my bed. I swear, she loves this child more than she does me. In fact, she arrives with another new rattle and a stuffed unicorn.

The baby has become a dominant part of both our lives. Sasha also takes my aunt's mind off the current political situation, which has driven her and most of her colleagues "to insanity," as she puts it.

I pay scant attention to U.S. politics, except to ponder that the divided nation to which I have returned reminds me somewhat of the six months of Peter III's reign. Then, too, opinions in Russia seemed evenly split: satisfied and enthusiastic or angry and worried.

My aunt admits she and her friends feel depressed. I cannot recall a national mood like this when I left in 1999; I may have been too young to care about politics. Presuming that the American Civil War was much worse, I'm confused as to how things became so politically divided.

"I would've assumed that what happened on September 11 should have brought the country together," I observe to my aunt. "I mean, I only read about it, of course—."

"You would think that, wouldn't you?" She frowns, massaging her forehead. She has been like this nearly once a week lately, her brow often furrowed with worry about everything from the environment and education to foreign policy and immigration.

Now she swoops Sasha into her arms and murmurs something to him in Russian.

"It seems odd," I note, "that Americans—and I hardly know if I can call myself one anymore—elected a liberal black president for two terms and then followed that up with a conservative TV host millionaire who seems to be loved by half of the population no matter how many mistakes he makes or laws and moral codes he breaks."

"He's an icon nowadays," my aunt muses, stroking Sasha's curly brown hair, so much like his father's. The baby seems to comfort her. "People would kiss his feet if they could reach him." As if to demonstrate she sucks on one of Sasha's sweet little toes.

When I share my comparison to Peter III, she offers an alternate way of viewing it. "Peter the Great inspired people that way, too, although *he* was in fact a great man. Nevertheless, half of the Russian people resented and detested him for all the changes he forced on the country. It pains me to make that comparison, though there really is more than one precedent for living in a nation that seems to be torn in half over its leadership. And then there's the Russian 'tsar,' Vladimir Putin . . ."

"Perhaps as powerful as Catherine was."

"Albeit not as benevolent," Aunt Roberta muses.

Staying uninvolved in politics away from home proves impractical, since I spend two days a week on Michigan State's campus. There lively and often heated arguments for and against immigration, the southern border wall, Black Lives Matter, and the #MeToo movement occur regularly when I study at the Student Union or International Center. A seemingly endless number of mass shootings, wildfires, hurricanes, and sex scandals also plague the nation and world. I'm uncertain how to compare the eighteenth to the twenty-first century.

After rapidly earning my high school GED during the pregnancy, I scheduled both summer and fall university classes around Aunt Roberta's teaching schedule, and this autumn signed up for advanced geology and art history. The latter was my aunt's idea, since we both know Catherine will at some point become an avid art collector.

Attempting to do homework with an infant and later a toddler on my hands proves more challenging than I imagined. I find myself rocking a crying Sasha in one arm and using my right hand to scroll through paintings on the computer in preparation for a quiz on the Dutch Masters.

"I'll take him," my aunt offers when I'm off to class or need both hands—not to mention some quiet—for homework. Most of the time, however, my ever-lactating breasts dominate life, so that even though I hire one of Aunt Roberta's teaching assistants to watch the baby when I'm in class, I cannot be gone long.

While breastfeeding, I listen to Russian language CDs. Just because I landed in the past fluent in the language, there are no guarantees the same thing will be true when I return. *If* I return.

Aunt Roberta also has started speaking Russian to both

me and Sasha. I pray my child will be with his father before he learns to speak too much English.

My aunt is dating someone. That shouldn't be a surprise. It's just that I don't recall her dating anyone while I was growing up. I'm happy for her. I find myself hoping he might be *the* one for her. If I manage to get back to the past with Sasha she will be alone again.

The man is an engineering professor named Thomas. "We serve on the same university committee," she explains over the wailing that indicates Sasha has another tooth coming.

"Sounds promising."

"He's just someone I have coffee with," she protests. "Nothing else. At my age there are few available men—or interesting ones."

He must be awfully interesting, because lately they've started going out for drinks and then dinner, and she arrives home later and later.

Between Sasha and my schoolwork, though, I pay little attention. It's a struggle to keep up with classes, especially History of Art.

"Not once has my professor mentioned a Russian artist," I complain.

"Alas, that's probably going to be the case no matter how many art classes you take," Aunt Roberta observes. "And don't forget Catherine will be buying art from all over the world, not necessarily from Russian artists. You'll have to study the Russians on your own. Remember when we went to the Pushkin Museum?"

I could scarcely forget. "Do you remember taking me to see the room with the portraits of the tsars and empresses? I didn't mention it then because it seemed so insignificant. Much later I recalled that when we left the museum, I felt a mysterious shiver down my spine.

Do you think it was a premonition? Is that the right word?" I ask.

"Or perhaps foreshadowing. There's another possibility, though."

"Well, I've exhausted all of them in the years I had to go over and over those final days before I, well, before I left."

"It's possible that you have some sort of susceptibility to time travel. After all, dozens of people must have handled that statue, and I doubt all of them now live in the eighteenth century. Or are running around the twenty-first, for that matter."

"I'm off to class," she announces, then sets her briefcase back on the couch and frowns thoughtfully. "There's another possibility, I suppose. For some inexplicable reason, you seem to have an almost supernatural link to Catherine. Her statue—or at least the mythological Minerva. Her court. Her painting. Maybe it's not just the sculpture, in other words."

"Maybe, since I cannot forget that my—or the other Maria's—parents were renowned sculptors in Elizabeth's court."

"I guess we don't have to figure out why, just maybe *how*."

"I'm so sick of trying to figure it out. I thought I'd come to grips with all this years ago. Now . . ."

OUT OF THE SHADOWS

Nevertheless, I tell her, "Maybe I'll go back to the portrait hall in the Pushkin Museum before I investigate the statue."

"Just be careful, okay? Don't get swept away again without it being your idea." She leans over and kisses both Sasha and me goodbye.

My trip to Russia is in the final planning stages. The first problem, though, is going to be finding a babysitter for Sasha, who I cannot believe I'm going to have to leave for so long. Aunt Roberta cannot be with him all the time. Still, I think if she had her way she'd cancel classes and devote all her time to her precious great nephew.

I've decided to go in spring before all the tourists pour into Petersburg, since my aunt tells me the main sites remain popular year-round with Russian visitors.

To my immense relief, two months after we apply, Sasha and I receive our Russian visas.

"Now we can go see your Papa," I whisper to him, gazing into those keen brown eyes that mirror Igor's.

Except for the day Sasha was born (blessedly after only four hours of labor), this is the happiest I've felt since arriving back in the present.

Chapter 20

(Catherine) 1765

"Glory lives, in our days, In the Empire of an Amazon . . ."
—Voltaire

Grigory paced back and forth in Catherine's sitting room, overflowing with enthusiasm for the new tasks she'd delegated him. One involved recruiting immigrants to farm the rich lands to the south. "I have placed advertisements in nearly every newspaper in every European country," he told her proudly.

"Including Prussia?"

"Especially Prussia. I must say, the terms are more than generous. I used your ideas and added some of my own," he said somewhat immodestly. "I've stressed the richness of the soil and offered an exemption from taxes for a number of years, depending on the arrivals' skills. I've also thrown in free seeds, livestock, and plows, at your request, my dearest."

"And a half year's free lodging?"

"As you wished, Your Imperial Majesty. And you would be thrilled at the response I'm getting."

Catherine didn't mind how much credit Grigory took for his efforts, as he seemed to thrive on coordinating the program, which already had resulted in caravans of covered wagons piled high with furniture retracing her own route from Prussia over twenty years ago. The thousands of new settlers cultivating the land would help feed Russia's growing population. She would have liked to award other lands to freed serfs despite the aristocrats protesting vehemently whenever she broached the subject. To avoid more conflicts, she reluctantly had excluded Jews from the immigration offer.

"I've invited craftsmen to come to our fine country to indulge their talents in porcelain and tapestry works, too," she told him now. "I'd like you to entice artists, writers, and scholars. There is no reason the arts should be confined to England, France, and Prussia. We need our own cadre of talented workmen and cultured artists and writers. Which is why," she added proudly, "I directed the purchase of two hundred twenty-five paintings last year. Even as we speak, Prince Golitsyn is accumulating many more in Paris—with our dear friend Diderot's assistance."

"Everyone's already talking about your designs for replacing old towns. I hope you don't wish to replace an old lover," he teased.

She laughed, grasping both his hands. "I could remodel him, too, could I not?"

He pretended to scowl, but by then she had turned back to her papers. Previously she'd drawn up a plan for revising the layout of all the towns that burned down—and already the constant fire threat had seen several places meet that fate. Each burned village or city, commencing with Tula, was to be redone in a somewhat Roman classical style rather than in their previous huddle of wooden buildings stacked higgledy piggledy. The creation of widened streets, brick or stone buildings, and formal squares also would diminish the risk of fire. She planned to order the creation of completely new towns, as well.

"I should summon some new jewelers, too," she mused. Jérémie Pauzié, her former court jeweler and creator of the magnificent coronation crown, had returned to Switzerland. She was still waiting for Igor Blukhov to present himself at court, with or without his wife Maria. "Will you check again on Blukhov soon?" she asked.

Grigory readily agreed, then began complaining about something else until she dismissed him. By this time their relationship had drifted into that of a married couple well out of the honeymoon phase, gradually morphing into a relationship peppered with minor disputes, occasional heated quarrels, and a modicum of boredom. Worst of all, she'd been forced to schedule their love-making time for one hour per day on certain days; Grigory had resigned himself to the fact that he would never be able to persuade her differently.

She admitted General Betskoy to her apartments, taking up her knotting or tapestry weaving while listening to him read from another of Diderot's newest journal issues. She planned to correspond once again with the French philosopher before dinner and wanted to refresh her memory on his recent salient points. Time permitting after neatly penning one of her usual ten- to twenty-page letters, she would make progress on a play she'd started. Her pen was never idle, so that at times her hands, head, and eyes ached simultaneously.

"Stop that!" she said without looking up when Betskoy waved his arm during a particularly interesting passage; this caused him to knock his wine goblet off the little glass table beside him, shattering both drinking vessel and table on the parquet.

"My apologies, Your Majesty," he stammered, then blithely continued reading while a servant rushed to clean the mess.

"Why do you keep doing that?" demanded Catherine. "I think you owe me about a dozen new tables and twice that many pieces of glassware."

"Yes, Your Imperial Majesty," he said, not looking up from the book.

They had the same conversation almost weekly, as Betskoy insisted her diminutive tables were insufficient in width for setting his own things down. Most of the tables cracked or split beneath his carelessness. The breakage was never billed to him. Catherine usually just sighed and ordered a new one.

During this hour with Betskoy, she permitted a court painter to sit unobtrusively in a corner and sketch her. She'd been unhappy with the last artist's portrait, which depicted her as an almost matronly and overweight woman with a high forehead, cold eyes, and a tight smile. She was more pragmatic than vain, though, well aware that successive pregnancies had thickened her waistline. Still, it seemed unfair to portray her in such a negative manner, and her pride in her appearance was bolstered regularly by compliments.

Her favorite portrait was one of the many that Vigilius Eriksen had done of her astride her stallion Brilliant after the coup. This equestrian portrait she had hung in Peterhof's throne room—the spot where her husband had abdicated. She'd ordered Eriksen to make several copies in alternate sizes and with different details so she could gift them to those she favored.

At times she feared she looked too masculine. On the other hand, she had often wished to possess the character and spirit of a man, as she tried to explain to Grigory. He didn't understand, and she doubted anyone else would either.

Now the mirror confirmed she was still an attractive if not ravishing woman with glittering blue eyes, straight white teeth, and a smile many described as "magical." Thus her countenance seldom worried her, although often when Grigory was gone to the chamber pot she examined her naked form for signs of aging. Evenings she traded her flowing daytime kaftan or the looser sarafan for an elaborate gown, then encouraged her maid to drape her in jewels.

Inevitably the jewelry recalled Maria Blukhova—her missing maid of honor—and she resolved to put more pressure on Grigory for answers. She had spoken to both Anya, her seamstress, and Tatiana, her senior maid of honor. Both had been close to Maria, and both had been sent to see Igor. Neither could get him to shed additional light on her disappearance.

Friends were hard to find in her position. Especially those she could trust. Already this year she'd lost one man who might've become her friend: the scientist and co-founder of

Moscow State University—Mikhail Lomonosov—who had died just before her thirty-sixth birthday. She mourned not only for the brilliant man who'd accomplished so much for the sciences and the arts, but for the polymath whose future had showed so much promise of accomplishing more. She would never forget him, nor the ideas they had discussed only the previous year.

With another sigh, she continued her knotting, forcing herself to concentrate on what she would write in her next letter to Voltaire and perhaps in another letter to fellow Enlightenment correspondent Denis Diderot, whose entire library she had recently acquired in order to help him out financially. At least the two of *them*, as well as others in their circle, showered her with compliments and praise for her accomplishments and her intellect.

It was her heart that was sometimes in need of more.

As far as she could ascertain, her son wavered between mediocre and successful at his lessons. Rather than showing an affinity for physics, astronomy, history, languages, drawing, or geography, however, Paul's favorite subject appeared to be dancing. The previous year he had brought the house down with his performance in the ballet *Acis and Galatea*, dancing the role of the god Hymen.

By contrast, he did not always charm his tutors or the government officials to whom Panin introduced him. Often his behavior appeared to foreshadow the man he would become, such as the previous autumn when he (according to his mathematics tutor, Semyon Poroshin) had gotten cross with an entire audience at one of the French plays Paul favored. "They clap before me and without my permission," he whined throughout the performance. In his daily report, Poroshin claimed that Paul stormed back into his rooms complaining, "In the future I will send away those who applaud in my presence when I am not doing it. It is not as it should be."

Paul knew well by now the role the five Orlov brothers had played in wresting the throne from the man he believed to be his father. He remained just a little less than rude to Grigory, in particular. From time to time he also made surprising statements about how he himself would someday rule, going so far as to promise one minister that he would appoint him king of Poland in ten years.

Nor did Paul lounge around. He rushed to do everything at breakneck speed, whether eating, finishing his lessons, or getting up in the morning. He raced around the dance floor, charming the ladies with his jumps and whirls, at the same time annoying his mother and her sense of decorum.

Poroshin kept the empress updated, and worried. As he observed in a report, "His Highness has a fault common to all those who are used to seeing their desires satisfied more often than frustrated. They are impatient, and demand to be obeyed immediately."

At times Paul reminded Catherine too much of Peter III, whose inability to remain still and tendency to make petulant demands also had been among his many annoying characteristics.

In one sense he differed from the young Peter III, however: Paul took an inordinate interest in women, particularly the maids-of-honor. Something, Catherine mused, would have to be done about that soon—and before he made inappropriate choices.

He was not a handsome boy. After one of his innumerable illnesses right before he turned ten, the boy had emerged with somewhat twisted, distorted features. Gone was the fair-haired Paul with the natural good looks that so often came with childhood. Having lived with a disfigured husband, she found it ironic and scary, as if Peter himself had come back as a ghost in her son's form. Except this was not *his* son!

At least the grand duke's health seemed to have improved, and he reverted to his tendency to gobble his food like a wild animal and without chewing. In addition to indigestion, he still suffered from headaches, for which he designed a classification system so he could discuss them endlessly by location and severity.

She did try to see her son at least once a day. Yet her time was so filled that usually she was able to dismiss her worries about the heir to the throne. Fortunately, Paul seemed thus far to lack a vengeful nature. For now that had to be enough.

CHAPTER 21

(MARIA) SPRING 2019

I check into a hotel situated at the confluence of several St. Petersburg streets, dubbed the Five Corners. It's across from a train station, near the metro, and steps from trolley and bus stops that make getting around easy. Half smiling to myself, I realize I miss the carriages, sledges, horses, and troikas that once moved me place to place—albeit, of course, at a much slower pace.

As anxious as I am to visit the Hermitage, I decide to allow time first to reacclimate myself to the city and the sites

I loved as a teenage visitor and then as home for the bulk of my adult life.

One of my favorite places—then and now—is the Alexander Nevsky Monastery or Lavra, situated at the opposite end of Nevsky Prospekt from the Winter Palace. Two cemeteries flank the entrance, with English signs identifying the graves of the most prominent, many of the oldest with faded dates from the 1700s and 1800s. On Tchaikovsky's sculptural ensemble of an angel hefting a cross above him and another angel reading on his lap, someone hanged a tiny nutcracker in honor of his most well-loved ballet. I've tried to think of some way to return to the past carrying a CD of classical Russian music. It's doubtful. And how would I play it?

Having remastered the Cyrillic alphabet, I can read the names on the elaborate funerary art, some pieces larger than a refrigerator. The cemetery hugging the walls of the Church of St. Lazarus across the way is more hauntingly beautiful, with tight cobblestone rows of sarcophagi, obelisks, and columns coated with green mold. Most dates and certain letters have faded into time, unlike when I attended funerals or visited holy relics here with Catherine's court.

Neither my aunt nor my parents brought me to church or provided a religious education. Still, this place somehow *feels* spiritual, as if a calming presence has touched me. And of course, I spent eighteen years attending church almost daily!

I search in vain for Catherine's baby girl's resting place. Nor can I locate her husband Peter III's grave where I distinctly remember it was situated; I remind myself to ask Aunt Roberta what happened to it. As for the sarcophagi of the empresses and tsars in the Peter and Paul Fortress, I resolve to avoid them. I still don't know the year of Catherine's death. Don't want to know.

Just as I did as a teenager, I seek a bench beside gardens encircling Kazan Cathedral—where Catherine and Peter married. Although it was a lovely cathedral back then, subsequent emperors had ordered an incredible new version with impressive colonnades and a massive interior. From there I enjoy the flowers blooming in Catherine Square, between the Alexander Theatre and outdoor art market. I distinctly recall once wondering who exactly the magnificent figure represented and what earned her such greatness. Now I know. A flower vendor sells me a bouquet of zinnias and baby's breath, which I lay at the foot of the enormous statue whose chiseled countenance looks so much older than the empress I left. I feel comforted at this evidence of her longevity.

On the third day I visit the Admiralty's garden, situated almost on the Neva's bank and a five-minute walk from the Hermitage. I bring a lunch, settling on a bench beside a fountain that sparkles in harmony with the building's golden spires and gilded mythological statues. It is then, gazing up at the statues, that I become obsessed with one of my earlier fears: "my" statue might have been moved from the Hermitage to another palace—or worse yet, into storage! Tossing the rest of my sandwich to the voracious, spoiled pigeons swarming the pavement, I determine to make my way to the Hermitage this very moment.

It is late enough in the day that the long line has disappeared, and since it's too early in the season for the tourist hordes, I gain entrance easily. Still, I'm painfully aware of all the cameras, security, and women with suspicious eyes monitoring each room. I must do this carefully.

It takes a long time to locate the statues, as they seem to pop up in all kinds of locations. I know it *must* be the right one: only Minerva—and that exact Minerva—will do. Eventually I find my way to a huge grouping of classical Greco-Roman marble statues. Zeus, Aphrodite, Hera . . . At first, nothing.

And then I am there, standing in front of Minerva. She is still here!

There is no way to describe my relief. Aunt Roberta has warned me repeatedly that the Hermitage frequently moves *objets d'art* to various locations within the museum, then hauls out "new" items from its massive collection to replace the old. As Aunt Roberta had told me, "These then go into storage facilities and vaults with security equivalent to Fort Knox." I hadn't considered that possibility in months.

For a few seconds, I yearn to touch Minerva. No, of course I cannot. If she takes me back to the past now, I might regain my husband—but tragically lose my son.

Swiftly I hurry upstairs to the Russian rooms on the second floor. There must be no temptation to go back until both I and my son are here. Only a few of the sumptuous rooms look familiar. I realize not only did Catherine have the Winter Palace redecorated, so did her successors. Feeling nostalgic, I peer into glass cases filled with utensils, tools, jewelry, fans, toiletries, and hairpieces from the eighteenth century. Ornamented silver snuff boxes, boxes for sweets, salt cellars, and sugar bowls recall so many formal dinners. Above all, the jewelry looks familiar, particularly the metal bouquet holders we ladies were so fond of wearing on our gowns. These were hollowed out to hold tiny real flowers, or nosegays fashioned from precious stones. I see a piece that looks exactly like one my friend Tatiana wore and another that I distinctly recall Monsieur Pauzié fashioning for Grigory Orlov to give to Catherine as a birthday present. The gems inevitably remind me of Igor.

Yes, right here are the cameos. Sapphire and amethyst varieties dominate the cases, though, and I hold my breath while searching in vain for the emerald one Igor created. There is a separate exhibit in what is known as the Diamond Chamber or Room that contains jewelry art from previous centuries, and I berate myself for not making a reservation. Alas, I also know that the Russian Federation displays her coronation regalia in Moscow.

A strange feeling comes over me—one I can only describe as homesickness. This was my life from my teens well into my thirties. Yet I need and want Sasha, Igor, *and* Aunt Roberta in my life. If I dared draw attention to myself, I would sit down and cry right here.

To break up the long stroll back to the Five Corners Hotel, I stop at Dom Knigi—the House of Books. Uncertain I'm doing the right thing, I purchase a slim volume that traces all the tsars from Ivan IV through Nicholas II, including photographs and brief blurbs about their reigns. I doubt I would—or will—ever dare show it to Catherine. Perhaps Igor might want to read it and look at the paintings. I make sure to buy one wrapped in plastic so I don't succumb to the temptation to open it until someday when the time might be right. Fully aware of the danger of bringing it and the plastic wrapping with me to the past, I resolve to keep it well hidden.

In the second-floor pastry shop, I savor a raspberry tart and espresso. Overlooking Kazan Cathedral's massive colonnade, the windows also provide a view below of scurrying pedestrians and impatient drivers on Nevsky Prospekt—the Great Perspective Road in what I consider "my" time. So many of the young Russian women seem dressed right out of *Vogue*. In contrast to their stilettos, short leather skirts, and expertly applied cosmetics, an occasional babushka moves more slowly in her sensible shoes, plain dress, and flowered scarf. Even in a so-called republic, I observe, there is little class equity.

Sometimes I laugh aloud at the sight of pedestrians with their eyes glued down at their phones until they crash into one another like bumper cars. I observe the same thing on campus, of course, where one day a student splashed me when she flipped over into a fountain.

I doubt I'll miss some aspects of contemporary life, which often seems frenetic and befuddling. I've been forced to adapt to so many new technologies—Wi-Fi, Kindle, iPhones, Windows XP or whatever version is out, whiteboards, HDTV, PDFs, Wiki, and especially Zoom—that I find myself getting headaches the way Catherine did after heavy reading.

At the university, too, I feel befuddled at terms tossed out so casually by fellow students: Snapchat, Linked In, podcasts, apps, blogs, Facebook, iPods, Blu-ray, Hulu, iTunes, and Blackberry. Fortunately, they usually attribute my ignorance to "old age." The rest of my generation seems to have adapted fine, though, and I do admit to growing fond of my camera phone for taking endless great pictures of Sasha. I don't have a Twitter account. I do like clicking on YouTube.

Personally, I'm content at the moment just to get my international phone service to work so I can call Aunt Roberta and give her the wonderful news—and listen to Sasha's ever-evolving vocabulary. No matter how hard I try, though, I cannot get through, let alone master all the apps—or applications, as I have learned—on my smartphone. This proves nothing so much as that I am a dumb, technologically inept participant in the twenty-first century. Maybe not as heedless as the drenched student walking into the fountain. Just barely able to function.

I don't care one iota. I will be home soon, to get Sasha and attempt what may be the impossible: returning to Russia and then back to our *real* home.

CHAPTER 22

(CATHERINE) 1766

"Her poor relations with Paul fell like a shadow over these first splendid years on the throne, and the shadow was to lengthen with her reign."
—Vincent Cronin

I'm almost finished!' Catherine announced proudly when Nikita Panin attended her one morning.

"With which project, Your Imperial Majesty?" he asked dryly, as if expecting some new scheme to revolutionize anything from beet farming or military uniforms to the banking system or bridge construction.

"With the *Nakaz*, of course.

"The treatise you've been scribbling away on for over two years?"

"You know it's my book on legal principles for the empire."

"Will I get to read this proposed new code of law soon?"

She reached within her favorite leather portfolio case, appliqued with mythological symbols. Undoing the clasp, surmounted by a large Romanov eagle, she extracted a stack of manuscript papers and placed it in his hands. "Not only will you be privy to it, I'm expecting you to edit and critique it."

Rather than groan at one more enormous task assigned by his sovereign, Panin appeared flattered as he looked down at the pages in French. "Just me? I am honored!"

"Yes, almost. I'm translating the first few chapters into Russian so I can get Count Orlov's perspective, as well."

As Panin lifted a bushy eyebrow, she hastened to explain. "Those chapters provide an overview of the state of our nation, and his recent work for me makes him uniquely qualified to edit and review them.

"You, my friend, I rely upon to do what you must to edit and rewrite if necessary the rest of the twenty chapters. Plus, I want you to glance through the six hundred fifty-five articles by others I've consulted and sometimes excerpted. They deal with proposed state, civil, and criminal laws, and should strengthen my arguments."

Even Panin was impressed. "And the serfdom issue? Did you discern a solution?"

She sank down on the divan in her drawing room. "It appears here and there in the document, just not to my satisfaction. You know how I feel, Nikita: It is against justice and the Christian religion to make slaves out of men, who are born to be free."

"Perhaps then," he said, "you should cease gifting your supporters with serfs."

She took no offense. "The answer obviously is hidden within an impenetrable labyrinth, and I may never find my way out." She picked up her quill again and began her usual habit of jotting notes in the margins.

"I must finish this letter to Frederick the Second." she said briskly. "Ideas are like hares; they so often run away that you must catch them at once."

Panin, rather than taking the cue that he'd been dismissed, shifted the weight of paper in his arms. "Again, Your Imperial Majesty, I am flattered to be asked to participate in the creation of this tome. My only fear, if I might be so bold, is that it could lessen my time overseeing the young tsarevich's tutors."

"Take some time away from court if you must. You and Grigory could work at Gatchina, the palace I gave him outside the city, where you could be relatively undisturbed. There's no one and nothing surrounding it except gardens and woods. And I will personally oversee my son's tutors. It's well past time I become more involved in the tsarevich's studies."

She had already selected Paul's texts, including *Telemachus*, *Natural History*, Voltaire's *Philosophic Dictionary*, plays by Racine, and works by poets from around the world. The rest would be assigned by secondary tutors she had selected. Still, Tsarevich Paul Petrovich was a far cry from the scholar his mother was, and despite following his proscribed routine, he did so glumly or resentfully.

This was becoming a concern, as the short, scheduled times mother and son spent together gave her scant confidence in his intellectual or social development.

He did dine with her frequently and she made attempts to educate him in current events, albeit usually with a larger but more intimate group. Sadly, the conversation rarely included Paul due to its lively pace on political subjects that bounced around the table as sporadically and unpredictably as billiard balls for an unskilled player.

Paul Petrovich remained a sullen-faced boy who barely attempted to mask his resentment about just about everything, especially his mother. This did not appear to have anything to do with any perceived claim to the throne, only to the way he now believed Catherine's lover had contributed to Peter's demise. He continued to reserve most of his coldness for the Orlov brothers.

Often he seemed more morose than resentful, and at times Catherine was tempted to tell him the truth about his father. His real one, that is, and as her son aged she could not avoid noticing how much his receding brow and short, turned-up nose—almost like that of a Pekinese—resembled that of Sergei Saltykov rather than her husband and all the other straight-nosed Romanovs. Still, in so many other ways he resembled Peter the Third, his alleged father.

Regardless of his true parentage, she could not feel love for him. Perhaps in part due to guilt, she began to make a greater effort to confide in him about affairs of state. She also tutored him in politics, which she presumed he would someday require.

Nonetheless, he remained stiff and prim while she talked,

and occasionally shrugged or yawned. Nothing seemed to interest him. If she didn't know better, she would believe he really *was* her late husband's son.

This year, however, she had discovered two things that excited him. The first was the shipbuilding mania engendered by her planned journey down the Volga River the following summer. The second was the planning of a great medieval tournament (called a carousel) to be held in Palace Square just after Paul's Name Day. Here they would put to use the huge wooden amphitheater constructed by the semi-retired Italian architect Rastrelli, whose Baroque masterpieces Catherine did not particularly favor.

Mother and son anchored the spectacle at either end of the two-hundred-yard stadium, with enough space to host the "knights" and their elaborately dressed ladies, as well as their opponents, the "beasts" (men who appeared in the formidable costumes of lions, tigers, dragons, and bears). Innumerable squires paraded behind them, hoisting shields and other paraphernalia presumably required by Roman troops led by Grigory. With its elaborate groups of costumed representatives from four ancient nations, the whole spectacle lasted all day and harkened back to the splendid performances once staged at Versailles.

For Catherine, the most exciting and impressive portion occurred when young women from the nobility opened the festivities by appearing in ceremonial chariots. They roared into the area like Russian Amazons, reminding the empress of a letter received from Voltaire in which he had compared her to the Amazon Queen Phalaestris.

"Were you pleased?" Catherine asked Paul when they

rejoined one another at the masquerade ball following the tournament.

"I should have been one of the knights," he grumbled.

"You may be too young now. If theater interests you, as it seems to, we can arrange for you to participate in the future." He turned away. Still, it was the first time in nearly a year she'd seen anything resembling animation on his countenance.

It was true her court rivaled that of her predecessor Elizabeth in entertainment and the arts. Unfortunately, supporting all the imperial theaters, a small acting school, nine full-time opera singers, French and Russian theater troupes, and a huge ballet company ate away at the annual budget. This didn't even include balls, court weddings, birthday parties, name days—and sometimes frivolous gifts like the Turkish costumes for fourteen men she'd ordered for Paul's tenth-birthday entertainment.

Catherine herself usually made only brief appearances at court events. She did continue the same dedication to the arts as that of her predecessors—and if that kept her son entranced as well, she was content.

Meanwhile, she continued to work around the clock. On Sundays she dutifully attended mass for two hours with her ladies, following that up with reading and writing all afternoon. Her desks inevitably contained piles of journals and reports, including those written by navigators, explorers, agriculturalists, and geologists. She always kept her quill handy, not hesitating to scribble notes and annotations in the margins. Seldom did she lack for interesting reading material. One Sunday Alyona and Anya entered the room just in time to hear her muttering in frustration over a pamphlet.

"What is wrong, Your Imperial Majesty?" Alyona asked.

"Nothing. Nothing except that this Danish code of law is so dull that if I were to toss it into Vesuvius's crater, it would extinguish any volcanic eruption!"

"I'm sorry," Anya murmured. "Would you like me to ring for some coffee? Or should I summon a lady to read you something else?"

"No, no. I shall check on the game. I am afraid that one of these days the archbishop will discover that my courtiers play cards on Sundays." She strolled down the halls to where several anterooms were occupied by whist players. As fond as she was of the game, she often wandered from table to table observing.

Noting that the room was chilly, she yanked a bellpull attached to the wall to summon a page. She also had just recalled an important message she wanted to send via Slava, the footman currently on duty.

She pulled again. And then again.

Turning aside, she entered the next room, where she spotted Slava hunched over his own cards with three other footmen. At first angry, she sauntered behind him and then kept moving to the other side of the table. Her features did not betray what she had seen. She suddenly understood why the young man had not reacted to the summons. Nodding to him as he jumped up, she took his seat and directed him to deliver the message. "Have no fear. I will play your hand until you return," she said in a measured tone. No one suspected that he was holding such a winning hand.

After the young man returned, she left again, reflecting that the players were dullards not to perceive that everyone had an agenda or a game face. Sometimes she wondered what percentage of people in court seemed willing to be pushed about like pawns on a political chessboard.

CHAPTER 23

(MARIA) 2020

We decide to wait until early January when Russians take holiday vacations. Aunt Roberta also assures me we'll be under less scrutiny with few foreign tourists willing to brave a St. Petersburg winter. Besides, at nearly two, Sasha is weaned, and my breasts have returned to normal size.

As if sensing where we're going, my sweet toddler miraculously does not cry or make a fuss on the long flights. He spends most of the time asleep in the middle seat between Aunt Roberta and me.

I devote most of my travel time to reviewing over and over

what I have done to prepare—and potentially anything I've forgotten. In a thrift store I located a mustard-hued, floor-length dress with just a little lace and no zippers. The best thing about it is a series of inconspicuous inside pockets where I plan to carry the dragonfly jewelry (in case I arrive needing money), two tins of penicillin tablets, the tiny book of tsars, and photos of Sasha in the tragic event that I make it to the past without him—a thought I persistently and resolutely shove to the back of my mind. I have a special gift for Igor as well, tucked in a flannel pouch in the deepest recesses of one of the two additional pockets I sewed inside the gown.

Aunt Roberta has sewn a toddler outfit for Sasha that transforms him into a little gentleman, albeit nothing modern that would draw attention to either of us in the contemporary world or the one where I pray we'll end up—hopefully in these same clothes.

I mentally review the plethora of vaccinations and preventatives the two of us got after dozens of trips to my doctors and the campus travel nurse, as well as to Sasha's pediatrician. The little guy has been poked with everything on the pharmaceutical market to protect him from any conceivable illness except one: since smallpox has been eradicated, the vaccines are no longer available to the public. This is one of the deadliest diseases in the eighteenth century, although Aunt Roberta assures me, "Catherine was a pioneer in what was a new vaccine back then. Just be sure to get it as soon as it's available. In fact, from what I've read, she will probably order you to take it."

I've also visited the dentist eight times: two newly filled cavities, three crowns, two pulled wisdom teeth, and four cleanings. Hopefully that will keep the dreaded pliers away from me.

For months, my aunt and I have repeated the same planning conversations and hashed over the possibilities.

A month ago, however, she stunned me.

"I want to go with you," she announced firmly.

"Of course. If I somehow lose Sasha, you will need to take him home and raise him. I thought we'd worked all that out." My stomach turns at the thought.

The idea of being forced to abandon my son is so terrifying that I almost missed her next statement: "No, I mean I want to go *into* the past with both of you."

"What?" I was incredulous, having never considered this option. I did, however, often hear envy in her voice when we discussed the past. I had fretted only about losing Sasha, not to mention facing the heartbreaking abandonment of my aunt once again.

"I've led a full life here, yes. However, as an historian, I cannot turn down such a possibility to live in that period. No matter how fantastical this all seems."

"But—"

"Maria, I've given this a lot of thought. If all goes as planned and our hands are clasped together, I could spend the rest of my days in Imperial Russia. I believe I could adapt. In fact, I *want* to."

I sank down abruptly on the couch, almost jostling poor Sasha in my arms. "How could you survive? And why would you want to take the chance? And what about your life here?" To me this made little sense, and I wondered if perhaps I had over-glamorized my life in the past to her.

"I'm getting closer to retirement anyway, and my disappearance would mean little to anyone."

"Except Thomas."

She blushed. Actually blushed. "I admit it would be difficult. It's not as though we were married—or have discussed that subject."

We talked for hours that day and off and on for the following weeks. I can only hope I convinced her of the risks.

Thankfully, she has now dropped the subject.

The nearer the designated date approaches, the more I dream about Igor. Not since the first months after my return have I awakened throbbing with need and slick between my thighs. My burgundy-colored nipples, no longer swollen from pregnancy or sore from nursing, now crave a different kind of suckling. More than once I fantasize while attempting to satisfy myself.

I also carry on long imaginary conversations with my husband, practicing what I will say and all the ways he might respond. Sometimes, taking out and fondling the dragonfly jewelry, I share facts and techniques I've learned in the present. "Did you know," I imagine explaining, "that geologists now discover nearly one hundred new minerals per year? That in one hundred years scientists will discover piezoelectricity in quartz crystals?" Then I rehearse how to describe the applications of this knowledge, starting with radio waves and then television.

"What would you like to see if we had such a television?"

I ask him one day while bouncing Sasha gently up and down in a valiant, albeit unsuccessful attempt to get him to sleep while he loudly protests the evident arrival of another tooth. "Would you like our son to watch drawings come to life on a screen?" I wonder if this is the best way to define animation and cartoons. Live television might be easier for him to visualize since we've both seen numerous plays at court.

The notion of explaining computers seems too overwhelming, though I look forward to attempting to describe electric rock tumblers and polishers. He already knows about faceting and grinding and types of gem cuts, of course, though not all the advances that jewelers have made subsequently. Sometimes I envision him hunched over his microscope, examining the facets of an emerald. And I imagine the amazement on his face if presented with a modern jeweler's loupe that could magnify his precious gems so much more than the small one he possesses.

"Your papa needs us," I assure a now sleeping Sasha. "And we need him!"

CHAPTER 24

(CATHERINE)

"Her spheres of activity encompass everything; no aspect of government escapes her . . . She's a living reproof to all those drowsy monarchs on their thrones who have no comprehension of the plans she is executing."

— Frederick the Great

Catherine again summoned Igor Blukhov to her apartments, ostensibly to examine his latest wares.

Having not seen him—only his apprentice—in a few years, she had to hide her dismay at his appearance. Yes, he had appeared haggard when she'd seen him shortly after his wife's disappearance, yet now he bore almost no resemblance to the handsome, virile young man she, Maria, and Grigory had known. No one had warned her that with his parchment-hued skin and skeletal limbs he looked as if he should be admitted to one of her new hospitals.

"How do you fare?" she forced herself to ask politely after he bowed and laid out his velvet cloths covered with glittering stones in magnificent settings. She then enthusiastically selected an amethyst parure, offering a generous price before he could set one.

"Business is excellent, Your Imperial Majesty. Perhaps if I had the ambition, I would open a second workshop." His voice lacked the enthusiasm she would have expected.

Catherine drummed her heavy sapphire ring on the marble table beside them. "I meant personally, Monsieur. Based on your somewhat . . .weary appearance, I surmise you never did hear anything about Maria."

He hesitated, lowering his eyes as if examining his unusually scuffed boots. "Alas, no. I do not expect I will ever see my wife again after so many years."

"Do you have reason to believe our Masha has met with foul play—or illness—then?"

"There has been no word whatsoever."

"Might we assume she has decided to remain in Italy," she mused, "or that something tragic happened to her traveling party on such a long journey, if not enroute, then on her return?"

He hung his head, revealing untrimmed hair that might have matched a snowy wig if he'd worn one.

"And you have no suspicions?" she pressed at his silence. "No hints? No correspondence from anyone whatsoever?"

He focused again on his boots and avoided his empress's keen eyes. "Nothing. I believe she is gone forever."

Catherine sighed heavily, then frowned as she absentmindedly fingered some of the other jewelry on the velvet cloth. "I cannot believe it. I cannot believe your wonderful wife—my charming, intelligent friend Maria Sergeievna—is no more." As a woman who had shed so many tears in her early years at the palace, Catherine now almost never wept, and had to dab at her eyes with a nearby piece of lace to avoid doing so now.

"Perhaps I just refuse to believe it, Monsieur Blukhov. Let us pray for our dear sister and wife. In the meantime, if you have any suspicions, please relay them to me. I should have sent an emissary to Italy long ago! In fact, I thought I ordered Grigory to do so."

Igor shook his head mournfully. "I appreciate your concern and your efforts, Your Gracious Majesty. I doubt, however, that after all this time anything will change."

"I'm truly sorry, Igor Igorevich. Which is why I hesitate to raise this matter . . . Have you at least considered the possibility of taking another wife?" At the stunned look on his partially unshaven face, she added hastily, "I only thought that you deserve some happiness. Not to mention someone to care for you."

"My Aunt Gina does her best. Personally, I have no appetite for happiness. No woman is going to alter that."

"What about children? Someone to whom you might pass down your talents and business in the future? If Maria is truly lost forever—"

"She could still return." His words, spoken barely above a whisper, carry no conviction.

"If you should change your opinion, my friend, there are two of my ladies who might interest you."

"I can only love once, Your Imperial Majesty."

"That is what you believe now, of course. However, I can assure you from personal and other experience that one *can* love again."

When a servant brought in a trayful of biscuits, preserves, and tea at Catherine's urging, Igor politely shook his head.

After making another purchase—a silver bracelet studded with shades of amber and a matching pair of earrings—she dismissed the woebegone jeweler. As he backed out of the room, she couldn't get over the sense he was hiding something. He had presented no theories, no suggestions, no speculations.

As soon as he left, she replayed their conversation in her head, particularly the part about loving more than once. Long ago she had thought she loved Saltykov, her first lover, before realizing that their relationship proved nothing more than one of lust and her urgent need for an heir. She had believed herself deeply in love with Stanislaus Poniatowski, too, although these days with him far away and king of Poland, she found she enjoyed exchanging correspondence with him, nothing more. And now she had Grigory, with all the fire and passion they'd shared for years. But lately she had had doubts . . .

Grigory and his brother Alexis spent more and more time away from the palace, usually hunting stags or partaking of their favorite challenge: boar hunting. Dressed in riding breeches, tall wading boots, and loose peasant shirts with wide sleeves for ease of movement, they would pursue their prey vengefully. With their combined physical strength, they rode on horseback with lances in a dangerous venture that kept them occupied sometimes all day and into the next. Catherine realized she seldom missed him.

With another deep sigh, she pushed Saltykov, Poniatowski, and Orlov from her mind and picked up her quill. She had much too much work to consider paramours, and if the truth be known, it was running her empire that unquestionably served as her first love.

For a year and a half, elaborate preparations had been underway for her Great Voyage. It was time she sailed down the Volga—Russia's Mother River—to visit and learn about her subjects and their cities. The long-awaited trip was planned for this summer. Catherine would sail all the way to Kazan, a Muslim city situated five hundred miles east of Moscow.

Captain Pushchin, who would command the expedition, had overseen construction of a luxurious floating galley for her needs. The fleet would consist of twenty-four other large vessels, eleven specially commissioned for diplomats and other crucial staff. She would be accompanied by over a thousand guards, sailors, and officers.

"It will be an extravaganza," Nikita Panin observed, reporting he had dutifully sent out advance teams of Cossacks to manage the logistics for each port and to break up several bandit gangs reportedly gathering along some Volga tributaries.

"To be sure," she agreed. "Be sure you also commission the Academy of Sciences to create a map for me—and a geographical description of each portion of the voyage plus a substantial overview of the features of each port."

She could barely contain her own excitement. Long ago she had made the lengthy journey from Prussia in a wobbly coach taking her to an unknown future. This time she would undertake a different long journey with flair and elegance aboard what appeared to be nothing less than a floating palace. This time she traveled as an empress, not a nervous girl. This time she was in control of her destiny.

CHAPTER 25

(MARIA)

It is Passport Control that frightens me most. The apple-cheeked young men—boys, really—prolong the process by examining passports and visas as if each of us is somehow guilty of something nefarious. Which I am—or will be. The boy stares down at the documents then up at my face, repeating the process a few times. He also stares down at Sasha. This does nothing to remove the nervousness that keeps my legs trembling beneath my dress. Fortunately, Aunt Roberta has attempted to prep me for this moment yet again.

After what seems like forever, the boy stamps my and Alexander Igor Blukhov's passports and gives a wave of dismissal. As I pull my son toward baggage claim, I start to breathe normally.

One hurdle down. One major one to go.

With the experience that comes from dozens of trips to the USSR and then the Russian Federation, Aunt Roberta scrounges up a luggage cart, snags our lightweight bags, and herds all of it and us through the green customs exit. She flags a cab, negotiates a price, and settles herself in the front and her niece and grandnephew into the back.

We've booked a hotel for several nights close to Palace Square and the Hermitage. We do not know how long it might take to accomplish our odd mission, nor if any museum rooms might be temporarily closed to the public.

We have little to unpack and must keep our traveling clothes clean until the right day. Sasha has several other out-fits, as does Aunt Bobbi, in case I'm the only one (heaven forbid) to succeed in returning to the past. Resolving to stop worrying about losing my baby, I nevertheless cannot get my stomach to agree.

Unpacking toiletries, I debate whether to take the birth control pills I'd brought. I had a shot of Depo-Provera a few days earlier, which will last for twelve weeks. If the pills obtained from a second GYN could take over from there—assuming they make it through in my pockets—I can prevent another pregnancy for over a year. This is optimism on my part, of course, in the event I'm fully reunited with my husband. I might want another child, and Igor presumably will, but will the time be right after I introduce his son to him? Nor am I convinced of the safety of the often unsavory and dangerous eighteenth-century birthing practices. At least my aunt insisted on dragging me to Lamaze classes throughout my pregnancy so I have something else to rely upon. And then there's my age . . . late thirties may put that option out of reach anyway.

In the end I toss the pill container in the trash.

We spend two days exploring the city, taking turns carrying Sasha and dodging falling icicles. I know I'll have to dress for warmer weather, since the museum's Cloakroom Nazis insist on making you check all outerwear and large bags. Since last time I left the present in the summer and arrived in the past during the dead of winter, I can only surmise that months don't run consecutively between past and present.

When the day arrives, we ponder whether it will be only the first of several days if we cannot get close enough to Minerva's statue. We dutifully purchase our tickets from a machine and stand in the frigid line with hundreds of Russians. Fortunately—or perhaps unfortunately—the line moves steadily. For perhaps the hundredth time, I resolutely push aside the fear that this won't work at all and that I will be stuck forever in this modern time.

We each take one of Sasha's hands and walk him through the second-floor Russia section first, trying to get him acclimated to the elaborate furniture. "Look, Baba!" he yells to Aunt Roberta every few minutes. Then he follows up by practicing a mixture of his Russian and English vocabulary. "Chair, Mama?" Other than yearning to touch things, he is a model child.

It is time to make our way to the statues. They don't seem to attract the hordes that gather around other museum artifacts, and providentially Minerva still perches on an edge of the great hall.

We've talked about this repeatedly, knowing that after a fast glimpse around the room for watchful room guards and curators, we'll have to move quickly.

"I love you!" I reiterate for the twentieth time to my aunt, and she to me. The plan is for her to release Sasha's right hand as soon as I touch the statue, and, if necessary, to create a minor diversion to take everyone's attention off the vanishing—or the fact that I still appear there, foolishly and dangerously grasping a priceless work of art.

Sure enough, a woman stands guard on one side of the hall, and so we casually pass the statue and pretend to look at others. When Sasha unexpectedly tugs at my hand and nearly gets away from me, it is all I can do to keep from grabbing him. I tighten my hand, and Aunt Roberta grips his other one.

Then, a streak of luck. The guard, chatting with a museum patron, moves away to point him in the direction of another hall.

It happens as my gloved fingers reach out.

Instantaneously a wall of darkness hovers in front of me, Sasha utters a little cry, and Aunt Roberta gasps.

I am in the Winter Palace. There is no doubt, although it takes a few moments to absorb my surroundings: crisp and colorful tapestries, two giant chandeliers, an enormous blue tiled stove, plenty of delicate gilded furniture, and one shocked servant rather than a museum guard.

Detaching from the statue—now the only one decorating what appears to be a large formal hall—I become conscious that the servant girl is shrieking and simultaneously losing her grasp on a tray of cordial glasses.

As shards of glass shatter across the parquet floor, I grasp two more critical things: my darling son has made it—and we are not alone.

"Aunt Bobbi?" I ask desperately.

"I'm okay. And so, I think, is our baby."

"How—?"

She grins sheepishly. "I held onto the hem of your dress."

"We discussed this! What if Sasha hadn't made it and had been left all . . ."

I start to stutter, collapsing with Sasha on a nearby divan, aware that the terrified servant girl remains. She trembles uncontrollably, rooted to the floor and unable to tear her eyes away from the three apparitions before her.

Before I can recover enough to ask her the date—or in what section of the palace we stand—she flees faster than a sole rabbit pursued by a hound pack.

Sasha tightens his grip and begins to cry, whether from the experience of going through time or fear of the splintering glass now at our feet, I don't know. My aunt and I manage to cradle him at the same time.

She gives me a wan smile. "I don't know where—or when—we are. I'm just so relieved the three of us made it. Together, I mean."

"Why?" I know she understands what I'm asking.

"It's not as if we haven't discussed it," she says crisply.

"Of course, but I thought . . . what about your life in the future?"

"The future, as you once put it, is over-rated."

"I did say that, only I meant for me!"

"Anyway, my dear, I'm here and I'm not going to—and probably cannot—return. Now, shouldn't we move? And quickly?"

I glance around speculatively. Recalling both past and present incarnations of the Hermitage, its design a labyrinthic pattern of linked rooms, I grasp Sasha's hand and look toward the opening where the servant girl bolted.

Passing the fireplace with Aunt Roberta close on my heels, I recognize the next room, serving as an outer office for the monarch's secretaries and visiting provincial representatives. Relieved at my disguise—accomplished with both dyed black hair and *sans* court-preferred cosmetics—I don't fear encountering anyone who might recognize me. As if to confirm this confidence, several servants bearing piles of paper or balancing trays of beverages and snacks scurry past, so intent on their errands they fail to look at our faces.

Unlike during my first unwilling catapult into the past, the three of us arrive fortuitously dressed in the same clothing we wore leaving the future. We look as appropriate as possible in this period, and I barely register what I should've noticed sooner: Aunt Bobbi, who now scoops up Sasha in her arms, wears an empire-style wool dress with a faux bodice and faux stays. The navy blue "gown" reaches her ankles—a major departure from her usual knee-length wardrobe of suits alternating with jeans or Native American garb. Had I taken

notice of her gown earlier, I might've suspected something—
or presumed she was invited to a period costume party!

"Yes, we do need to get out of here." I spy another exit
which, if I recall correctly, leads down two flights of stairs to
a servants' entrance.

We stumble outside into a sunlit courtyard, and after
ensuring Aunt Roberta and Sasha are behind me, I allow my
eyes to sweep the various fences and servants' quarters for
a way into the city. To the right the gilded statues atop the
Admiralty sparkle, and with relief, both my aunt and I know
exactly which direction to take.

Within minutes we reach familiar territory, an intersec-
tion that leads both to the market and to a handful of elegant hotels frequented by the aristocracy. Lacking a coach, I
assume a confident air before approaching the front entrance
of the most modest building. Having rehearsed this part
mentally for months, albeit for two people rather than three,
I know exactly what to do and say.

"We will require apartments for the duchess and her son.
Oh, and one lady's maid," I amend the request.

"You may put this on the account of the jeweler Igor
Blukhov," I continue airily. "Or charge it to the empress's
account." I wave expansively in the direction of the Winter
Palace from which we just fled, praying that there really is an
empress on the throne.

"Madame, it is our pleasure to accommodate you. Any
relation to His High Born is welcome on our premises. I have
fine apartments available."

Relation to whom? No matter. I elect not to pry rather
than blunder into incorrect or suspicious-sounding assump-

tions. It doesn't matter, as long as we end up pawning off the bill for our accommodations on someone. We have so few legitimate rubles that any defrayed expenses are a necessity until we can sell some gems.

Fortunately, the innkeeper asks no further questions.

Aunt Roberta has no such compunctions. "Do you know, my good man," she asks in her flawless Russian, "whether Her Imperial Majesty is in Petersburg at present?"

I hold my breath. Yes, of course we must ascertain if we can turn to Catherine if Igor is absent from the city—not to mention whether she still wears the crown. What if he answers that it is held by an *emperor*?

"No, *mesdames*. Our Little Mother has just departed on a long voyage across our great Volga River, so I'm afraid you will not be able to gain admittance to the palace for many months. Perhaps her servants at Peterhof could accommodate you."

"*Spasibo*." And then my aunt makes an obvious, incredibly regal turn toward the staircase that presumably leads to our rooms.

The elaborate mantel clock announces that it is approaching midnight and hence—based on the sky outside—it will stay light for hours yet. Still, I am eager to go to Igor.

"Me eat!" Sasha announces just then, and I order room service from a servant who has just arrived, as if anticipating my son's relentless toddler hunger.

He possesses nearly a full set of baby teeth now, yet I take no chances and order him kasha ("ah, buckwheat porridge," my aunt tells him with approval), mashed potatoes, and chocolate cake. Delighted with this meal, he stammers an assortment of halfway unintelligible, mostly Russian words. He then falls promptly asleep in his chair.

Our own meal arrives just as I finish tucking Sasha into the second bed and stroking his brown curls and chubby cheeks until he falls asleep.

Dinner consists of roast hare, potato soup, au gratin potatoes, fruits, cheeses, thick rye bread, and strawberry tarts. "I'm ravenous. You need to eat, too!" Aunt Roberta scolds, putting down her spoon when she notices I'm sipping my wine quickly while barely touching our repast.

"I can't. Too nervous."

"Wait!" my aunt stops me as I move toward the door. "You cannot go out now."

"Why not?" I frown. True, this is not exactly how I'd planned it when envisioning Sasha and I moving briskly along Great Perspective Road and pushing open the entrance to the House of Gems: Igor's shop. And mine. Admittedly the hotel was and is a great idea, and this way my poor husband will not have to deal simultaneously with both my return and the appearance of a son he never knew he had.

"It is late. Although it appears to be approaching the season of the White Nights, you have no escort. And more importantly, you have no alternative plan. If your husband is not there . . ." Her voice trails off, and I finish the sentence mentally: *Or if he has a new wife with him, then what will you do?*

What could I do? I listen, though, insisting only on going down to the lobby to request some additional information.

"Be careful," Aunt Roberta warns unnecessarily.

A night clerk is on duty, bowing slightly as I approach the

desk. Confident now of having fortuitously and miraculously regained my Russian fluency, I lean confidentially over the counter. "The duchess has been invited to a ball at Peterhof soon. She would like to commission a gift that could be crafted in time for our Little Mother's return. Might you have any recommendations?"

Flattered at this attention and request for advice from a lady, the clerk is more than happy to oblige. "Madame, I could not say for certain, yet I have heard that Our Gracious Sovereign collects many things, just as her predecessor, the great Peter the First, did."

"Such as?"

He taps his pipe on the elaborately carved desk. "Snuff boxes, I believe. Rocks and minerals. And jewelry, of course."

"Ah. I—she—brought jewelry on our last visit only a couple years ago. For her coronation. We should not want to duplicate any gift for our Little Mother. If she recalls it, which she may not." I look questioningly at the man dressed as if he himself were a nobleman in a gray silk coat and breeches.

"She most assuredly would not have forgotten, even if a few years have passed. They say she has a memory sharp as one of those giant elephants that were a gift to our late Empress Elizabeth Petrovna. Or perhaps it was Empress Anna Ivanovna." He winks in a too familiar manner. "I would recommend the House of Gems just around the corner," he adds as I back up. "Monsieur Blukhov works nearly exclusively for the empress, and he would know what she needs or desires."

Biting my lip to resist the temptation to ask more, I merely say, "*Spasibo*, Monsieur. You have been a great help. I shall not select jewelry as a gift from the duchess then—unless I consult Monsieur Blukhov."

Unable to contain my excitement, I return to find my aunt wide awake and finishing off our wine.

"Well? What did you discover, my Masha?"

"You know me too well, Aunt Bobbi. I discovered my husband is alive and working for the empress *and* that it is in fact Catherine who rules and it has only been, according to my new admirer downstairs, 'a few years' since her coronation. So I did it!"

"Brava!"

"Now I just need to determine whether Igor is in the city, convince him I am not a ghost, beg for forgiveness, tell him he has a son, and prepare him for an introduction to his new aunt from the future!"

"One day at a time, dearest."

"I know. And Aunt Roberta?"

"Yes, my child?" she replies sleepily.

"Tomorrow we will also get to the bottom of how you pulled this whole thing off, and what the hell is going to happen in the future when both of us disappear!"

She dismisses my words with a wave. "First let us get some sleep so you may go to that beloved husband of yours in the morning. Sasha and I will wait for you here."

"And what if I am not back by lunch?"

"Maria, I know the *modern* city—and I'm absolutely dying to get acquainted with the version I've studied. If you're not here, Sasha and I will walk Nevsky Prospeckt—the Great Perspective Road—and try to 'charge' some new gowns at Gostiny Dvor. Despite landmarks that don't yet exist, I believe

I can find my way around just fine. Oh, have the summer gardens opened to the public yet in this age? I'd like to take Sasha there, and of course—"

"Okay. I get it," I laugh. "Just don't go too far. Without coins for a carriage, you might find yourself toting your nephew back to the hotel."

"I *can* still lift him, you know. However, he is starting to weigh more than a huge sack of potatoes."

I'm scarcely listening now as my aunt lists all the places she wants to see. I only want to see one.

CHAPTER 26

(CATHERINE)

Everyone advised her not to go. That leaving Petersburg invited attempts to usurp her in absentia. That the empire would collapse into chaos. That her safety during flooding season presented an unreasonable risk. This was Russia's heartland, however, and she burned with a desire to meet and mingle with the people, to make up her own mind about the various ethnicities reportedly inhabiting such a fruitful, historical area.

When the galley leading her imperial flotilla of twenty-four vessels was buffered by strong winds and high waves, when the skies unleashed perpetual rain, when the melting ice chunks ramming the hull threatened to shake everyone to the core, when freezing rain pounded the decks . . . Catherine dismissed it all as "maritime adventure" in her copious correspondence. She wrote most frequently to Panin, who along with her son Paul and most of her diplomats and ministers had been left behind—the latter to ensure uninterrupted business in the empire. An array of couriers from Moscow fought the frigid weather to catch up with the boats daily to provide urgent messages and supply her with the paperwork on which she thrived.

She also dealt with the unruly climate and frustrating delays by playing endless card games. "You win all our money," Grigory complained. He turned to his brother Vladimir. "We have played a thousand wasted games to fill my lover's coffers." Catherine merely smiled at the two Orlovs.

That morning, after working on translating a Byzantine historical novel written in French into Russian, she'd lost her footing on deck when the boat rolled more than usual. Other challenges included inexplicable noises that nearly panicked her and terrified her ladies. Maneuvering frequently from the large riverboat to a substantially smaller boat that bobbed up and down like a tiny cork presented more problems and added to their anxiety.

The card games with her ladies and gentlemen soothed and distracted the empress. The weather was destined to calm down, and until then she refused to admit her fears to anyone—including Grigory.

It is a metaphor for my rule, she thought. She might stumble, miss her footing, and risk drowning in order to maneuver the flotsam of politics bobbing on the river. Nevertheless, Catherine vowed somehow to maintain the fortitude to sail onward and even to excel as she rounded each unfamiliar bend.

Nothing less than enchanting, the town of Uglich greeted the ship from a Volga promontory. Heavy clouds, a persistent drizzle, and pewter sky still could not dim the small, elaborate red-brick cathedral with its sky-blue domes spangled with gold stars.

"It's the Church of Dimitri on the Spilled Blood," Vladimir Orlov exclaimed in awe.

She had read about it. This is where it all had started: the awful domino-effect power struggle known as the Time of Troubles that followed Tsar Ivan IV's death. His sole heir, an eight-year-old son, allegedly had been stabbed to death on this very spot. The world still assumed murder (as opposed to the alternate theory of the boy's accidental fall on his knife), likely ordered by Boris Godunov, the most famous of many later usurpers of the throne who would threaten peace, stability, and the future existence of the vast Russian empire.

The mystery of the child's death intrigued her, as did other unexplained deaths in history. This one was somewhat personal. Were it not for the boy's gruesome death—as potentially evidenced in 1591 by the discovery of the tsarevich's bloody corpse in the courtyard—there would have been no Romanov dynasty. No Peter the Great. No Elizabeth. No Catherine—at least not on this throne.

As usual when her dream galley, the *Tver,* docked, it was trailed by a suite that had swelled to a contingent including nearly two thousand officers, navy sailors, guards, and servants. A gala reception of regiments awaited her inspection. Monasteries and churches had been spruced up in anticipation of her visit, and at each port they moored at one of the hastily constructed quaysides, decorated with red or green cloth. Atop each, a newly built triumphal arch decorated with the empress's monogram and image faced the river. Seminarians chanted newly written verses, village choirs entertained, nobles vied to offer hospitality, hundreds of subjects crowded around in hopes of kissing her hand, and bureaucrats vied for attention and offered invitations. Kettle drums, French horns, and trumpets heralded her arrival.

This pattern continued as she sailed downstream, and aboard the *Tver* Catherine carefully monitored her maps of the river and tributaries as closely as she read the background on each of the villages and towns on the itinerary. She charted her progress religiously, and in the eagerness to move on fretted when the schedule continued to go awry.

Thus far the weather had unleashed ceaseless downpours and storms on the flood-swollen river, buffeting the boats as they encountered ice pellets and sleet. Today remained frigid, so she donned her cloak and disembarked onto the carpeted pathway that would pave her progress throughout shore visits.

Inside Uglich's famous cathedral, a series of massive gold-trimmed paintings had been commissioned in her honor. She would discover similar creations for the remainder of the trip, repeatedly thrilling to the marble sculptures, gilded frescoes, and bejeweled icons inspired by her visit.

During an early morning approach to the next port, a ruby

sunrise penetrated the clouds and spilled over the water's surface, simultaneously illuminating the golden domes ashore. Little could compete with this beauty: this peace that she attempted to gather within herself—intending to use it to sustain all her future days.

Drinking it all in, she felt as though gemstones were shining from her secret soul.

Chapter 27

(Maria)

An opalescent dawn—confirmation that we are approaching the season of White Nights—peeks through half-open brocade curtains. Resolutely I rise from the bed in which I've tossed and turned all night, punching pillows as I anxiously anticipated the long-awaited reunion with the husband I thought I'd lost.

Neither Aunt Roberta nor Sasha, curled up together in a second bed in our well-appointed rooms, stirs.

Recalling Igor prefers to rise at dawn, when he claims to be most productive, I quietly brush off and then don my only gown. My entire body tingles with anticipation as I envision being wrapped in my husband's welcoming arms in only a few minutes' time.

Aunt Roberta may caution "one day at a time." I, however, have waited nearly three years for this, and am dismissing her advice. I do not intend to delay another moment.

Intent on my destination, I barely register the once familiar aromas and sounds of the city: vendors hawking scrumptious meat-filled *piroshkis,* the heady scent of lilacs, carriage drivers wielding whips and hollering warnings to pedestrians who scurry across the cobblestones, and the ever-present odor of horse dung. Technically it does not get dark at this time of year. Still, today candlelight shines from between shutters or through poorly ventilated walls.

The sign on the shop looks the same, with only the façade repainted pastel blue. Flanking the entrance, pierced metal candleholders create angled patterns of light that confirm it is still not quite dawn.

I brush my newly black hair with my fingers, hoping I appear as young and attractive as he might recall me. Although I'd imagined and practiced this moment for so long, it takes me a full minute to push open the door.

Standing alone as if searching for someone just inside the entrance, I pray again that it is not Aunt Gina who sees me first—if she is still alive. I say another prayer that my sudden appearance doesn't bring on a heart attack if she is.

Hearing a noise from the workshop that sounds like something rattling, I move slowly to that door.

I'd know him anywhere, even in profile.

He is standing on a ladder, stretching to grasp a pile of

small boxes from a high shelf. I cannot see his face, only that his figure appears thinner and his unpowdered hair reveals new strands of gray.

Deciding it will be prudent to wait until he climbs down and sees me, I am startled when a voice behind me exclaims, "Maria Sergeievna! You are back!" She is speaking in Italian, and louder than her usual tones.

As I whirl around to face Aunt Gina, she crosses herself and then reaches both arms out for a two-cheek kiss.

Simultaneously, a loud crash reverberates through the workshop, and I whip back around just in time to see Igor and the ladder crash to the floor.

Aunt Gina and I rush to him, sprawled with one leg tangled in the ladder rungs and everything surrounded by countless gemstones spilling from the fallen open boxes.

My mind registers only two things: the awful expression on Igor's open-mouthed face, and the chaotic tinkling of thousands of rubies, sapphires, emeralds, and diamonds still cascading in a glittering fountain from ceiling to floor.

I don't think a few moments have ever before seemed closer to an eternity.

As we hasten to lift him, Igor impatiently brushes us away.

Once standing, he opens and closes his mouth, wordlessly as a fish. He brushes Aunt Gina away when she attempts to examine him for injuries.

Not knowing what to do at this silent rebuff and somewhat

unexpected reaction, I bend to retrieve and rebox some of the gemstones.

"Don't!" he says, staring at me. I watch nervously as his features undergo a series of changes, at first what appears to be love and joy, then something like sadness, and then what looks more like anger. His arms, initially reaching out to me, drop to his sides.

"Go!" he utters at last.

"I have just arrived! I came to you at once, my darling. I know it's a long story—"

"I don't wish to hear it. Stop picking up the stones and just go."

Shaken and confused—perhaps as much as Igor is—I turn to Aunt Gina, who is already ordering a young girl who must be a new servant to bring some tea.

"No need for that," Igor argues with his aunt. "She cannot just disappear and then prance back into my life five years later as if she had never abandoned me."

"Five years? It's been more like three, and you know it. And I did not return from . . . from where I was, alone!"

"Of course not. Why should you care what your husband has been enduring and his grief through all this time?" He fairly spat out the word "husband," and my eyes brim with tears.

Does he truly not want me anymore? "Is there . . . is there a new woman?"

"You are crazy!" he exclaims, moving toward me and putting his hand on my arm as if to confirm that I am real. Then he gently pushes me in the direction of the door! "Go, please."

Helplessly I turn toward Aunt Gina, who openly weeps and

clings to my other arm. "Nephew! You cannot do this. You know you don't want to throw her out."

Igor turns his back to us before moving the ladder and then stomping out the side door.

"What am I to do?" I plead with Aunt Gina for answers.

"Give him time, my darling. He needs to remember what he has lost, although I don't believe for one moment that he has ever forgotten."

I have no choice. Reaching into one of my pockets, I pull out the small photograph of Sasha that I risked bringing just in case we became separated by time. Placing it gently on the worktable, I hope she merely will assume it is a realistic painting on unusually glossy paper.

"This is our son," I say tearfully. "We—he and I—will be waiting for our husband and father." I explain where we are staying before leaving, much faster than I want to, unable to control the sobs now shaking me and tears spilling down my cheeks and chin.

"Tell him . . . tell him I have never stopped loving him."

Aunt Gina, now crying just as openly, nods before reluctantly removing her trembling hand from my shoulder. She leans over to stare in fascination at Sasha's photograph.

And then I am gone.

CHAPTER 28

(CATHERINE)

On the left bank, a flotilla of smaller boats adorned with flags greeted her. Their empress devoted several minutes to delighting at the sight of a seemingly endless row of cathedrals and monasteries whose flamboyant towers, domes, and cupolas sparkled along the riverbank as if Yaroslavl were determined to decorate its neckline with jewel-like charms. Exuberant cheers of the townspeople, local dignitaries, and notable residents of surrounding towns and regions seemed just as impressive.

Here her schedule included touring factories, landmarks,

and monasteries, as well as inspecting two productive silk works before wearily retiring to her elaborate floating apartment where she hosted the diplomatic corps. Over the course of inspecting the city's layout, she had ordered numerous changes, while overall pronouncing the city "very pleasing to everyone."

The next day Catherine exhibited some weariness by the time they reached the port of Kostroma, its kremlin founded in the early twelfth century. Here the empress toured Ipatievsky Monastery and admired its white wedding cake façade. From this historic place sixteen-year-old Mikhail Romanov had accompanied the boyars who'd traveled here to invite him to rule Russia in 1613, thus ending the Time of Troubles. Now it is mid May, the lilacs opening in purple and white starbursts that frame the river, and all is calm.

The morning after providing the entourage with a gala reception, the city administrators, still reeling from a recent fire, presented Catherine with the new reconstruction plan they had drawn up.

After looking it over, she had a better idea. Pausing in the main square, which was covered in the usual canvas sheeting prepared for her to step on when ashore, she summoned Grigory to her side. Suddenly and deliberately, she dropped her open fan on the ground.

"What are you doing?" her lover asked, and others crowded around to listen.

She pointed to the unfurled fan. "It seems to me no fewer than seven streets could and should radiate from a horseshoe-shaped square right here." Turning to the ever-present city officials trailing her like goslings, she spread her fingers over the fan and commanded, "Let it be so."

"*Brava!*" Vladimir exclaimed.

None commented on the small groups of "worshippers" who regularly preceded them. Dressed in rags, they walked backward, pausing regularly to kiss the ground without dropping their precious lit candles—as if she herself were an icon. She had been slightly embarrassed the first time this happened, until one of the local priests assured her, "The peasants in these forests never before have laid eyes on God's anointed sovereign. To them you not only represent the deity; you are God Almighty Himself."

Even for her, this was a humbling idea.

Not only did city planning issues annoy Catherine, so did some of the clergy she met. Greeted in tiny Gorodets by pious women strewing silk shawls and scarfs before her and calling her their "little apple," "benefactress," and "ray of sunshine," she nonetheless found this reverential welcome mitigated at the Fëdorov Monastery. Having already toured a dozen monasteries, she easily distinguished between the well-organized, reverential ones and the disorganized, corrupt ones. This one, with its deceivingly impressive new façade, fell into the latter category and thus irritated her.

"Katya," Grigory whispered as the consecration ceremony dragged on. "At least attempt to show some interest."

Seething, she could not hide her feelings, even in this holy place where Alexander Nevsky had died in the thirteenth century. "It's not as if anyone can hear me!" she hissed back.

Truthfully, the doddering and obviously incompetent abbot could not manage to conduct a proper liturgy. This was troublesome enough, but the disrespectful monks and priests kept making loud corrections and cussing at him just as noisily.

Normally she fattened each church's coffers with a donation when she departed. This time she left a pitiful one.

Naturally suspicious of any institution that threatened her Enlightenment ideals, Catherine also found it upsetting to learn that there was frustrating divisiveness between the area religions. "In this place," she continued to complain to Grigory and Vladimir Orlov, "we have a simple bishop surrounding himself with more simpletons. No wonder they are losing their flock to the Old Believers who settled this area after Patriarch Nikon split the church."

"That was a century ago," Vladimir Orlov pointed out. "Surely they should have come to terms with one another by now."

"One would assume. However, now I am hearing that the priests refuse the holy sacrament of baptism to both the schismatics and the Muslims."

"You cannot have your fingers in every pie," Vladimir commented lightly. Then, simultaneously receiving a warning glance from his brother and noting the glimpse of blue fire in his empress's eyes, he hastily added, "Your Most Gracious Sovereign cares so deeply about her subjects that it must be impossible not to worry about such things."

Between ports and paperwork, she wandered impatiently along the *Tver's* aft, where gold domes glittered from the riverbank after nightfall, as if sending a message heavenward. She thrilled as clouds parted to reveal thousands of stars twinkling back.

"Behold, the Little Dipper," she pointed out one night as Grigory joined her portside. "And so many stars I feel as if I could scoop up handfuls of silver!"

"More correctly, my dearest, it's called the Ursa Minor." Grigory, an avid astronomy enthusiast, set up his telescope there, and most evenings thereafter the two of them star-gazed.

In his enthusiasm, Grigory sometimes forgot to retire early enough to awaken his lover, who needed to sleep at least a few hours before rising at four or five a.m.

"You are the brightest star of them all," he assured her repeatedly before turning back to his other passion. "In fact, your star is definitely in the ascendant!"

Catherine only smiled and kissed him chastely. "The shooting stars may not honor your humble Katinka, but they most definitely illuminate our mind."

CHAPTER 29

(Maria)

"I don't understand! Not anything!" I cry to Aunt Roberta while pacing our small sitting room at the inn. I returned this morning grateful to find the place empty so I could cry myself to sleep. Now it is late afternoon.

"Try to get control of your feelings, my dear. I know it's almost impossible. You must think, however, of Sasha."

She is right. My baby has retreated to the corner, huddling with a runny nose and tear-stained cheeks that bear evidence of the emotional damage I'm surely inflicting on him. I have no right to vent my feelings in the rooms we all share. When

I run to wrap him in my arms, he seems half afraid of me!

"My God, how can I let one man destroy me—not to mention my child?"

Aunt Roberta shakes her head sadly and sighs. "The ways of love are as mysterious as the stars. You must, I think, give your man time to accept your return. And begin to forgive you for your long and what must seem mysterious and cruel absence."

Drying my face and bouncing a reluctant Sasha in one arm, I manage to take a seat and sip some of the tea my aunt ordered earlier. "That's just it. To him it seems as if I've been gone so long that he actually accused me of leaving for five years! Somehow I have to bring Sasha to him, and maybe—"

"Maria," Aunt Roberta interrupts gently. "There's something you obviously do not know."

"I *know* a lot of things. I *know* my husband doesn't want me back."

"What you don't know is the year, do you?"

"Not exactly. When you and I figured it out, we assumed it must be 1764 or more likely 1765."

"It is the year of our lord 1767." She says it firmly before explaining that she has been chatting with babushkas and mothers on benches in the summer gardens. "Catherine is in fact firmly entrenched on the throne. It's just that nearly five years have passed since you . . . since you fell back—or forward—into the future."

Unable to grasp this information, I feel no real shock, just confusion. Seventeen sixty-seven? And I left in seventeen sixty-two?

And then it hits me.

"Sasha! My God, he was born less than a year after I left. He's just two!"

"I'm afraid so. And that means, of course, that—"

"That I cannot show up with a baby so young when five years allegedly have passed!"

"Exactly. Thankfully, your child is long and big for his age. But he would have to be at least four for Igor to accept him as *his* child."

I don't know how to react. What to say. What to do.

"Can't I just explain? No one really knows, after all, how time travel works. Certainly not me, apparently, let alone Igor."

"Given an opportunity to think for a while, he might accept that. You must know, my dear, it *will* take time, I'm afraid. Who knows how much?"

"Whoever said 'time is the enemy' knew what he or she was talking about," I say morosely, pulling a rope to summon the maid again.

I'm afraid I will need something stronger than tea tonight.

A full day passes before I am calmer—let alone coherent enough—to really talk with my aunt. "You must tell me what possessed you to make this leap into the past," I insist over breakfast, and she nods slowly.

She seems relieved I asked, perhaps as much due to her desire to sidetrack my thoughts as an eagerness to divulge her thinking. "There was some subterfuge involved, of course," she begins. "You see, I started planning this a couple months ago."

"So I assume, from what you've said already. What I don't understand is *why*?"

"Let me try to explain, my dear niece. I had it all. Everything I wanted or needed in terms of a career, anyway: tenured for twenty-five years, full professor for twenty, a half dozen books, more articles and conference papers than I can count. My vitae runs nineteen pages. The only steps left were department chair, which I turned down twice already, or a move into administration—which makes me yawn at the thought."

"Surely there must have been something else you wanted to do. . . Or maybe someone you wanted to be with in all these years?"

"Just a handful of damaged relationships. Nothing I regret. No one I miss. I only missed you, my sweet."

Neither of us is eating now, and we remain silent as the maid clears the dishes.

"Why would this be any different? This time and place, I mean?"

"It *is* different. I already know and see that. And I no longer need professional recognition or to prove my competence. That's all been accomplished, and the idea of a career change at this point doesn't interest me."

"You loved what you were doing, though. I *know* you did!"

"I did. And have no regrets. Still, I'm too young to retire and my career seems stalled, you might say. I had no more ambitions when you showed back up—other than being an aunt and then a great aunt, that is."

"You surely don't mean to live for us, Aunt Bobbi. I know that would not make you happy."

"No, it wouldn't necessarily be enough. Who knows what kind of life I can build for myself in the eighteenth century? Don't I owe it to myself to try and find out?"

"Please don't get me wrong, and I hope I haven't glamorized it too much. I'm accustomed to living without running water and toilet paper and cars and who knows how many other things you will miss! You didn't spend eighteen years getting accustomed to these ways—not to mention attitudes toward women and the poor."

"Somehow I don't think we will be poor, will we?"

I attempt a smile. "Hopefully not."

"And as I've told you, I made arrangements to cover our disappearance in case we never come back. I've also planned in case we do—or did. Return, that is." She lowers her voice while Sasha plays on the floor. "I have a safety deposit box key in case either of us ever goes back. It contains identities, money, documents—and it's paid up at one of the most dependable banks for twenty-five years."

It will take awhile to digest all this. It will also take me more than a little time to figure out what to do about Igor's rejection of me. For now, Aunt Roberta must find her own way in this very new, albeit very old world.

Aunt Gina is announced at the hotel the following morning.

It doesn't surprise me that she's come, given what I know must be her hunger for a grandnephew or niece all these decades since she helped raise Igor after his mother (her sister) and then father died. She may be overcome with happiness when she meets Sasha, but it is me she hugs and kisses repeatedly.

"How is your nephew?" I ask eagerly. "Is he recovering from the shock?"

"I fear not, my darling. I did show him the odd shiny portrait. He says unless it was painted at least two years ago, the child definitely is not his." She looks embarrassed, and I hastily make her comfortable on the couch with some tea.

I guess it is fortunate that Aunt Roberta figured out the chronological quandary for me, or I would be in more shock than I already am. "Of course, it is his, Aunt Gina. You *do* know that, don't you?"

Her eyes crinkle and her face radiates joy as she looks delightedly at my son. "He has the look of his father, to be sure," she laughs, crouching on the floor and opening her arms to Sasha.

Surprisingly, he releases his hold on the couch and takes a few tentative steps toward her, then, giggling, launches himself into her arms. I've never seen him react so enthusiastically to a stranger before. Still, I'm not surprised. Aunt Gina exudes a maternal personality, whatever that undefined nature might be.

Yes, he might be starting to resemble his father. Until now I've only noted similar nut-brown curls and jasper-flecked eyes. Relieved that Aunt Gina has pronounced him "her great nephew," I can only pray his own father will claim him, too— eventually.

Aunt Roberta arrives, and within minutes she and Aunt Gina alternate fawning over Sasha. It is readily apparent that he will be overly spoiled by two doting aunts.

The two women also find themselves engaged in conversation, and I observe them quietly as they trade the child back and forth. I had no idea if they'd warm to one another. Now another rock-like worry falls from me. I will need them both to survive here, to share in the care of their mutual nephew—especially if I'm to be denied acceptance by my own husband.

It is not a matter of *if,* I vow. It must be a matter of *when.*

Meanwhile, we must have money to survive. I have no idea if Igor will assume responsibility for our rooms here, and anyway, we must eat and find suitable attire for all three of us if we do not plan to wear the same outfits daily.

The two women barely notice when I leave, bound for several jewelers that I recall in the hope that one might be willing to do business and not ask too many questions.

In the end, the thick-set Prussian with a curly black wig and matching beard does not recognize me, having newly emigrated here. "Do stop by if you have more to sell," he offers as I depart with ruble coins carefully wrapped in a pouch.

Weighted down with the coins, I refuse to mourn the lightness in my other pocket, which until minutes ago contained the dragonfly brooch thickly decorated with peridot and blue opals.

"It is what you must do," Aunt Roberta confirms a few days later when, over a lunch of borshch and blini, I tell her my plan.

We each ordered three suitable day gowns from a seamstress who serves the inn's guests, and they are to be delivered today.

"Tomorrow I will go to the palace," I confirm. "Her Gracious Majesty may not be there, but it is time I renewed some friendships if possible. And finding work is now essential." *Perhaps I could serve my dear friend Anya in the atelier,* I think hopefully, at the same time mindful of my previous unpleasant experience there, not to mention my ineptitude with needle and thread.

"Might she take you back? Catherine?"

I sigh heavily. "I don't know if she would accept me into her service again. She does not like to be betrayed, although she does possess a forgiving soul. I will write and send a messenger to deliver the letter on the Volga.

"There is another possibility, however: my other dear friend Tatiana—assuming she will forgive me. She would have been the last person here to see me before I disappeared, and I owe her something for what she must have endured. Perhaps I could serve in some capacity in her—well, her mansion, I guess you could call it. She and her Danish count live nearby in a home resembling a small palace."

"Maybe you could find a position for me," Aunt Roberta suggests hopefully.

"We've already discussed this, and you know I need you to look after Sasha. Besides, you have no bonafides, no background that might make you acceptable. Unless we can concoct a suitable one, that is."

"And I've already told you," she counters, "that no one will question me if I'm an immigrant from, let's say Moscow, and eager to work as a tutor or secretary."

"Remember, though, that we have to maintain your 'cover.'" I bracket the air with both hands. "Once a countess, always a countess. Perhaps," I add thoughtfully, "a duchess, like we've been using, would be less conspicuous—and you don't know any of the aristocracy in Moscow."

"Nor do I have any true royal ties."

"Then let us say you emigrated here from Yekaterinburg."

"Siberia. Yes, that might work. And the city was founded by Peter the Great in honor of his wife Catherine the First," she grins.

"And it doesn't hurt that it is rare for someone of the nobility to travel all the way here from the Ural Mountains. Igor has talked often of going there, though, since it is a city rich in minerals and gemstones. He might ask questions."

"You forget that he will know who I really am."

"True. And I don't believe he will betray you. It might work. Here it is usually nobles who serve the royals above them. Countess Tatiana must by now be one of the empress's closest ladies, or at least she was when I left. I think we must come up, too, with some way to account for your fluency in English—even use it to your benefit."

So we begin to fabricate a story to explain my absence—now necessarily a much longer and more complex tale since discovering I must account for five years rather than three. And for Aunt Roberta's presence. By nightfall, we have discarded the Ekaterinburg story as being too risky and continue to explore alternates. Besides, Aunt Gina told Aunt Roberta that she is quite certain Igor told the empress that I left for Italy to visit her family, so perhaps I will have no choice but to concoct a story around that.

In the end, Anya is on the river with the empress and thus unreachable. Tatiana, however, welcomes me back with open arms, and accepts my story—a convoluted, poorly plotted fiction—with nary a whisper of doubt.

Learning that Aunt Roberta speaks English, my dear Tatiana hires her immediately to tutor her three sons.

Aunt Gina jumps at the opportunity to come to the inn several times a week to take care of Sasha—without telling Igor—thus delighting her and freeing both me and Aunt Roberta time to earn some rubles.

And now I must wait. For Igor. For Catherine. For my life to reassemble and resume in a way I can accept.

CHAPTER 30

(CATHERINE) MAY 1767

"I beg that you remember that I have often accommodated
myself to the present, without closing the path
to a more favorable future."
—Catherine II to Frederick the Great

From shore came the sound of galloping horses attempting to catch the waterborne flotilla. Catherine waited impatiently as her riverboat bumped the bank to receive her messages. Flipping hastily through the pile, she stopped in surprise. One of the thickest packets contained a letter from her former lady, Maria Sergeievna Blukhova—posted from Petersburg, not from the Italian provinces.

Frowning, she tore it open first. Quickly scanning the letter, she eyed the French penmanship suspiciously. "It says here," she announced, turning to Grigory, "that Maria Sergei-evna has a son! And that she was detained enroute to Venezia by Prussian officials in both directions after she spent months trying to get to the Adriatic Sea."

"And the baby?"

"Born near Venetia almost immediately after she arrived. I cannot imagine such a long journey, which she says she was compelled to make with little notice to assist Igor's ailing uncle."

"She sent no word!" Grigory protested. "Not to Her Gracious Majesty, and apparently not to her long-suffering husband, either. Hmm. I would not respond! Something smells about this story."

"I'm inclined to agree, Grisha, yet the fact remains that she is safe. It appears that she could not leave Italy while attending the old man and then having Igor's child. After that she fell seriously ill herself for nearly two years—both she *and* then the child."

"And after that?"

"After that she was detained by a long-lost relative—an aunt Igor did not know he had, who had been living in Glasgow and then traveled all the way to Venezia to meet Maria."

"And then?"

Catherine read further along. "It seems she then traveled some one thousand kilometers back to us—and brought the aunt with her. She claims to have sent several letters to Igor Igorevich Blukhov during her prolonged absence, but apparently none reached him."

"Nor you!"

"To be sure. And she claims to be eager to rejoin my service!"

"How could you consider such a thing?" he protested.

Catherine dipped a newly sharpened quill into the bejeweled inkwell she used for her voluminous correspondence. "We shall see. I will send for her at once and demand more details to account for what has now been nearly five years."

"She should consider herself fortunate at Her Gracious Little Mother's Benevolence."

"I should like to assume so. We shall see," she repeated before summoning one of her messengers.

Bombarded by petitions from soldiers, farmers, and recent converts now demanding more land, Catherine wondered how she ever could have found herself with so much free time at the beginning of the Volga voyage. Some of these hundreds of petitions—including wrongful ones—were from serfs denouncing their masters, and no matter which way she dealt with them, unrest seemed to break out. She also encountered accounts of peasant rioting, serfs boycotting their responsibilities, and nobles demanding she order these same serfs flogged.

Each time she sighed heavily, painfully aware that any earlier ambitions she'd had to free the serfs seemed hopeless, naive, and fraught with significant pitfalls. In fact, Chapter Eleven of her *Nakaz,* which had taken her two years to write, dealt with the issue of serfdom and thus far was proving to be the most controversial section. Since the final document was due to be delivered to the large, newly elected Legislative Commission in mere weeks and comments and revisions kept reaching her on board, she could not get its future reception off her mind.

Grigory tried not to yawn when she attempted to discuss her woes with him while they watched the stars at night. Alternatively, she found herself often turning to his brother Vladimir when she wanted a sounding board.

"Is it so wrong," she asked him one evening after they had retired from an early game of cards, "to want the humblest of men and women to be treated as human beings? Members of my senate and the nobility insist on slicing up my *Nakaz* as if it were a giant wheel of cheese that should be whittled down to bite-sized portions. Perhaps that is not the correct analogy . . ." Although she seldom drank in the evenings, she ordered a brandy.

"It seems to me, Your Majesty," Vladimir Orlov said thoughtfully, "that even a benevolent autocrat sometimes must make concessions to those whose support she requires to maintain power." He held his breath then, uncertain whether he had overstepped his boundaries, as he had in the past.

Catherine lifted her cordial glass to him in a toast. "Touché. Some of my French friends no doubt would compliment me for my democratic approach, although thus far the issues have only frustrated me. I had no hesitation offering drafts first to my ministers, then the senators, and then to selected noblemen. I had no idea they would gut my treatise and send it back with gaping holes."

"So more like Swiss cheese, Madame?"

"Exactly. Every part of it evoked division. I let the senators erase what they please and they struck out more than half of what I had written. Then I submitted it to educated noblemen and they removed half of the remaining articles. Ultimately I fear it will comprise only one quarter of my labors. I strongly believe that serfs should not only be permitted to purchase their freedom, but that such servitude should be limited to six years maximum. And once a serf is free, he or she should so remain."

She drained her glass and added bitterly, "I fear that these two articles regarding serfdom that I have added shall never see the light of day."

Totally forgetting Vladimir's presence, she turned and headed for bed, feeling a sense of defeat unlike anything she'd experienced thus far in her reign.

CHAPTER 31

(MARIA) 1767

Aboard a riverboat trailing the empress's massive galley, *Tver,* I float along with several dozen ladies and servants. Only I, however, must await an imperial summons before approaching Her Gracious Majesty Catherine II, Empress of All the Russias. My trip overland down to Tver and then all the way south to meet the flotilla at the confluence of the Volga and Oka rivers proved uncomfortable. At least the weather cooperated for me and my two escorts, our horses, a somewhat rickety carriage, and now a swiftly sailing boat.

I've observed Catherine from up close and afar, of course, and don't doubt she has seen me. Her mood has been less than cheerful, as she detests the heavily populated market crossroads where I embarked. I was close enough to hear her complain to a minister, "This town is beautiful in its situation, abominable in construction! I have issued orders to rebuild everything from the governor's house to the spirits and salt warehouses."

She appeared to be speaking with one of her ministers I do not recognize (as has been the case with most of her staff). Later I learn that this incredibly handsome man is Vladimir—Grigory's brother and, although youthful, the newly appointed president of the Academy of Sciences. I listen while appearing not to do so as Catherine commands the formation of a trading company whose investors will foster trade in grain and other valuable commodities with St. Petersburg.

Her energy seems boundless, and her memory sharp as always. "Granted, Nizhny Novgorod boasts four cathedrals, three monasteries, two convents, and thirty-nine churches," she observes to her ever-present listeners. "Now I look forward to our next mooring at a village of merely one tiny church," she continues from quayside. She stands atop canvas that protects her brocade slippers, her voice ringing out as strongly as I remember. I have forgotten how petite she is—perhaps five foot two or three to my additional five inches in height.

Both here in Nizhny Novgorod and in a few smaller ports we've met up with groups of Old Believers, or schismatics, who complain bitterly to their sovereign of abuse and denial of sacraments by the Orthodox and even the Muslim clergy. I've known the pragmatic empress for over twenty years now, and suspect she is not as spiritually devout as she appears. Several times I've noticed her eyes roaming around a church's décor rather than staring straight ahead to contemplate an icon, as custom demands. However, she seems genuinely distressed at all the religious and ethnic tensions in rural Russia. She seldom openly criticizes the Orthodox Church, but possesses zero patience for its intolerance of other religions.

On the other hand, her enthusiasm for the unfamiliar cultures we encounter almost daily is contagious. One afternoon I realize that I haven't thought about my husband, son, or aunts for an entire day! This disturbs me, and at the same time seems somewhat soothing. Catherine has kept us so busy lately that I scarcely know what to do next.

In Cheboksary, which Catherine almost immediately pronounces "superior in every way to Nizhny Novgorod," we reach the unofficial capital of the Chuvash territory. A delegation of female dancers in traditional red and white embroidered attire greets us, lined up with upraised arms to form a rainbow-like bridge we each pass under as part of the welcome parade.

I have befriended a newer maid of honor named Alyona, who seems to know much more about this area and the people's Turkic roots than anyone. "The hats are called tukhya," she notes while standing beside me, gesturing toward a host of helmet-shaped headdresses with pointed tops. They are covered with decorative beads and coins. "See all the rosette appliques on the sleeves and aprons? They indicate that the woman is married," she explains. She also points out the foot cloths that reach their knees and their birchbark shoes.

Later we sneak away for a bit to speak with one of the most elaborately garbed girls, who admits to being dressed for her wedding. I should have figured that out, as she is literally covered with hundreds of gold and silver coins from ears and neck down to the sashes that fall to her knees.

"Sometimes we pass out from the weight," she admits, struggling with her Russian to find the right words. "Each dress can weigh up to sixteen kilos if all the metal is attached."

This reminds me of the imperial dress that Catherine wore so long ago for her nuptials. I recall how the young grand duchess begged to have the gem-laden crown removed for just a few minutes that day. She must have looked incredibly splendid at her coronation, and again I wish I had witnessed it.

In the Holy Trinity Monastery, Alyona and I cover our heads and attempt to catch up with Catherine. This means following the carpet rolled out through the area like the yellow brick road in Oz albeit headed for the emerald roofs of the monastery and its churches. Catherine's feet will not touch the ground.

"I feared we might not be welcome here," Alyona whispers at one point, and then proceeds to fill me in on the recent history of this part of the Volga region. It turns out that over 400,000 non-Orthodox minorities were forcibly baptized or massacred only twenty-five years ago.

"It reminds me of the Holy Crusades," I remark, and she nods knowledgeably.

"My tutors taught me of this period. The Muslims have endured much."

I consider mentioning what has happened to the Jews—or will happen. Of course, I cannot. Aunt Roberta will be interested, however, and I admit to being in a hurry to get back to my family.

We are nearly to Kazan, marked already by glorious mosques alternating with sumptuously decorated cathedrals in testament to the area's diversity.

It was here, I recall, that Ivan the Terrible, or Ivan IV, defeated the Tatars once and for all—a victory that prompted him to order the design and construction of the incredibly flamboyant St. Basil's that still dominates Red Square.

I observe as much to my good friend Anya, now the head seamstress who orders around an entire staff on the river and who upon my arrival expressed boundless delight at seeing me again. Both she and Alyona generously share their quarters with me.

"And do you recall the legend of the Cathedral of Saint Vasily?" Anya asks, using the famous landmark's Russian name as our smaller barge maneuvers to port side to await Catherine's grand ship to catch up. "How Ivan the Fourth ordered the eyes of the two architects who designed the church cut out?"

"Why would he have done such a thing?" I ask in horror.

"Because when he questioned them, they claimed to be able to create something yet more beautiful if so needed," Anya replies matter-of-factly.

Alyona shudders and crosses herself. "It sounds like something our late departed Little Mother Elizabeth Petrovna might have done."

Knowing she once worked for Elizabeth, whose fierce temper I recall well, I don't question Alyona's assessment.

"*Nyet*, I do not think so," Anya says. "Nor Our Most Gracious Majesty, who abhors violence."

"Since I am currently in disgrace," I put in lightly, "I only pray you are correct in your assumption."

Alyona says nothing, and for the first time since my return to the past I experience a twinge of fear. I vacillate between hurt, disappointment, resentment, and anger at Igor's rejection of me. Somehow it never occurred to me that Catherine—usually so forgiving—also might reject me.

"She will send for you," Anya assures me, as if reading my mind while motioning away the two young seamstresses who had finished measuring me for suitable court dresses.

"Remember, my dear friend, that Her Imperial Majesty must uphold her reputation, and it is well known that you quit her service without leave."

Somewhat eerily, her prediction comes true shortly thereafter. As the *Tver* approaches the dock, I am summoned to balance unsteadily across a plank to climb aboard.

Catherine greets me formally while I curtsy so low in my new gown that I stagger to rise again.

"Congratulations on the birth of your son," she says after motioning for me to relax. "I write to mine daily, although I hope you and your little Alexander will maintain a closer relationship than the tsarevich and I do."

Murmuring something that sounds vaguely regretful, I try not to glance around too noticeably at elegant quarters that simply could or should not exist on a river vessel. Seeing my eyes alight on a small marble table, Catherine smiles. "Those are gifts from a local inventor in Nizhny Novgorod named Ivan Kulibin. Some sort of a protégé of an Old Believer merchant, I believe, who presented me with both this lovely microscope and the jeweled telescope. My dear Grigory covets the latter, of course, although I mean to keep it for myself." The microscope, I notice, is far larger and more ornate than the one I recall Igor using in his shop to examine inclusions in gemstones.

I also notice her escritoire boasts a golden snuff box enameled with an image of Peter the Great. "*Da*," she says, noticing me gazing at it. "This is always in front of me when I work."

She walks over to her escritoire and points to a long, detailed map. "Here," she places a bejeweled hand on a spot. "We are close to where our mighty Volga curves in a ninety-degree turn south. The entire province of Kazan serves as the crossroads of Orthodoxy and Islam. Thus far my welcome to the edge of Asia has been affectionate," she says proudly, "and I would like to look my best."

Then, as if I have not been absent without word for nearly five years, she commands me to select her day's jewelry from the elaborately carved wooden boxes in her quarters. Apparently, any further conversation will wait.

She turns and sweeps out of her apartment and onto shore. I trail behind, just as I once did, and other than noting a wary eye cast in my direction by Grigory, am relieved no one protests or seems the least bit surprised at my presence.

Children and women greet our contingent with silver trays of wriggling fish and the traditional hospitality offering of bread and salt. The welcoming music is almost deafening, and I can hear nothing more as I follow the imperial entourage to a local church and then monastery. Inside, the clergy point out miracle-working icons and other objects deemed appropriate for someone they associate with princely glories.

We stay here an entire week, impressed by the intent and respectful attitudes of those worshippers beneath the slender, graceful minarets of the mosques we visit. Catherine notes that "the humility of the Muslims portrays a great contrast to that of our own often disrespectful worshippers." Later she orders a new mosque constructed here.

Sometimes we are treated to entertainment by a diverse group of local peoples ranging from Mordvins and Votiaks to Tatars and Chuvash. I confess to not being able to tell one from the other, and their varying costumes help little. "It is a kaleidoscope of peoples," Alyona comments enthusiastically. "How can all of us be Russian?"

"Yet we are," I say, running my fingers down the smooth royal blue gown Anya has ordered for me. Anya herself, busily supervising her staff as they make alterations and ready gowns for the women accompanying us, is unable to attend all the festivities.

"Sometimes that is a blessing for you," I joke, describing to Anya how for an entire day Alyona and I shadowed the royals as they visited Tatar children at a seminary, received a delegation of newly baptized converts to Orthodoxy, met with the Cossack khan, and hosted a group of nearly five hundred merchants who've traveled all the way from Siberia with their petitions.

Evenings I seldom join the card games, and usually wearily retreat to the boat to which I am still assigned with Alyona and Anya. Alyona usually comes aboard much later, however, as it is her duty to attend the games. That is when I begin to be grateful for my "isolation" from the courtiers and their endless round of activity.

"It was much quieter earlier on the voyage," Anya tells me, looking up from her needlework and watching sympathetically as I rub my weary feet. "The Orlovs loved it, I believe. Only the empress fretted at the inactivity."

"I have noticed that both Grigory and Vladimir seem invigorated when the crew members point out the best hunting areas along the river."

"Oh, yes. I believe they have already founded several new fishing enterprises—as if they need more wealth."

I fall asleep quickly, and do not hear Anya anymore.

At the end of our visit to Kazan, the royal contingent is invited to a ball, and I am to be included. After sorting through Catherine's jewels and selecting for her a parure of rubies and diamonds—resisting the temptation to ask her if it was Igor's design—I let a servant girl, Olga, assist me with my own gown. It's the first time I've been dressed so formally since I left in 1762, and I have forgotten about the nuisance of so many layers. Not only have I not missed stays and their tight laces, which Olga pulls so tightly I can barely breathe, I forgot about the discomfort of the foot-long ivory busk that runs down my chest to my navel. Still, I feel lovely twirling around in a lavender silk gown over a pannier, both of which will probably leave me sweating by midnight if I don't pass out from lack of lung power.

"Borrow any of my jewels that you wish," Catherine told me earlier, and so I selected a simple teardrop of amethyst and matching earrings that dangle as long as my hair (thankfully still not showing strands of gray). Unfortunately, the dye is growing out and my auburn roots must be hidden by an upswept hairstyle. I don't have a mirror available on the boat. Nevertheless, Anya and Alyona assure me I look "stunning." If only I'd been dressed like this when Igor first saw me . . . yet I doubt it would have mattered. Resolutely thrusting that thought to the back of my mind, I meet Catherine's retinue on the quay.

Local dignitaries, merchants, clergymen, seminarians and all their wives shower the empress with the usual array of gifts, which she passes to Alyona and a servant to sort and store on the ship.

Following Catherine and Grigory, I find myself strolling beside Vladimir Orlov, who takes matters into his own hands and introduces himself. I respond formally, as a married maid of honor should, especially seeing his eyes light with interest.

The entertainment takes place outside of the governor's home, my first real event since returning to this century. No one advised us that the local officialdom would be wearing masquerade costumes. Since our traveling party is not, I suppose it is an honor—and perhaps less expensive for the attendees than ball gowns and men's formalwear. The dancers and singers alternate entertaining with costumes, music, and steps that reveal the cultures of an array of peoples of non-Russian descent. Introductions are made in Russian, and I wish Alyona were here to distinguish between Cheremis, Tatars, Votiaks, Chuvash, Mordvin, and Mari ethnicities.

After a dinner indubitably fit for an empress, fire-works explode high over the Volga. It is then that Vladimir approaches me and strikes up a conversation. "I understand you have been many years in Milan," he says politely.

"Venezia, actually." I close my fan to signal I'm in no mood for conversation. While staring up at the explosions of color sparkling the sky, I wonder if he was sent to entrap me in lies.

"I have never been there, although I'd welcome the oppor-tunity," he continues, apparently undaunted. "I understand there is a significant scientific culture. But it is the wealth and richness of its painting, sculpture, glassmaking, and other fine arts that lure visitors from as far away as London."

"I was ill and secluded for most of my visit."

"That really is a tragedy. Did you get an opportunity to participate in the famous carnival held there?"

"I did not. Excuse me, I must attend the empress." It is a weak excuse, since Catherine and Grigory are wrapped up in themselves. I simply will not make up impressions of a city I have never visited!

"Ah, I understand. I have heard that many women move about unhampered by restrictions there—wearing masquer-ade cloaks and various disguises."

I shrug and then gamble. "Of course, that is true. However, I had a baby to raise and little time for frivolities."

He excuses himself then, and I wonder if the Imperial Library in Petersburg contains writings on Venice. Hopefully so.

On quieter nights, I listen to the haunting notes of the Volga boatmen who sing as they sail beside us whenever we approach or depart a town. The river provides its own entertainment, particularly at sunrise and sunset when the ship's wake shimmers in an array of hues. At such times I can imagine the wide ruffled water as the empress's train of pink brocade unfolding behind us.

Sometimes the river gleams like an emerald or sapphire carpet leading us in a downriver waltz past other vessels and onshore onlookers. We are all floating in the cleavage of hills now dressed in spring dandelions and rapeseed, while silver birch spectators line the bank, clapping in the breeze or sometimes prostrating themselves on sandy shores. Drinking it all in as we glide past medieval churches boasting cupolas shaped like gold droplets poised above earth, I sip tea in imported silk and grant imperial waves.

I've never been here, of course, but sometimes it feels as if I have. Thinking back to all I know from more modern times, I imagine a passionate Levitan on shore, honoring Russia's watery mistress by dabbing paint on canvases that, albeit not yet created, will outlast us all.

Every few miles we pass something or someplace of beauty, and it is as if Mother Volga now courses through my veins and overflows the banks of my soul.

Catherine summons me once again as we are packing for Moscow and preparing to disembark a bit prematurely from her seven-hundred-mile downstream journey.

"These people are spoiled by God," she remarks after visiting Simbirsk. "Everything you can imagine is here in plenty, and I don't know what else they could need. I will tell Panin, whose people live here, the same."

We have stayed at Ivan Orlov's nearby estate, and Catherine continues to brim with enthusiasm for the richness of the flora and fauna.

For a short while we talk, I basically repeating my story and she nodding. Occasionally she shakes her head. "Unbelievable," she comments at last. "However, we are prepared to forgive you, and hope that your woebegone husband appreciates your tale and can do the same."

I hesitate before confessing: "Igor is not pleased at my return. He doubts my account of such a long absence."

When she expresses some sympathy for my plight, I feel more confident that my soft grilling might be over. "I will speak to him, Maria Sergeievna. He has a son, and with that comes a grave responsibility. Did he tell you that I have named him a baron—and you, of course, a baroness?"

I stammer now, overwhelmed by the generosity of someone who thought I had abandoned her. "It was the summer you left," she explains, "nonetheless still well-deserved."

My thanks seem inadequate. Now, though, I recall the innkeeper referring to Igor as "His High Born"—what I considered a slip at the time.

"As for your current circumstances," she continues. "I will expect you to remain in my service, at least until your husband gets the windmills out of his head. I could use your assistance. And your advice is always welcome."

I curtsy again, agreeing to all the terms she sets forth.

"You were once my reader," she continues, "and I value your insight into literature and perhaps at times into my thought processes. For example, I'd like to hear your ideas on my current letter to Monsieur Voltaire about this place."

"It would be an honor." My heart trembles, my relief palatable.

"*Da,* of course. Let me tell you what I wish to relay to him." She begins to read from her favorite gold-edged parchment: "There are twenty peoples of various kinds in this town, who in no way resemble one another. And somehow we must make a coat that will fit them all. It may well be possible to discover general principles, but what details! I might say that there is almost a whole world to be created, united, preserved. I may never finish it!"

I murmur something congratulatory, adding, "You *do* have the chance to finish it, Your Gracious Imperial Majesty."

"Perhaps," she replies, waving at a servant to pour us more coffee and serve the delightful, honeyed pastries endemic to this area. "So much work remains that I cannot see how to fashion that coat—or all the coats necessary to bring such a vast empire together."

"Like Joseph's coat of many colors."

"Exactly." She smiles affectionately, and I feel myself warm to her, as well. "We have come a long distance, you and I, Maria. My circle is quite small now. When I enter a room at court, you would think I had the head of Medusa the way they act petrified and all stiffen up. I want to screech like an eagle when that happens. Well, I can tell you that the more I screech, the less they are at their ease. In fact, Lev thinks it's quite hilarious to wear fake snakes dangling from his wig to do an impression of me! You remember Lev Naryshkin?"

"Of course. He used to divert attention from you and Grigory so you could speak alone. And didn't he help you sneak out of the palace many times?"

She laughs. "Indubitably. He remains part of my inner circle. I have no real position for him, so now he is Master of the Horse. He is still a joker, though, who is rarely seen in the saddle."

Turning serious again, she adds, "There must be no more than ten or twelve people who put up with me without constraint, and I hope to count you as one of them again. Now I must go back to Moscow, like it or not. I suspect you and I have a lengthier and more extensive trip ahead of us."

Hopefully she is right, I reflect later, my last glimpse of the Volga reminding me of the empress herself. The river has always been viewed as feminine—a woman of various moods carved through forested hills to engrave Russia. She has seen centuries of invasions while maternally welcoming seagulls, skiffs, and barges. We float along as if between this empress's benevolent bosom, interrupted only by sandbar nipples while defying all other attempts to tame her. On shore the burnished gold, silver, and green domes appear sporadically but predictably, reminding me of accumulating charms for my childhood bracelet.

Catherine has (most generously) permitted me to return to Petersburg until she concludes her business in Moscow; this, as I understand it, will include the reading of a treatise, the *Nakaz* or *Instruction*, she has written to the Legislative Commission.

When the empress races on horseback for her seven-day

return to Moscow's elaborately carved wooden Golovin Palace, I begin a more leisurely route with Anya to Petersburg. "Be glad you are dismissed for a while," Anya teases. "It is not unlike Her Imperial Majesty to set out hunting two or three times per week—nearly as often as our late Empress Elizabeth Petrovna."

"What does she hunt?"

"Mostly game birds. In the capital her birding staff has grown to forty-nine! In Moscow she is frequently much more restless, and there are predictions that she and her falconers will journey out many times per week. I, on the other hand, have a pile of gowns assigned to me and my sewing staff."

"Thank you for the warning. I'm not a hunter," I laugh, and then, more soberly, add, "I, too, have business to attend to in the place where my loved ones await—at least all but one awaits me."

She looks at me sympathetically. "Do you regret the weeks you spent on the river?"

"Not at all." In fact, it is a voyage I know I'll never forget. The journey ahead of me—my life here and now—remains the giant question mark.

Chapter 32

(Catherine) 1767-1768

"An autocrat in Russia, she was a republican in France. Her courtiers were, on the one hand, nobles who defended serfdom, and on the other, philosophers in love with liberty. And she played this double game effortlessly, now letting her heart speak and now her reason, now her taste for Western order and now her tenderness for Russian irrationality."
—Henri Troyat

It required five sessions of her newly-established Grand Legislative Commission to hear Grigory, Yelagin, and Volkov alternate reading her great *Nakaz* or *Instruction* aloud. She had every reason to be proud, she knew, yet still regretted those chapters she'd been convinced to edit or even omit.

Chief among these, as she never stopped bemoaning, was the idea that serfs should be able to accumulate enough property to buy their freedom. She'd been shocked to hear Alexander Stroganov, whom she considered "gentle and humane, kind to the point of weakness" passionately defend the cause of slavery. No less a surprise came from the lips of Panin, who declared she had written "maxims to bring down walls."

"It is my understanding that our empire includes nearly twenty-eight million serfs, none of whom are permitted to own property. And we have approximately half a million members of the nobility who own most of these serfs. There is a problem of balance, Count Panin, not to mention equity."

"The system cannot be altered without bringing the empire to its knees, Your Gracious Majesty. You should know that by now."

She sighed heavily. "There must be a way. If not today, if not this year, then in the future."

"And don't forget that many peasants keep half of the fruits of their labor. They are tied to the land, albeit land owned by someone else. Such earth-shattering changes must be kept for the future."

"And meanwhile?" she demanded bitterly. "Prince Golitsyn provides an extraordinary example of the wasted talents of all these people. Rather than contributing to our great society, they are so little valued that Golitsyn's fashionable horn music now requires forty serfs: one each to blow a single note of music. This is their sole *raison d'être!*"

"I agree it is outrageous, yet look around your palaces, Your Majesty. Is it not true that one servant is assigned to open and close each door?"

Catherine guiltily pretended not to hear him. "Thank God my great predecessor Peter the First at least had the presence of mind to ensure peasants could work their way up the class system through service, not merely via the fortunes of birth."

In the end she had rewritten the offensive chapter of her great treatise. She also issued a condemnation of the mass enserfment of free people and exhorted masters to treat their serfs with humanity. For now, that would have to suffice.

On other topics in the *Ukaz*, she met with success and accolades, particularly her stances on crime and punishment. She sought to mandate fair trials, consistent sentences, clear penal laws, and crime prevention through education. She abhorred capital punishment and insisted on reiterating the importance of the presumption of innocence until proven guilty.

On this legislative mission, her coterie also included a young man she had met briefly at her coronation, and who steadily had worked his way up the table of ranks and into Catherine's circle. His name was Grigory Potemkin, and in addition to his political and military acumen, obvious admiration for Catherine, and blond good looks, he possessed a keen sense of humor. One night when Lev Naryshkin invited Potemkin to join him and Grigory Orlov to play cards with Catherine, they begged him to exhibit some of his famous mimicry. Potemkin replied that he could not do so in this company; however, he said so in Russian by mimicking Catherine's distinctive German accent. Everyone waited anxiously for her reaction. And then Catherine laughed uproariously.

Her triumphant mood continued through the fall and winter. With her *Instruction* so successful both at home and then abroad (in Europe both autocrats and philosophers had received it enthusiastically), she felt little surprise when a contingent of delegates formally offered her the titles of the Wise, the Great, and the Mother of Russia. Just as formally, she refused the honor, insisting that "Such things should be up to posterity to determine."

Nonetheless, she could not help feeling honored. She had reigned for just over five years, and this accolade only stirred her onward with her agenda. It was time to return to her true home in Petersburg.

The empress's prospectors arrived in Petersburg with stupendous news: the discovery of huge silver deposits on the Mongolian border. "What a boon!" she told Betskoy. Perceiving a lack of enthusiasm, she reminded him, "You cannot deny that Russia suffers a severe shortage of silver ruble coins."

Others took a much keener interest. When she summoned Igor Blukhov to consider his latest pieces of jewelry, he reacted eagerly to the metallurgists' forecasts—unlike his estranged wife Maria, who sat in the same receiving room appearing to concentrate fiercely on her knotting.

Knowing both shared her own avid interest in mineralogy, Catherine glanced at her handsome maid of honor and cleared her throat.

Maria looked up belatedly. "Who knows, Matushka, what other wonders the prospectors in the Ural Mountains will find?" She used the informal Little Mother form of address, which her empress recently had permitted.

"Absolutely correct, which is why I have sent geologists across Siberia and the deserts beyond in search of more ores and precious stones." Catherine turned to Blukhov, standing with his back to his wife. "I plan to turn over any newly discovered mines to the merchant class. People like yourself, for example. And soon, when I have some moments, I intend to establish a School of Mines here—Russia's first—to train additional geologists and engineers, all sorely needed."

Igor appeared even more interested. Maria looked longingly at her husband rather than at her empress.

"If I could be so presumptuous, Your Gracious Majesty," Igor said, "we might consider simulating a mine right here so that technicians could train under realistic conditions."

"Splendid! I discussed this long ago with Monsieur Lomonosov before his tragic death. Ever since I have considered such a possibility based on something similar happening in Saxony, where only a few years ago the prince regent established such a mining institute. I can imagine a 'real' underground mine with tunnels and shafts."

"It may be that the metals and minerals the earth protects and holds dear will prove pertinent and valuable to our future," he said eagerly.

"Exactly. Therefore, I hired a scientist—Francis Aepinus— to teach my son. Did you know, Igor Igorevich, that he wrote an entire treatise on the electrical properties of tourmaline?"

The two chatted about tourmaline and other gemstones and minerals in which Catherine, as an avid collector, took a keen interest. "On Sundays after mass I read the geological reports, and last month I learned that . . ." She went on enthusiastically, failing to notice that Maria appeared to barely listen.

Then Catherine said casually, "Igor Igorevich, I would

not object if you were to send your son—Sasha Igorevich—to study eventually with the Tsarevich Paul. They are of course far apart in age. Nevertheless, Monsieur Aepinus already has agreed to tutor the child in material appropriate to his level when he reaches a certain age."

Igor turned as red as the silken Turkish carpet beneath his feet, momentarily looking as if he would protest. Then bowing, he said, "Whatever Your Imperial Majesty desires."

"Excellent. I also assume you might groom him to some-day work with you—maybe to become a partner in your business when he reaches adulthood."

Neither she—nor presumably Maria—missed it when Igor's jaw clamped so tightly they could hear his teeth snap together.

"Thank you for your generous offer," he said hoarsely before repeating the bow and then begging leave to attend the remainder of his palace customers.

After he left, Catherine turned to Maria. "It seems the two of you remain far apart as the planets."

"Alas, we are. And as I told you last month, Matushka, only recently—very recently—he has begun to treat the boy like a son, albeit without acknowledging his paternity."

Catherine sighed. "This has caused us much pain. Anyone can see from a glance who the boy's sire is. Isn't that what Grigory commented the first time he observed Sashenka?"

"He did. My husband is a more stubborn man than I had imagined when we married. He does not like to admit he is wrong."

"That is to be expected, given the length of your absence and the boy being so small for his age." Sensing Maria's discomfort, she asked, "Shall we begin our lesson now?"

Appearing relieved, Maria followed her empress into a more private study. Here they would practice conjugating verbs where no one would overhear them.

Recently Catherine had discovered that not only did Maria speak English fluently, but that her maid of honor Countess Tatiana had hired Maria's own aunt—or perhaps it was Igor's aunt—to tutor her children. Thus far she had not met this mysterious aunt—apparently a countess or duchess who had been educated in Glasgow and whose arrival in Italy had further detained Maria from returning to Russia. She looked forward to the introduction.

Despite possessing a keen memory and confidence in her linguistic abilities, Catherine dismissed two servants standing by. She did not want anyone to know if she faltered over a new vocabulary word—nor to overhear what she was undertaking a few hours per week. It would not do, she reflected, for the British ambassador to discover she was attempting to master at least the rudiments of his language. Let them all believe she spoke only French, German, and Russian. She smiled to herself, imagining how many comments she might overhear.

"My son is nearly grown," Catherine mentioned to Count Panin when he joined her for coffee and cakes. She said it almost casually, as if observing the weather. By now, though, he knew her well. The empress seldom indulged in light conversation, especially during the workday.

She had summoned Panin to join her, ensuring the servant girl brought him tea rather than her own preferred beverage. "My favorite pastry," he noted briefly, picking up a slice of raisin-and-almond-filled pie.

"Such treats are just one aspect of what makes one happier, am I correct?"

Wiping crumbs from his waistcoat, Panin looked up and noted the look of intent in those fiery sapphire eyes. As if suspecting this would be a serious conversation, he pushed his still steaming tea glass aside. "To be sure, there are things we all need to enhance our satisfaction with life."

She clapped in delight. "My dear Nikita, you know me well. That is exactly what I want to discuss."

"Pie?" he asked wryly.

"No, sex."

Panin started coughing in an alarming manner, and a servant rushed over and began patting him on the back.

"For him, Nikita, for your pupil—my son! Now, take some sips of wine. I'm afraid you choked on an almond."

After Panin transformed back to a scarlet-faced, wheezing guest gulping wine, Catherine laughed.

"Truly, my friend, this conversation about my son's sexuality must occur now. Surely you realize that the boy approaches his fourteenth birthday—and is exhibiting a tremendous amount of attention to the young ladies at court."

When he had recovered, Panin sputtered, "Yes, mistress, of course. Of course. Must we discuss this now?"

"We must." She deliberately set her coffee down.

"Might we not wait another year perhaps?"

Dismissing the idea, she waved her long-sleeved arm and

turned earnest. "I was his age when I arrived in Russia, and Peter not much older. I absolutely refuse to leave nature to take its course. This is the mistake our late and beloved Empress Elizabeth Petrovich made, and I won't have it!"

"Don't you mean we must find him a wife first, though?" he asked hesitantly, clearly uncomfortable with this conversation.

"Yes, we shall instigate a search for a suitable bride for Grand Duke Paul soon. That will take more time and interviews, however. Perhaps months, perhaps years. Meanwhile, I want to ensure he is well prepared to perform his conjugal duties when the time comes."

"And you expect me . . . me? To accomplish what exactly?" Catherine nearly laughed again at Panin's discomfort, manifested by an overall shaking and his downcast eyes—not to mention a face still red as the raspberries on one of the cakes.

"No, no. I will leave that to Grigory. He and his brothers can procure the right woman to initiate my son into the mysteries of sex. Not that I don't trust you, with all your vast experience, Nikita Ivanevich, to explain things thoroughly." She suppressed a grin, and his blush deepened.

Panin had just ended an affair with Count Stroganov's estranged wife (making him the butt of endless court jokes) and was now head over heels in love with one of Catherine's maids of honor, Countess Anna Sheremeteva. The engagement had regained him a modicum of respectability, which he did not wish to squander. Nor did he want to annoy his empress. The direction of the conversation thus caused him to squirm. He took several deep breaths and appeared to be formulating an answer.

"You are dismissed, Count Panin, lest you have an apoplexy in my chambers!"

Three weeks later, Grigory informed her that a suitable widow, Sophia Chartoryuzhkaya, had been located and that she was honored.

"Grisha, you must advise my son that no matter how pleasant or enchanting a woman she is, he must not take the liaison seriously. In fact, we should sever the relationship after a couple of months at most. Nature, I believe, will take care of the rest."

"Katinka, that might not be so easy once he gains a taste of . . . well, the pleasures of the act."

"Admittedly. However, before his first mistress is introduced to him, I want you and only you to inform him—both of them—in no uncertain terms that the relationship must be temporary. Nothing must stand in the way of making an appropriate marital match for him. I fear what might happen if he cannot disentangle his emotions from this woman."

"But—"

"This is not negotiable. You must make him swear it on the Bible if necessary. When the day comes that I introduce him to his bride-to-be, whoever she may be, he must not profess to be 'in love' with a mistress. This happened to me repeatedly with my own fiancé, and I will not accept it from my son!"

Seeing how strongly his lover felt about this, Grigory promised. And then he convinced her to make time for their own lovemaking.

Tragedy struck the court when Count Panin's fiancée caught smallpox and died, only increasing Catherine's fears of the disease. Attempting to elude the pox for herself and her son, she flitted from one suburban summer palace to another. Nothing could alleviate her fears, not even attempts to distract herself by boating, riding, and hunting.

"At least you are getting some well-needed exercise," Grigory said.

"Of course, after you accused me of being 'stuck in an eternal armchair.'"

"You were—or are—especially in the winter when you seldom hunt or ride. You must stay healthy, Katinka."

After periods at Gatchina and Catherine palaces, she settled at Peterhof, where a fresh ocean breeze, as she pointed out to Grigory, might continue to provide what she believed could help dissipate the effects of the disease.

"It's simply grist to my mill to have a pretext to stay in the countryside," she told him, at the same time bemoaning the state of Peterhof, into which she had invested a ridiculous amount of money for upkeep.

She had every right to fear smallpox, since its ravages had affected not only commoners but other courts in Europe. Maria Theresa of Austria and several key Hapsburg family members had contracted the disease, in some cases fatally. Long ago in Russia, Peter I's grandson, the fourteen-year-old Tsar Peter II, had succumbed to the disease. Nor would she ever forget that it was smallpox that took her own uncle, Empress Elizabeth's fiancé, a circumstance that had resulted in a lack of heirs. Consequently, she had summoned her nephew the future Peter III to Russia as her heir. It also had been Elizabeth's sentimental attachment to her late fiancé's family that had prompted her to invite his niece to Russia as a candidate to wed Peter. So both deaths had set off a chain of events that had indisputably changed history. Despite counting herself as the unexpected beneficiary of those events, she remained terrified of the disease.

That summer word came that Empress Maria Theresa had risked a new inoculation for smallpox that Catherine already had been researching. "We shall send her a gift to herald her courage," she told Maria. "Please see if our dear Igor Blukhov can craft a rosary made of the most precious stones so that Her Majesty may give thanks for her survival."

As for putting her own plan into action, she needed only to await her own expert, Englishman Dr. Thomas Dimsdale, to arrive. If there was a cure or at least a preventative made possible by science, she would avail herself of it. To do otherwise seemed irresponsible and ignorant.

CHAPTER 33

(MARIA) 1767-1768

Since my return from the Volga region, Igor and I have spoken no more than a half dozen times—none of them satisfactory, let alone cordial, conversations.

"I cannot forget that you left me on purpose," he told me the last time we met when I was permitted to bring Sasha to visit an ill Aunt Gina. "Nor do I accept this baby," and then, emphasizing the last word, he added "as my own."

"He is yours, of that I am certain. I had no idea when I . . . passed through . . . that I was pregnant. He was born seven months later. My Aunt Roberta will verify this, of course.

Neither of us knows anything concrete about the vagaries of time travel. I've told you all this before!"

On each occasion we stood in the entry to his main workshop, in the exact same spot where I had first shocked him as he removed boxes of gemstones from the shelf. I do note that as my unwelcome visits progress, the place begins to look more and more immaculate. So does Igor himself. Aunt Gina confides, "Regardless of whether or not he accepts or believes you, my dear, he acts, dresses, and looks as if for the first time in years he has something for which to live."

If so, I cannot tell. His tone remains harsh. Recalling the loving manner he took with me throughout most of our marriage, I am as hurt to hear this as I am to see the new expression chiseled like granite on his features.

At least there apparently are no more doubts in his mind regarding my truthfulness about arriving here inexplicably from the future the first and now second time. It's only the matter of Sasha's age that he cannot reconcile.

This morning I am visiting to bring some broth to Aunt Gina, who has recovered fully. I fear, though, that she does not take good enough care of herself. To her disappointment, I allowed Sasha to accompany Aunt Roberta to Tatiana's palace, where he adores watching the horses and playing with her dogs. Aunt Gina is pleased to see me, and I apologize for the fact that without a kitchen, the hotel's broth is the best I can manage.

When she retreats into her own kitchen, she does not return.

I decide to take matters into my own hands, bravely opening the door to the main workshop. "We need to talk some more," I tell Igor. "You have never permitted me to explain more than the basic facts, nor share with you the time I spent in the twenty-first century."

"Fine!" He pulls out a chair for me in the shop while he hunches over the set of bejeweled spectacles he is decorating with diamonds. So, I think wearily, he is not even going to give me the courtesy of eye contact.

"Are those for the empress?" I ask politely, knowing she suffers from an unusual number of migraines, especially when reading.

"No. I promised her that when she is ready, I shall adorn a pair for her with rubies and diamonds. Right now she does not want anyone to know she needs them."

I smile, though he does not look up. "This is true. Most of her ministers have advised her against wearing spectacles, as they fear they will detract from her imperial persona."

"Nonsense. As far back as Emperor Nero, people wore them for reading. The average human eye cannot sustain perfect vision with age."

"You sound like one of her scientists."

"Well, she should listen to them. Especially Dimsdale, the British doctor."

"And which one is he?" I ask casually, grateful for the moment that at last we are sharing a normal conversation and not arguing.

Igor pauses and looks across the wooden table littered with tiny tools and pieces of garnet and silver. "He is a friend of Baron Cherkassov, the president of the Institute of Health. He has been advocating for a newly discovered inoculation against the pox, a subject he's written about widely, and the empress has urged him to come to Russia. I hear he might arrive next year."

"Truly? A cure for smallpox? I thought that wasn't—won't, I mean—be developed so soon."

"This Dr. Thomas Dimsdale believes in introducing the disease intentionally into the body so one could build up some kind of resistance to the disease later on."

"We call that a vaccine or an immunization. An injection with a needle—a shot that protects you from something like the measles."

"Hmm. Maybe. I believe, though, that he actually cuts the person's arm open and inserts the live disease from a smallpox patient. I fear Her Imperial Majesty will incur the wrath of her subjects over such an idea—if she implements it, that is."

"Look around us, Igor. From what I hear, recent years have been deadly. And if there is a way to protect our Sasha—"

"Do you want some wine?" he asks, abruptly dismissing the subject of the son he does not claim.

Sighing, I agree, and we move into the dining room. There is no sign of Aunt Gina, only pleasant smells emanating from the kitchen.

"Tell me your story then," he says, albeit without the bitterness ever-present in his tone these past months. "From the beginning," he specifies, and I sense that his primary interest is why I left in the first place. He pours us glasses of cabernet, and I relax a bit.

I recount as much as I can, making no attempt to shield myself from blame. The discovery of the statue. The entire bottle of wine. The hour or so I sat contemplating the possibilities. My overwhelming curiosity. Then the confidence that just a touch would not remove me from this life I loved.

"Did you once, even for a moment, think about me before you . . . left?"

"Yes, of course I did! Not solely about you," I admit. "I also thought about my aunt, and what had happened to her in the future. I didn't know where and when I might end up. I guess I just had to try. Perhaps subconsciously I was thinking, too, that if I were to have the opportunity to go back, I should make the attempt then and there rather than wait until we— until we had children."

Tears seem to fill both of our eyes at once. "I was shocked and devastated when I ended up back in the museum—the palace, I mean—in my own time. Eighteen years later, in fact. I knew I had made a horrific mistake, my love, yet I could not find a way to return to you."

"Another day you must tell me exactly how it was it took you so damn long!"

"I couldn't come back while I was pregnant, and certainly not until Sasha was old enough to walk. And you have no idea what both the Russian and American authorities thought about my sudden reappearance."

"That you were insane?"

He sounds calmer than before, despite the intensity of his words, then stands and removes the wine glasses from the table. I understand our visit has concluded.

I dare not look at his precious face again. I dare not call out to Aunt Gina to say goodbye. Nor do I dare hope this might be the beginning of something verging on reconciliation.

I am worried about Aunt Roberta. Although she may have come to this period of her own free will, I'm afraid she might not be happy here. Or now.

"Do you regret coming with me?" I ask bluntly one afternoon.

We remain at the inn as Duchess Meekhof (having decided elevating her to countess was too risky) and Baroness Blukhova, with Igor paying for our lodging for reasons I do not explore or question. My small salary at court and Aunt Roberta's tutoring earnings permit us to keep the three of us clothed and fed. There is no question that our fortunes might change if Igor would welcome us into his home. No doubt the entire court has an opinion on our estrangement, as they surely did on my disappearance.

"Regret?" she asks, as if befuddled by the question. She is sipping tea in front of the fireplace and Sasha has sprawled out asleep on the divan.

"You gave up your entire life. Not just the comforts of the future, your career! Not to mention a man who seemed to adore you." I only met her suitor once. However, Thomas did seem to wear his heart in his eyes.

She sets down her tea and moves it deliberately aside. "I didn't love him. Not the way you love Igor. I did trust him, which is why I turned over my affairs to him."

"Meaning what? Your apartment? Your possessions? Your money?" I have wondered about all of that; however, since our arrival I've pushed aside my guilt over what I consider as literally dragging her into the past. My prior attempts to get more than meager details from her have failed.

"I wanted to be with you, Maria. And with Sasha. Don't

feel as if you should reproach yourself for that. I planned this for months. I know," she adds quickly as I open my mouth to protest.

"I arranged things so that if I disappeared and never returned, no one would suspect anything or search for either of us."

"But your job!"

"I was close enough to retirement that no one objected when I asked for an extended leave of absence. The Board of Trustees approved it just after Christmas. I just never told you."

"Now I feel worse. The university was your life! And what if you hadn't been able to come through—into the past—when I did?"

"I planned for that, too. And you're right, teaching *was* my life. I wanted a new one. And if that meant an opportunity to live in a period I'd researched since I was in my twenties—and could be with my niece and grandnephew—all the better. Contrary to what you might believe, my dear, I am content. Now, if only I could meet the empress!"

"Aunt Roberta, this is what I planned to tell you today. That Her Majesty has sent a message inviting us to live in the palace as soon as she returns to Petersburg next month—if we want to, that is."

My aunt smiles—a radiant smile I've not seen since I brought Sasha home from the hospital.

"So we will need to call upon your friend Anya and get some dresses made, correct?"

I laugh and pull the cord to summon a maid. "We should toast to our good fortune."

Good fortune, indeed. At least as good as it can get until Igor welcomes me back into his life and acknowledges the son he helped create.

Several days later we visit the House of Gems and get to celebrate again when I introduce Aunt Roberta to Igor. He is polite, albeit noticeably wary.

As if sensing our happiness, Sasha emerges from the back room with Aunt Gina and immediately races to hug my legs until I pull him up.

"We are leaving in a couple months for lodgings at the Winter Palace," I tell Aunt Gina. Seeing the beginning of a frown, I add, "you are still most welcome to care for Sasha there. If your nephew permits your visits," I add in a lower voice.

She mutters something in Italian before adding in Russian, "This is not his decision. It is mine."

A short time later, the three of us toast with vodka and blini slathered with caviar. On the rug beneath our feet, Sasha plays with a pile of wooden blocks, secure in the love of the women surrounding him. Igor has disappeared again.

So much has changed in the massive Winter Palace in the past few years. Catherine obviously has had it redecorated, as well as expanded. Now I and her other twenty maids of honor (all wearing fancy white caps) live upstairs in the southwestern part, accessible by a literal warren of corridors and staircases. Catherine's staff, readily identifiable by their dark-blue woolen uniforms and brooch with her initials in diamonds, tell me they will trade for pale blue linen attire in the summer. Most of us also wear ornate gold badges trimmed with diamonds and the empress's monogram beneath a tiny crown. The badges each have a loop for a ribbon where we can keep necessary keys. So far I have none.

The empress's apartments overlook the south, or what will someday be known as Palace Square. She receives ambassadors and other dignitaries in the green damasked audience chamber, while its counterpart along the Neva River hosts large banquets. The green and gold dining room converts most evenings to a billiard hall. The empress's state bedroom doubles as the Diamond Room—home of the royal regalia. In actuality, the designer who catered to Catherine's neo-classical principles has arranged for this room to serve as her salon, or the place where she entertains and plays cards. Her smaller boudoir is linked to it, flowing into her study, the library, and eventually the chapel to the north. With over one thousand rooms, over a hundred stairways, nearly two thousand doors and an equal number of windows, the palace makes it impossible to find one's way around. I despair of ever locating Sasha if he gets lost!

Only a few months after settling in our room (we have been given one with three beds), I'm summoned to Peterhof, one of three suburban palaces where she fled to escape the smallpox ravaging the city. Aunt Roberta has been included in the invitation. I'm delighted to have her with us, and relieved she will not be exposed to the disease due to her assurances she was vaccinated as a child. As for Igor and Aunt Gina, I can only pray for their health and safety.

One morning I find Catherine seated at her rosewood writing desk wrapping up a meeting with a fine-looking gentle-man who eyes me with interest. "And is this the daughter of the sculptors you mentioned?" he asks.

"It is. Maria Sergeievna Blukhova, this is Monsieur Eti-enne-Maurice Falconet. He is working on my artistic tribute to our great predecessor, Peter the First."

I curtsy politely, eager to hear about my so-called parents. Alas, it turns out he knows them only by reputation.

After his departure, Catherine complains, "Despite all his ideas and a fine reputation, thus far his proposals have been a disappointment."

Falconet. The name should mean something to me, I think, and then it clicks. He is the man who designed—or will design—the gigantic Bronze Horseman statue that will someday serve as the symbol of St. Petersburg.

"I'm certain he will come up with the right idea, given time," I assure her.

"Perhaps. He is renowned in France. Now, my dear friend, it is time for our lesson—and maybe you will indulge me later by reading. My eyes ache today, and Monsieur Diderot has just written to me. She hands me several pages as well as her quill. "If I interrupt you, it's so you can note something in the margin."

I can only imagine the look on Aunt Roberta's face when I tell her I have read the Russian empress a letter from the great Diderot. "Your Imperial Majesty," I dare interrupt. "Might it be possible for you to someday grant an audience to my aunt? She is a highly educated woman, and perhaps more informed about Peter the First than anyone I have met—excepting Your Imperial Majesty, of course."

Her eyes glimmer with interest.

"She is something of a scholar despite being a woman," I hasten to add. If I'm correct, this will deepen her interest.

She leans forward slightly. "How marvelous! And how did your aunt acquire such a repertoire of knowledge?"

"She left Italy as a young child to study in Britain, where she also became fluent in English." Careful to keep "facts" to a minimum, I find this keeps me from contradicting myself. Since Aunt Gina is tutoring my aunt in Italian, I hope this all sounds at least somewhat plausible.

"And how does she desire to proceed in our empire, now that she has emigrated?"

"You would have to ask her, Matushka. I believe she is most interested in exploring Peter the First's collection at the Kunstkamera, as well as the imperial archives."

She takes a long sip of her strong coffee. "We shall arrange for an audience with the duchess and then determine what access might be granted."

Relieved, I drop a curtsy. "Thank Your Gracious Majesty. I know she will be honored." The rest will be up to my aunt, who may have to fill in more details about her mysterious past.

Grigory Orlov makes one of his flamboyant entrances then, barely repressing a frown when he sees me. I know he remains suspicious about my lengthy absence from court; hopefully he will come to believe at least part of my story.

What else can I expect when my own husband doesn't believe what I tell him?

I am not present when Aunt Roberta meets the empress. They remain secluded in her chambers for over an hour. A good sign, I reflect, restlessly awaiting my aunt's return to our quarters.

When she arrives, dressed in such a fine gown that no one in the twenty-first century would have believed it was her, she can barely speak.

"This," she nearly sputters, "this is why I am here. I know that now. This is the most wonderful—no, the most enlightening—moment of my life. Thank you, my dear daughter. A thousand thank you's."

After that, my aunt gets summoned regularly, though she often dodges my questions about the specifics of her conversations with Catherine. She also remains busy tutoring Tatiana's children, who have accompanied her and their mother to Peterhof, as well as teaching Sasha to read.

I warn that her fictitious past in Scotland may get her in trouble. Thus far, however, she has worked her way around the fact that not only is Catherine's personal physician from University of Edinburgh, the empress employs Scottish scientists, architects, and other craftsmen.

Igor and I meet a few more times, usually because I am sent to the shop on jewelry business for Catherine (a situation I suspect she manipulated). Still, we've not seen each other since I moved here. So I'm surprised one day to see his familiar figure approaching where Sasha and I are ensconced in the garden below Peterhof's cascade of fountains. His steps slow and he pauses to await the carriage beside him to stop before tenderly lifting Aunt Gina out near one of the fountain's gilded statues.

He does not appear startled to see me, and barely sup-
presses a grin when Sasha, tossing a cloth ball with me,
shrieks in delight at the sight of Aunt Gina. "Baba!" he cries,
nearly run over by the carriage as he races for her, the two
of them both speaking excitedly in Italian. Although I knew
Aunt Gina had been teaching Sasha her native language, I did
not realize he had retained so much. Now he chatters away
too fast for me to follow, and I resist the urge to interrupt
them in English to admonish him for the umpteenth time
to be more careful around horses and carriages. Since Aunt
Roberta and most of the staff speak Russian, it seems I have
a tri-lingual toddler.

Igor seems to have the situation in hand, grasping the reins
of one of the horses and chastising the carriage driver loudly.

After greeting the two, I motion for a servant to bring
several of the elegant, foldable red chairs used for sitting on
the grounds. The three adults settle in them. Sasha cannot
release his hands from those of Aunt Gina.

"We have come to beg a favor," Aunt Gina says as another
servant appears with a tray of cold beverages.

"*You* have," Igor mumbles. "Don't forget that initially you
merely told me you wanted to come for a short visit and might
need assistance getting back home to the shop."

Aunt Gina has the audacity to laugh with only a trace of
guilt, and I notice how spry she looks compared to years past.

As if reading my mind, she picks up the ball and tosses it
to Sasha's outstretched arms. "The boy gives me energy, don't
you Sashenka?"

Sasha giggles and throws the ball back, barely missing a
fountain landing. "Enji," he attempts to repeat.

"Energy," Aunt Gina repeats slowly, and my smart little guy repeats it perfectly.

Igor clears his throat. "It has occurred to my aunt that you might be extremely busy now, moving from one summer palace to the next."

"So we thought maybe—" Aunt Gina jumps in.

"*You* thought maybe," Igor says wearily.

"Yes, *I* thought maybe he might come and stay with us for a few months. You know, to give you some time and freedom to attend the empress."

"But—"

"My aunt is right," Igor interrupts. "This palace life is not the best environment for a child, and we could supply him with round-the-clock care and attention."

I resist the urge to retort that letting us live in a hotel followed by the palace for a year wasn't conducive to our child's upbringing either. Then, too flabbergasted to think clearly as the offer sinks in, I go on the defensive. "He has plenty of children to play with here, and numerous servants to tend him when I am away or up late at night—which I seldom am, incidentally. There's no need to yank him from his home."

"You don't exactly have a home, though, do you?" Igor arches one eyebrow in a way I used to adore. "Her Royal Majesty summons you at all hours of the day, and you constantly move from Gatchina to Tsarskoye Selo to the Winter Palace to here at Peterhof. It's not a stable upbringing."

"My Aunt Roberta is here!"

"Is she? I don't see the 'duchess' right now, and from what I understand she is quite busy with other duties."

I can hardly argue with that. Before I can say anything

more, Aunt Gina interjects, "Might he not stay with us at least until he begins his math and science lessons? I am much too old to be traipsing off to four palaces to see the boy."

She does not look that old these days, and I can sense that the only reason Igor is not protesting loudly is because he recognizes how much my son means to her.

"Remember, my dear aunt, the boy is *not* yours," Igor leans over to say.

I can almost see her thinking: *No, but he is yours.*

"And people might talk," Igor adds, frowning.

Aunt Gina pushes a silver curl behind her ear and reaches out for Sasha again. "Let them! I merely stated that we have plenty of room and I have plenty of time." Then she speaks rapidly to Igor in Italian again, and I despair of understanding.

When the tone of the conversation changes—Igor's to one of resignation—I know that his aunt has won.

Tempted as I am to refuse, I am secretly pleased. If it has occurred to Igor that this is Aunt Gina's way of manipulating him into spending time with the boy he denies is his son, he wisely refrains from accusing either of us of such a thing.

I make one last—and the most important—protest. "What about the pox in the city? That, after all, is why Her Gracious Majesty has spent months in the countryside."

"I assure you he will be protected," Aunt Gina assures me.

"How? Even members of the imperial court are not protected. Did you hear that Count Panin's fiancée has died of the disease?"

Igor puts a hand on my arm. "Rest assured, Maria Sergei-evna, the boy will never be exposed to ballrooms or palace crowds—nor market or street crowds. And unlike so many others who see the highly discussed inoculation as the devil's work, I promise to get Sasha to this Dr. Dimsdale the moment Her Imperial Majesty gives her approval."

So it is done. My son will go to stay with his father for the remainder of the summer at least, and I will be a childless woman separated from her husband. The idea holds little appeal; I can only pray that father and son form a bond.

I wait as long as possible to visit Sasha—not to mention Igor. By early August I can stand it no longer. A child needs its mother, regardless how many court ladies entrust theirs to servants and governesses. At least I can see him for a while.

Sending a message in advance ensures they will be ready for me, and grudgingly I admit that it also gives Igor the opportunity to be away during my visit if he so chooses.

Thus I am doubly relieved when Igor himself opens the door to House of Gems as soon as my carriage pulls to a stop.

Perhaps to cover his embarrassment at lifting me down, he immediately informs me, "My aunt has prepared your favorite dessert."

"Tiramisu?"

"*Si.* The Duke's Pudding, as it used to be called."

As we enter the shop, neither of us mention what both of us must be recalling: that originally the famous dessert was served as an aphrodisiac.

"I had it once in the—the future," I tell him now. "Not nearly as tasty as Aunt Gina's, though." In truth, Aunt Roberta and

I rarely went out to dinner in the States, unable to risk being captured on camera by an army of phone-wielding observers.

Sasha greets me joyfully, and for the first time I realize he now comes up to my waist. How old is my son—really? Do I count the "missing" years? I had presumed he turned three this spring, although he exhibits the height and vocabulary of a four-year-old. This is more than a little disconcerting, and while Aunt Gina makes us all comfortable, I find my eyes unexpectedly tearing up.

"What is wrong?" Igor says quietly as Sasha retreats to his room to pull out his things one by one to show me.

"I don't know. I guess I just fully realized that I might be past forty now. Well, not if I am on *future* time, which means I am in my late thirties . . ."

He does not look surprised. "And so?"

"And so, I can hardly have children anymore. What the hell was I thinking?" I stand, prepared to depart and take my three- or four-year-old son with me.

"Stay." He says firmly. "It's not as if you were *planning* to have more children, is it?"

"I had *hoped* so! Or at least one you believe is yours!"

This is not going at all well—at least not the way I had anticipated the visit. I barely notice Aunt Gina surreptitiously slip from the room with Sasha.

Igor heaves a sigh, moving closer to me on the divan. "First of all, my dear Maria Sergeivna, you don't look anywhere near forty. And if I were you, I would take at least five years off that before revealing your age to anyone. Lest you arouse suspicion, if you understand—."

Putting my hand up with the palm toward him, I interrupt.

"Don't *you* understand? That's not the only problem! I was two years older than Her Imperial Majesty when I arrived . . . back here. How can I now suddenly be younger than she is?"

"I doubt anyone will recall or make inquiries about your age. What I meant to say is that you don't appear too old to bear a child. However, the problem for me is that I admit to fearing childbirth might be too dangerous."

"You *fear*?" I reach for the handkerchief he gives me and blow my nose.

"Yes, I do. Regardless of whether this is my son or someone else's—." When I raise my tear-filled eyes in protest, he covers my mouth gently though firmly. "Please allow me to continue."

Unsure whether to be angry, relieved, or just curious, I wait. "I have come to a decision that might—just might—work for you. For all of us. I am willing to adopt the child and raise him as my own. Including as my heir."

Dumbfounded, I do not respond. Should I be thankful? Insulted?

"Why?" I finally manage.

"Because he is *yours*. And he needs a father. And because you are mine. I think?" He stares down at me with penetrating eyes sparkling with a hint of tears.

"I've been yours since the moment I saw you in Empress Elizabeth Petrovna's chambers selling jewelry."

"And I yours, my love. I'm not certain how long it will take for us to get back to where we were when you left—or disappeared—yet I would very much like us to attempt such a feat. I have lost too much already."

We don't kiss. When he envelops me in his arms and I

breathe in the once familiar scent of him, I accept this as an overture, perhaps a promise.

Somehow even after all this time, it seems much too soon. For both of us.

"Perhaps," I hesitantly suggest. "Perhaps we could court first? The way we used to?"

His eyes crinkle in a grin, the first one I've seen on him since my arrival. "That would be marvelous. Shall we start now? Next week is the ceremony to lay the foundation of the new cathedral."

"Named after St. Isaac of Dalmatia. I know. Her Majesty has invested 64,915 rubles on marble secured from the shores of Lake Ladoga. An Italian—the great sculptor Antonio Rinaldi—is to design it."

"So Aunt Gina informs me daily," he laughs. "According to her, Russia owes half of its achievements to Italian craftsmen."

"Yourself included."

"Of course. I am her favorite Italian. Come, let us tell her that we will attend the event together."

CHAPTER 34

(CATHERINE) FALL 1768

"The Turks have declared war!" the messenger announced, and Catherine dropped her quill, splattering ink on the letter she had been writing.

"Tell me what has happened," she demanded, simultaneously ordering her maid to summon Panin, Grigory, and Procurator-General of the Senate Prince Vyazemsky.

"Your Imperial Majesty, your own ambassador is now a prisoner of the Ottoman Empire." The messenger, kneeling and trembling, obviously feared the news might reflect on him personally. "The entire embassy staff is imprisoned in Constantinople."

"Dispatches must be sent. Please await them," she ordered.

It was Alexis Orlov whose message explained what had happened: "The Cossack troops sent to suppress those Polish Catholic rebels have crossed the border into the Ottoman Empire. They sacked the frontier town of Balta, massacring Jews and all Balta's citizens along the way. Now the sultan has retaliated."

Her Imperial Majesty groaned when she read this, as much from the idea of what a war would cost as from her anger over the actions taken in her name. War itself she did not fear. Fiscal irresponsibility she did. A mere few years ago she'd extricated Russia from the seven-year-war with Prussia, and only now could she begin to repair the financial damage.

Nor could the timing have been worse in so many other ways. For one, recognizing a need to establish a foothold in the Black Sea, she recently had ordered the decrepit ships in the Baltic refurbished. She had hired British officers to command them, planning to send them on a long journey to commandeer a position in the Black Sea. Alas, the ships had not set sail yet.

Her relationship with Louis XV had reached rock bottom, deteriorating to the point that, besides calling her a usurper, he refused to refer to the new empress as Her Majesty. Long ago when she had tried to secure a loan from him prior to her coup, he had judged the affair too risky. That was his own diplomatic folly, she'd long since decided, fondly recalling that the British had contributed one hundred thousand rubles. And now, as a traditional ally of the sultan, Louis surely would cheer this Turkish victory. Not only would there be no hope of an alliance with France, she feared that now France might declare war on Russia.

More importantly, she was preparing to have Dimsdale secretly carry out her long-awaited smallpox inoculation. For days she'd forgone meat and wine, increased her exercise and fresh air, and faithfully swallowed eight grains each of powder of crab's claws and calomel, plus an eighth of a grain of tartar emetic. This laxative concoction prescribed by Dimsdale was followed by a morning dose of Glauber's salt.

The infected peasant child whose smallpox matter would be injected into her had been selected and would be brought to her. Neither she nor the doctor believed the current theory that a donor of the disease would die.

"Nothing can be more important than ensuring I am alive to rule and to fight as many wars as necessary for the empire," she assured the ever-hesitant Dimsdale and his apprentice son Nathaniel. She had tried repeatedly to convey the urgency to the Englishmen, practicing her meagre English on them when they demurred, delayed, or failed to understand her.

On October 12, she summoned Dimsdale, his interpreter Alexander Cherkasov (who also headed the medical college at Cambridge), Panin, and a Holsteiner from Paul's household. Grigory happened to be away on a hunting expedition.

Since no mention of Dimsdale's arrival appeared in the official court records, she assumed that her brave action would be a secret. Nonetheless, people knew the whom and the what—just not the when. Only Catherine controlled that knowledge, taking pains that no one try to dissuade her from what the Sorbonne had banned as an act against Providence.

Dimsdale cut the skin in both her arms before carefully inserting the smallpox pus from an infected peasant boy named Alexander Markov. It didn't hurt terribly, and she did not complain. She recalled the awful period of her late husband's case during the early days of their relationship; she still regretted visibly recoiling the first time she saw his pock-marked face and distorted features. It was a moment that most likely severed whatever goodwill there was between them. This must not happen to her own son and heir.

Afterward, she retreated to Tsarskoye Selo for her recovery.

She continued to take the awful bedtime laxative Dimsdale ordered, crushing it into powder and disguising the taste with syrup or jelly.

A week after the inoculation, marks appeared on her arm. She sweated throughout that night, and in the morning Dimsdale discovered new pustules circling the incision site. Determined not to worry, since the entire point of injecting her with the disease was to ensure she contracted a mild case of smallpox, she played cards and walked the Great Hall of Catherine Palace, with its splendid golden enfilade, array of gilded windows, and massive painted ceiling that nearly rivaled that of the Sistine Chapel.

The spots, including one on her forehead and two on her wrist, disappeared rapidly, leaving not one scar. When she developed a sore throat, she gargled with black currant jelly.

Throughout her convalescence, she continued to work as much as possible and to maintain an active correspondence.

In Catherine's opinion, Baroness Maria Blukova risked her own life by tending to her mistress. "My family is safe," she assured Catherine, "and I can at least read to you and assist with papers and letters."

Maria's help proved to be a godsend. And with Maria and a few other ladies confined to the spacious and beautifully landscaped grounds of Catherine Palace in Tsarskoye Selo, the empress heard no complaints. She kept them several meters away from her, though, joining them on garden strolls. Gradually she worked back up to her usual ten miles per day, measured by her pedometer, while she stared at the palace's elaborate green and buff façade and calculated ways to improve it someday. Unlike her predecessor Elizabeth, she detested pink, and left the Winter Palace apple green and planned the rest of her renovated palaces to be done in colors ranging from golden yellow to cherry red.

Maria and Tatiana made no secret of looking forward to getting their own inoculations, vowing to stay with Catherine until she was ready to have her courtiers mildly infected with the virus. Maria offered her Aunt Roberta's companionship, as well.

"Absolutely not," Catherine replied. "I am endangering too many lives here already, including your own. And absolutely no one except Grigory undergoes this experiment until the heir does." They were all waiting for young Paul to recover from chickenpox, as both she and Dimsdale adamantly agreed that introducing a second virus to his young body would be risky.

In response to Dimsdale's persistent nervousness about killing the empress of Russia with his methods, Catherine had reassured him beforehand that she'd provided for that eventuality. "I admit that certain sensations render me apprehensive about my life. You are correct in surmising that my subjects would hold you responsible for any accident that might befall me." She waited a few moments for Maria to translate, as she wanted no errors.

Continuing, she assured the doctor, "I have stationed a yacht in the Gulf of Finland, on which you and your son should embark as soon as I am no more. The boat's commander, in consequence of my orders, will convey you out of all danger."

As the empress continued to recover, she had no doubt that the escape plan would not be needed.

Meanwhile, Maria assisted with correspondence, even though her penmanship could not compare to the empress's large and elaborate script. When Falconet chastised Catherine for defying the Sorbonne, she directed Maria to reply, "They often decide in favor of absurdities, which in my opinion should have discredited them long ago. After all, the human species are no longer goslings."

The archbishop himself led a Te Deum in the palace chapel on November 2, when Paul received his uneventful inoculation. After that, Maria joined Grigory and over a hundred nobles and ladies who followed suit. To demonstrate the safety of the procedure, Grigory decided to go hunting again the day after his own. Attitudes shifted rapidly after Catherine's heralded survival, especially as the most beautiful court women no longer feared disfigurement.

On Catherine's Name Day, November 24, she made Dimsdale a baron and titled the little Alexander whose smallpox had been injected into her. Both also received handsome monetary rewards.

By year's end, Catherine wrote merrily to Voltaire in response to Empress Maria Theresa's boasting of having inoculated a few patients in the Austrian court: "More people have been inoculated in Russia in one month than in eight months at Vienna." Catherine was determined to have as many thousands of her subjects as possible follow suit, regardless of the required time and organization.

Meanwhile, confident in the health of herself, her son, and basically the entire court, she could delve into other matters of significance. These included not only the nascent war, but her burgeoning art collection for the Small Hermitage, significant architectural projects, tax reform, spontaneous revolts in the Balkans, educational reform, an overhaul of the currency system, and the new journal, *All Sorts*, that she'd just founded and edited.

Catherine also had a passion for British literature, which Baroness Maria often read to her in Russian when Catherine's eyes were too weary to read the French or German translations.

"We must see to it that more world literature is translated," she mentioned to Maria over the days that she listened to her translate Laurence Sterne's English novel, *The Life and Times of Tristram Shandy, Gentleman*.

"You are correct, Matushka. It is reading and literature that have made you as great as you are, and everyone should have access."

After several similar conversations, the empress commissioned one of her highly educated secretaries, Grigory

Kozitsky, to translate her own *Instruction* or *Nakaz* into Latin. He also would translate the Greek and Roman classics denied to Russian readers, beginning with Ovid's *Metamorphoses*. These comprised his first duties in his new appointment overseeing Catherine's latest creation: the Society for the Translation of Foreign Books.

Always bursting with ideas, she continued to resent hours wasted asleep.

CHAPTER 35

(MARIA) 1769

"S he is a maniac about collecting," Igor observes one day while we await Sasha's return from the summer gardens where Aunt Gina had taken him to play.

At first I think he refers to Aunt Gina or Aunt Roberta, seemingly outdoing one another purchasing the whimsical wooden toys my son loves so much. The cleverly crafted and often animated toys come in so many variations that no child could ever get a duplicate. Sasha's favorites include a dancing bear and another that saws wood; a woodpecker knocking his beak on a tree; a sleigh pulled by trotting horses, and a miniature palace complete with tiny people carrying trays in and out.

"He's young, and now that he has tutors, he deserves his fun," I say casually.

Igor stares at me a moment and then laughs. "I am referring to Her Imperial Majesty—our empress who cannot stop ordering things built or purchased to add to her growing and already enormous collections. Do you not agree?"

Now it is my turn to laugh. "Of course. Not only have I assisted the empress in labeling hundreds of paintings to fill the newly constructed Hermitage addition, under her direction I've reorganized the Diamond Fund in what I think of as the master bedroom (which she claims is exactly three thousand steps from the Hermitage). Her appetite for artistic objects does seem endless, though one can scarcely criticize her luxurious purchases considering all her societal and political achievements. And she does find bargains. Sometimes I see a painting she acquired for almost nothing, and I *know* it will be considered a masterpiece one day."

"Does *she* know that it will?"

"Sometimes. She spends a lot of time these days devouring everything ever written about the European art market. She also studies catalogs of the paintings she purchases."

"Do you have favorites yourself?"

"Oh, yes. Recently she acquired this amazing group of paintings from Dresden. I love one of the Rubens, 'Perseus and Andromeda.' It's full of cherubs and this magnificent right half of the painting dominated by a Pegasus that looks incredibly real; it's as if you could reach out and stroke him. Anyway, I've rambled enough about the art. It's just that the collection she puts in her new Hermitage is getting huge."

"And your own aunt feeds into this collecting compulsion, does she not?"

"She does. Not in paintings, though. Aunt Bobbi keeps showing up with gifts that delight Catherine. I suspect, however, that *she* is the one who's really in love with the inkstand flanked by gilded swans and the clock encircled with cupids."

"And don't forget all the rebound books she finds for her. I'm no book binder, though I can tell you there are some fantastic gems on the covers. Is she hoarding money or just lucky? Or perhaps Roberta has a benefactor we don't know—"

As if sensing she's being discussed, Aunt Roberta enters, grasping something so large that I don't understand why she didn't entrust it to the groomsman. "Look what I found in Gostiny Dvor!"

She unwraps the item slowly, as if unveiling a piece of art—which in fact it could be. "Another samovar? How much tea can four old people drink?" Igor teases.

"Ah, Your High Born, this one is not for *you!*" Aunt Roberta points to the three-foot-high silver samovar that has occupied the dining area since Igor's father gifted it to his bride over forty years ago. "Yours is beautiful, and your aunt keeps it steaming all the time. I just wanted my own."

Hers is squat, almost octagonal, and very wide; it appears made of bronze with curved legs and elaborate decorations of mythological figures, fruits, and leaves. "This is for my room at the Winter Palace. Do you realize that all my life I have coveted one of these? The antique ones—or what we will call them someday. Unfortunately, in my time the Soviet and then Russian authorities never permitted them to leave the country—especially not with a foreigner."

I can understand my aunt's long-term desire for a genuine Russian samovar, though her new predilection for ornamental objects surprises me. I've always thought of her as someone who is content with her books, and our apartment was never cluttered with *things* other than a few Russian souvenirs.

Igor appears puzzled, although he seldom quizzes my aunt on her peculiar statements about the future. It is as if he is absorbing and then trying to decide what he believes.

"Perhaps you should have purchased a traveling one, you know, one of those cube-shaped varieties," I suggest. "After all, we are always moving from palace to palace, and unlike her predecessor, Catherine does not believe in hauling everything except the kitchen sink from place to place."

"The kitchen sink?" Igor again seems confused, and then shrugs. "Enjoy your purchase, Mademoiselle."

"That's Roberta to you," she reminds him.

"Roberta then. Your niece and I were just discussing the empress's obsession with collecting. Which reminds me, the metalworking is amazing at court, not to mention the porcelain dinner sets she has accumulated. If it weren't for her passion for gemstones, I might not be able to earn a living!"

"Don't worry, Igor Igorevich, she also collects rocks and minerals," I remind him.

"Just like her predecessor, Peter the First," Aunt Roberta chimes in. Lately she has spent hours taking notes and making drawings at the Kunstkamera, coming back to the apartments with tales of the oddities, absurdities, and grotesque body parts that Peter collected for his museum.

"Have you seen Her Majesty's gem collection?" I ask her. "I swear her entire bedchamber resembles a priceless jewel case."

"I'm trying my best," Igor says.

"Yes, darling. Imagine, when she was a teenage princess, I used to take care of her things in just two boxes. Now she has literally an entire store in there! The walls are lined with glass cabinets full of treasures, and then she has this giant crystal globe for examining everything in detail. If she wants to choose a gift for someone, she goes through the entire collection and pulls out a diamond sword belt or a ruby snuff box or signet ring. She's almost what we would call in the future a 'hoarder.'"

When Aunt Gina and Sasha open the door and let in a blast of late winter air, Igor's aunt insists on settling us all down for gingerbread cakes and tea from the samovar in question.

"Smells wonderful!" Aunt Roberta exclaims, then wrinkles her nose. "Can I assume then that this is not one of those endless fast days and weeks that get me in trouble all the time?"

"We're fine," I assure her before turning to Sasha. "How was your lesson?" Sasha frowns, for all the world resembling his father when he doesn't like a piece he is working on. "I like reading. It's my science tutor who does not want to teach me anything *I* want to learn."

"Like what, young man?" Igor asks, and the two of them retreat to the kitchen to check on the progress of the gingerbread.

Within a half hour, all of us are sitting around the dining room table—newly expanded, I note—and savoring Aunt Gina's creation. "Igor's mother taught me this recipe," she tells us. However, it is obviously for her great nephew Sasha that she has created the pastries in the shapes of boats and bears.

"I remember one event hosted by our late Empress Elizabeth Petrovna," I tell everyone. "They had a cake that must have weighed as much as that front door, and all in the shape of a double-headed eagle. Then there was a top layer that was baked into a replica of Peterhof!"

As we laugh and share aspects of our days, I feel the proverbial lump in my throat. Is it possible that after all this time we are almost a family?

Crossing my fingers beneath the table, I feel more like smiling than I have since the three of us were transported here. Aunt Roberta polishes her new samovar while Sasha plays tag with the puppy (perhaps a shepherd mix) his papa brought home for him.

Across from me, Igor seems to be reading my thoughts, and his eyes are sparkling with something that I suspect is yearning.

Now it is his move.

I do not have to wait long. It has been nearly two years since my return when my husband takes our "courting" to the next logical step.

"I want you back in my life," he says softly. His carriage

driver has just picked me up at Tsarskoye Selo, from where the two of us will travel to a party hosted by Grigory and Catherine to show off renovations at Oranienbaum.

Surprised at his timing and not certain I really heard him (rather than what I *want* to hear), I stare down at my fingers and the amber and citrine rings sparkling above the folds of my tangerine-shaded chiffon gown. Although Anya was hired to design the dress, Igor had ordered it secretly. I could not be more pleased with it, nor with the orange and red shades of my tall kokoshnik headdress.

"Very well, we should talk after the event at Oranienbaum," he replies to my silence.

I nod and turn to smile at him, handsome as usual in breeches and a cutaway coat that reveals citrine buttons to complement my own outfit.

The long ride to what is perhaps Catherine's favorite palace passes in light conversation, with the two of us mostly exchanging anecdotes about Sasha. "You should see him with Catherine's greyhounds," I tell him. "They swarm him when he pretends to be asleep on the floor, leaping over him like circus animals—and him giggling the whole time as they kiss his face, hands, and ankles. The only time they abandon this play is when Catherine enters the room, and they all line up like obedient attendants waiting for pats on the head."

"He has learned to glue gemstones, did you know?"

"Probably hereditary," I say without thinking. Then, when Igor does not react negatively, I rush on. "Plus his mother took classes in jewelry making in the future. With all modern tools."

"You never told me this!"

"There really has not been an opportunity," I half scold, smiling so he knows I don't mean this as a rebuke. "In fact, I smuggled something back from that time for you. I've been holding onto it to give you at just the right moment."

Then I produce it from my reticule, where it fit so snugly this afternoon when I decided that two years was too long to deny him such a gift.

"A loupe? This large?" He exclaims in wonder. I know he has several, of course, mostly dangling from his apron or neck in the shop, albeit nothing to rival something with such a powerful lens.

I lean over and adjust the flame on the coach's brazier, giving him more light. Slipping my two-carat citrine ring off, I hand it to him so he can try the jeweler's loupe.

"Oh, my darling. This is magnificent! I would not have believed that so much magnification was possible."

"There are many other tools that will be invented, of course. I couldn't fit them in my pockets, and I was holding Sasha tightly with one hand."

"I'm so relieved he made it with you," Igor says quietly.

For most of the remainder of the trip I tell him about my jewelry lessons, and then the university classes I took in art history and geology. It is the latter, of course, that intrigues him the most.

We discuss the war, too, and I am so relieved my estranged husband is not required to be conscripted.

"I couldn't leave now," he says simply. "Incidentally, have you heard that she awarded that Potemkin courtier the ceremonial key of court chamberlain?"

"It's a high honor, of course. I think she watches his career carefully." I don't tell him that, while I know little, I do recognize the name from something in the history books. "Perhaps he will become one of her generals," I speculate.

It is amazing how quickly the time goes on such a long trip, not to mention with the man I love.

Nonetheless, we arrive weary and ready for a short nap before the night's events. The highlight will be a tour of the recently completed Chinese Pavilion, designed at Catherine's behest by the Italian court architect Antonio Rinaldi and completed the previous year. Unsure whether I am relieved or disappointed, I follow a servant to the separate rooms assigned to Igor and me. I don't know how he feels about this. He does take my hand and leave a lingering kiss on the palm before retreating to his own quarters.

Catering to his empress's attachment to all things Chinese and the artistic style known as *chinoiserie*, Rinaldi designed a distinctive building with a gable roof and an alabaster balustrade embellished with decorative vases. Statues of mythological gods occupy the grounds, and I feel a sense of relief that statue-hunting is no more a part of my life.

Inside, not only are the rooms richly ornamented with gilding, inlays, parquet patterns in exotic woods, stucco moldings, carvings, and wall murals portraying scenes from Roman mythology, the ceilings are breathtaking. Catherine points each one out, proudly naming the outstanding Italian artists who painted them. "My favorite," Igor tells me as we enter the Great Hall. The painting by Torelli, entitled "Apollo and the Arts," portrays the god surrounded by allegorical figures representing Sculpture, Painting, and Architecture.

"Mine, too," Catherine, who is almost next to us, smiles at

Igor. "Stefano Torelli is a genius. Shall I show all of you the nine patronesses of the arts—the Muses—and his painting, 'The Triumph of Venus,' in the Hall of Muses?"

From there we wander into the state rooms, and as the party moves toward the hall where we will dine, I cannot move. This—the Mosaic Chamber—ranks as my favorite. Igor, who lingers with me, cannot tear his eyes away either. It's small and much more intimate—maybe classic, with its blend of chinoiserie vases, French chairs, and silk embroideries. Catherine also refers to it as the Bugle-work Cabinet, with good reason; the entire room (or cabinet) shimmers so much it appears to move due to a dozen wall canvases covered with bugles made from threaded glass tubes. These are set into elaborately carved golden frames shaped like palm trees and topped by dragons.

"Our dearly departed Monsieur Lomonosov supplied two million beads. Rinaldi hired nine needlewomen to sew them on the panels. I cannot imagine how long it must have taken those poor women." Catherine's voice is almost hushed with awe. "And see the glass mosaic tables he designed—using no fewer than ninety colors?"

Besides Japanese and Chinese subjects, the amazing ceiling depicts an allegory of Catherine as the Roman goddess Fortuna pouring medals, coins, and jewels from a horn of plenty.

We dine near the Picture Hall, a circular room lavishly decorated with five dozen paintings by European masters. Throughout dinner, Igor and I speak little, as if our minds are both elsewhere. At opposite ends of the table, Catherine and Grigory talk so animatedly to the guests on either side of them that all I must do is pretend to listen.

Igor speaks up only once, to express how impressed he is by the gigantic three-story roller coaster midway through construction outside. "Ah, the Sliding Hill," Grigory responds. "I think sometimes it is Her Imperial Majesty's favorite project."

His brother Vladimir, who appears to have given up his attempts to woo me in favor of a much younger lady-in-waiting, leans across to address the entire table while he spells out the completed and planned features. "It is of stone and wood, painted a sky blue and white, as you can see already, with flights of spiral stairs on either end. The height of all three levels increases as if one is rising, with the entire edifice topping thirty-three meters high and the rectangular length of the slide itself a full five-hundred and thirty-two meters. We shall have a demonstration tomorrow if it is working."

Oohs and aahs greet this information, followed by a chorus of questions about the science of its functioning. "You can already see the carved carriages in the attached pavilions. They are gilded and shaped like ancient chariots or gondolas," Catherine interrupts animatedly. "I believe one is a bear with a saddle. We, my dear guests, will soon spend our summers exceeding all expectations for the winter sledding versions throughout Russia. Rather than just fly us one third of a mile, the tracks will keep us rolling up and down all year. It shall be wonderful fun!"

"A side rail will bring you back to the top!" Grigory adds enthusiastically. "One never knows what our marvelous empress will decide to create next!"

"I cannot take the credit, of course," Catherine says. "Antonio Rinaldi has once again outdone himself, and he promises it will be completed within perhaps two years. Ah, so long to wait!"

After dinner, Igor and I trail behind everyone up the stairs to the Grand Palace, with its façade reminding me of the color of orange segments. A servant again leads us to our adjoining rooms, and I turn toward my estranged husband to wish him good night.

I am thus surprised when at long last, he takes two steps forward. Falling into his arms the way I've longed to do for so many lonely years, I scarcely notice when he waves the servant who escorted us away.

Without removing one arm from my shoulders, he opens his own door and gently pulls me inside.

My returned kisses and the way I wrap myself around his still muscular body convince him he need not ask for permission. Within what seems like a moment we have fallen together onto his bed, and I have no recollection of how my gown and stays get removed.

After such a prolonged period of celibacy, the first time is quick and lustful. For both of us.

The second and third time and all the rest over the following day, we leisurely explore one another's bodies. "You are still the most breathtaking woman I've ever seen," he whispers at least once every few hours.

When I open the door leading to my own chamber to change clothing, I discover trays of food with silver covers and piles of fruits and pastries. Other than that evidence that someone had been there, no one knocks or disturbs us.

At times we nibble on the food—but are only ravenous for each other. We do talk a little about Sasha, who Igor repeatedly refers to as "our son" or "my son." I decide more conversation can wait.

We completely miss the following day's tour of the Sliding Hill, also known as the Switchback Pavilion.

Neither of us cares.

CHAPTER 36

(CATHERINE) 1769

*"The Turks and the French have taken it into their heads to awaken the
sleeping cat. And now the cat is going to run after the mice . . . and
now people will talk about us and be surprised at all the uproar
we make, and now the Turks will be beaten and defeated . . ."*
—Catherine II

Urged on by the French, who favored the Turks, the battles raged on. Catherine had faith in her military, at the same time fully aware of its lack of supplies and weaponry, as well as some disorganization. She was confident these weaknesses could be overcome, especially after she had appointed Alexis Orlov commander of the Russian fleet now bearing down on the Black Sea. Nevertheless, she hurled a glass against a damask wall when she heard that Frederick II had called this "a

war of the blind against the paralytic." The infidels or paralytic, she assumed, were the Turks, who continued to lose
battles throughout the year. *We'll show you who's blind,* she
vowed. It had been a long-time dream of hers to wrest away
the Crimean Peninsula—preferably at the same time as Constantinople. Peter the Great had tried and failed. She believed
she could carry out her idol's goals.

Campaigning seriously got underway just before her fortieth
birthday, and she summoned everyone into the dining room
to give them good news: "The Turkish camp is taken, along
with a great number of trophies and prisoners. Our losses
were almost nil since the enemy cannon fired over our heads."
General A. M. Golitsyn, her commander-in-chief, sent word in
early May that the Russian troops—mostly conscripted—had
defeated another thirty thousand Turkish soldiers.

Kissed by the spring sun, the piles of snow evaporated, and
everyone ignored the war to stroll the grounds of the various
palaces. Catherine managed to host a number of private enter-
tainments, often beginning with a theatrical performance followed by dinner at one of the two mechanical tables—called
a table *volant* or flying table—she had ordered constructed
at the Winter Palace, including one in her beloved new Hermitage. Her Thursday night dinners at the latter included
seventy or eighty people who were then treated to charades,
poetry readings, art conversations, music, or dance.

Now, however, it was time to move to Catherine Palace
at Tsarskoye Selo, where the original mechanical table had
remained a source of merriment since Elizabeth's reign. No
servants presented themselves, as each dish was raised or
lowered to a guest by a complicated system of pulleys. Each

person ordered by scrawling an order with chalk on a round slate left under each plate. When he or she rang a bell, the slate could be dropped via a rope to servants waiting below. Catherine and her guests often amused themselves by ordering oddities for someone at the end of their table who had left momentarily.

The highlight of Catherine Palace was her favorite: the Amber Chamber. Relaxing amidst its rich palette of oranges and yellows illuminated by gilded statues and golden trim, she scarcely wanted to leave. Sometimes she invited her closest friends to play whist on the parquet floor, confident that the cards fell her way whenever she played in here.

Baroness Maria Blukhova and her son Alexander were on the grounds with the empress and two of her beloved dogs when Vladimir Orlov showed up to reintroduce Catherine to Ivan Kulibin, the inventor she had met on the Volga trip two years ago. As they sat in one of the hanging gardens, Kulibin demonstrated a new clock he had designed. Shaped like an egg, it struck each hour with Easter tunes. To little Sasha's delight, it also opened to display the Resurrection, enacted by miniature gold and silver figures who acted it out. Just as enchanted, the empress opened and closed it several times for the boy.

"Papa make!" Sasha cried, pulling on his mother's hand.

"Perhaps," Maria smiled down at him. "He thinks Igor can do anything," she commented to the group, which now included Paul and his science tutor, Professor Aepinus.

"My son is wrong in this case," Igor, rounding the corner just in time to hear all the excitement, laughed. "He thinks I can move the moon in the sky."

"This clock is only a trifle that you could certainly imitate," Kulibin said modestly.

"*Au contraire*," Catherine protested, and ordered him a reward of one thousand rubles.

"Speaking of science—and engineering," Grigory said, "when will we get the opportunity to see the progress of the Thunder Rock that will support Falconet's statue of Peter the First?"

"Go see Thunder Rock!" Sasha begged his father, who laughed.

Aepinus shook his head. "Not quite yet, I'm afraid. They are building a special road, and don't expect to start the progress until November."

"Papa, wanna go!" Sasha insisted.

"You heard your teacher," Igor tried to sooth him. "They say it most likely will move at the pace of a turtle, despite copper balls beneath it. Do you remember what a turtle looks like? We will have a lot of time to see the Thunder Rock later this year. And look, Your Imperial Majesty is wearing a pair of earrings made from the rock."

Catherine obligingly showed them off to Sasha and everyone. "I had another pair made for the queen of England, King George III's wife."

For months, residents of the area have been obsessed about observing the potentially endless progress of the monolithic boulder. They claimed it weighed nearly sixteen hundred tons after stonecutters had struggled to whittle it down to a more manageable size before it left its original resting place half submerged in Karelia. Catherine had advertised to find someone with a mechanical imagination who could come up with a reasonable, workable way to transport the giant rock to Petersburg, and now that an engineer had been appointed, her enthusiasm knew no bounds.

Catherine herself had selected the massive granite boulder—shaped somewhat like a wave and allegedly once struck by lightning—to occupy Senate Square overlooking the Neva. There it would serve as the plinth to support the huge equestrian statue of Peter the Great that would take Falconet many more years to create. To most people, the logistics of the enterprise seemed far-fetched, primarily due to all the manpower required and a specially constructed barge flanked by two tankers to haul it to its final home.

"We shall all go and see the rock on my Name Day in November," Catherine said merrily, patting Sasha's head. No one was surprised that she so eagerly awaited the sight of "her" rock—and the mainstay of her tribute to Peter the Great—rolling slowly along the road and pulleys made for it, before being floated down to the Neva River and then to the city. No one expected it to arrive in its final resting place in less than a year or maybe two, even with over four hundred men assigned to the task.

Science came to the forefront once again in late May, when Aepinus set up a telescope for Grigory, Lev, Praskovia Bruce, and Zakhar Chernyshev to join Catherine to watch the long-awaiting transit of Venus. It was to be a world event, with Russia one of the prime viewing sites on earth.

Almost at the last moment, Vladimir Orlov came running

up to Grigory's observatory situated atop the empress's apartments.

"This is how the late Imperial Majesty Louis XIV of France observed solar eclipses," he explained, fitting a piece of smoky glass atop each telescope's lens. "If you do not do this, you could lose your eyesight."

As they all took turns peering through the telescope, Catherine marveled at the sight of the darkening orb moving for hours across the face of the sun.

"It's as if one planet is attempting to overshadow and subdue the largest of them all," Grigory said in awe.

"It's not what I expected, however," Vladimir Orlov said, at the same time scribbling down measurements and notes. "Venus appears as nothing more than a small blemish crossing such a massive sun."

Viewing it all through the special lens, Catherine felt a thrill run from her neck down her spine. Rather than willing the small planet to slow much as the other observers did, she found herself commiserating with the temporarily darkened sun. She rejoiced at this largest star's ability to survive and elude the elongated shadow that was Venus. When the transit ended, the sun once again splashed its golden orb of brilliance on the earth.

Just like me, she thought, knowing she was being vain, yet beyond worrying about that anymore. Then she turned and invited her small party to come inside for a worthy celebration.

When a Great Comet similar to the one she'd witnessed on her journey to Russia twenty-five years ago appeared overhead two months later, she dismissed her subjects' fears that this foretold a loss to the Turks. She was convinced that once again a comet heralded more good things for the empire of Russia and for her life.

CHAPTER 37

(MARIA) 1770

Enamored of early military successes, both large and small, Catherine spends more and more time in consultation with her ministers and military leaders. Taking advantage of this break, I decide to spend early spring moving some of my things into Igor's house and shop. The empress will summon me if I am needed.

Aunt Roberta has declined Igor and Aunt Gina's invitation to move in, preferring to remain in the Winter Palace directly across from her new job. To her delight, Catherine has appointed my aunt to oversee the Imperial Library, situated in one wing of Peter the Great's Kunstkamera museum.

"Now *this* is a worthy position!" she exclaims, arriving at the House of Gems frequently to share her latest finds. She also prefers Aunt Gina's cooking to the endless courses accompanying palace dinners. "Today I located not one but two books Her Imperial Majesty has been longing to read for ages. First, though, I directed the bookbinders to restore them."

Just then Countess Tatiana's carriage arrives to drop off Sasha from an outing with her own children, and I promise Aunt Roberta we will discuss her job soon. She smiles and reaches over to squeeze my hand, and I honestly would never believe that she is a day over my age. Since arriving here and meeting the empress, her eyes sparkle as brilliantly as aquamarine and any hair strands once resembling gray seem transformed into a shimmery silver.

"Don't ask me what I miss most about the future," she leans in to whisper to me. "It's definitely mosquito repellent!"

"I concur," I say ruefully, watching her aggressively scratching her arms and ankles.

As we mercifully assemble as a family, it is difficult to avoid war talk altogether, especially just after Alexis Orlov has sailed right into the Ottoman navy moored in Chesme Harbor and destroyed the sultan's entire fleet. "Can you imagine?" Igor shakes his head. "They claim that over eleven thousand enemy sailors drowned."

Aunt Roberta sets her spoon down. "What's more gruesome is what Rumiantsev did farther north on the exact same day! Can you believe that twenty-five thousand of our countrymen succeeded in killing one hundred twenty-five thousand Turks at the River Larga? Her Majesty is elated at the dual victories, of course."

"*Basta!*" Aunt Gina insists, motioning to the girl we employ that she may clear the dishes. "No more war talk in this household. Now, I want to hear more about Roberta's position. Not," she adds sternly, "about those monsters our late Imperial Majesty Peter the First collected for the Kunstkamera."

"Agreed," Aunt Roberta laughs. She often explores the Kunstkamera before or after her shifts at the library. "I'd rather talk about the binding and refinishing work, anyway." She then launches into the first of what will be many discussions on the process of preserving old books and manuscripts.

"Peter the First amassed thousands of volumes on his Grand Tour of Europe. They are still not cataloged, though. And years later many are grimy, with loose pages that must be glued back in and fragile covers that require stiffening."

"Are the covers made of leather?" Igor asks.

"Mostly calfskin, yes. They touch them up with a bit of birch oil to preserve them, and the ones with jewels usually require securing again."

Now she had garnered Igor's interest, and they talked excitedly about how the prayer books were the most well-used so that reapplication of their gilded edges must be done often. "I understand some have cameos embedded in the covers. Have you seen those?"

"I have indeed, Igor. Most of them are on great big old Bibles."

"And what stones are they carved upon?"

"Sapphire, emerald, amethyst, and topaz, mostly. Occasionally mother of pearl or abalone. Nothing as gorgeous as the one you made for Her Majesty."

"I didn't know you'd seen it."

"Oh, yes. She shows it to everyone. I do notice that she's rather sly about where she hides it when she is ready to put it away. Of course, cameos are getting more popular on everything from snuff boxes to signet rings and bracelets. I'm afraid you've created something that has fueled her desire for more cameos, though."

"Perhaps," I suggest, "you could create for her a cameo on a snuff box. Those are probably two of the three things she loves most."

"Fine idea, my dear wife! What is the third? Could we manage to combine them all to present her on her next Name Day?"

"Stationery," I reply promptly. "She told me she is 'like a drunkard' when she confronts a piece of blank paper. You've probably noticed that she uses that special thick paper bordered with gilt."

"No, though I did notice one day while waiting for her that she always uses her right hand to write. She does other things with her left."

Aunt Roberta laughs. "I know exactly why! I heard her tell Monsieur Betskoy when he asked one day why she takes snuff with her left hand. She told him she does it so all the people who kiss her right hand won't be offended by the smell of tobacco."

Talk then evolves into Catherine's other pursuits, which include her belief in public education for every child, regardless of gender. "It will take a long time to get this underway in our empire," Igor remarks.

"Thank goodness our boy is so smart and has access to schooling," Aunt Roberta says, rubbing the top of Sasha's head. My son, who has concentrated mostly on the delicious dishes Aunt Gina has prepared, is nearly asleep at the table. "I think we've bored the poor child," she notes.

"Of course you have," Aunt Gina scolds. "All this talk of dead people, advanced jewelry making, tobacco, and education—not to mention book binding, of all things. Let me put him to bed."

"I'll do it," Igor interrupts, and with Sasha's hands wrapped around his neck, my two men with matching hair that blends together retreat to one of the back rooms.

"While he is away, Maria Sergeievna, I want to show you something," Aunt Gina says, ensuring that they are out of hearing before she rises. Moving more swiftly than normal, she reaches the top shelf of the armoire and retrieves something that resembles a photo. For a second I think it is the one I left her so long ago, and if so, it's dangerous to have it where someone might wonder about the miracle of photography.

I am astounded at what she shows me. So is Aunt Roberta.

"My nephew has never seen this—at least since he became an adult," Aunt Gina confides. "I've been hiding it in case I needed it. Thank the Good Lord I didn't need to."

The miniature painting depicts a boy Sasha's age standing stiffly near a horse and carriage who strongly resembles both Sasha and Igor. "Is it *him*?" I ask in wonder.

"His father had it painted before he died. I think Igor is about eight or nine there."

"Why didn't you show it to him?"

"No need. I knew my stubborn nephew would come to his senses eventually. I'll show it to him soon enough."

I am weeping, as is my aunt. The likeness is astounding. No one in the world could see that painting and not know it is my husband, and that he is unquestionably the father of my son.

"Stop that," Aunt Gina chides. "He is coming back. Or should I say he is back? Into your lives?"

I excuse myself then to regain control of my emotions. And to rejoice. All this time I had the proof, yet having my husband love the boy unconditionally while uncertain of his paternity makes him a special man. A man I can forgive for the time it took him.

Sasha has learned to read and excels at his lessons, with science and literature being his latest favorites. Catherine, who has never been able to warm up to her own son, does at least take an active interest in Paul's education. Now for some reason she does the same thing for Sasha, including gifting him a collection of imaginative French tales. "My dear governess Babet read these to me all the time when I was a child," she explains while stitching on a tapestry she is creating. "Not only did I get fluent in French at a young age, I enjoyed all the stories of wolves and princesses and magic and thorned-in castles."

It is true, I realize as I pick up reading halfway through "Little Red." If Sasha doesn't know what a word means, he asks.

"When did you become so good at French?" I ask, surprised, though I know everyone at court speaks Russian, French, or both.

"Papa teaches me sometimes. We don't tell Baba, though, because she says Italian is *bellissima*. The best language, she says. I get a gingerbread boat if I do well. Papa gives me sugar candy, too. It's a secret." He places his finger over his lips. "Will I get dates or nuts if I don't tell them I can speak French now?"

I pretend to be upset about his inevitable trip to a dentist sooner than I'd planned, then laugh with him. "You are a pistol," I tell him in English. When he looks puzzled, I don't translate—exactly.

⌘

It is time for an after-supper walk, and when Aunt Gina insists she must assist Sasha with his lessons, Igor and I set off for a stroll. It is early July, and the White Nights still have not shortened. As we pass the Admiralty sparkling in the endless night, I cannot help pausing and turning toward the sight of the Winter Palace, its own façade mirrored in the calm river.

The pale facades of other Petersburg buildings and palaces mix splashes and swirls of color as they reflect on canals and the Neva's gray-green surfaces. At times all of Petersburg resembles a giant watery canvas with scenes reminiscent of the Monets and Manets my art history professor showed in his Power Point presentations. Especially now, the city transforms into a living Impressionistic painting. I struggle to explain schools of art and my own classes to Igor, and he struggles to understand how we can study paintings without seeing them in person or in books.

"I cannot promise to understand all this, my lover," Igor says in wonder. "I can tell you that I've often imagined that when the sunset and sunrise colors blend and merge, I feel as if we are living beneath a giant agate sky."

"Exactly, my beloved. It's observations like that that first made me fall in love with you. Remember when you used to call me your precious opal?"

"It's just as true now as it was then," he says softly, and takes my hand.

For a while we stroll in silence. There is something on my mind, though, and I have to say it. "Sometimes I feel cheated out of the past. Part of it anyway."

"I feel the same way." He squeezes my hand. "I spent nearly five years without you, not to mention missing out on your pregnancy and the first two years of our son's life."

Tears threaten to spill from my eyes. "I've never been certain you believe me. I don't *know* how time travel works, just that apparently I missed all those same years with you. I can never get them back."

"We will have to make up for them by living our lives to the fullest, my sweet. There's no question Alexander is my son, regardless of all the court gossip about his age."

"There is nothing we can do about that," I say sadly.

"It doesn't matter. What matters is that we are all together. And our son will have four adults to love him."

We are approaching the area of the palace that houses the Hermitage, where this spring we often took Sasha to visit Her Imperial Majesty—or rather her dogs. Before leaving Russia, Dr. Dimsdale gifted her with two small whippets, named Duchess Anderson and Sir Tom Anderson. Although they had special servants assigned to take care of them, the sleek, loveable dogs spend most of their time in Catherine's apartments. She permits Sir Tom to sleep in her bed atop a woolen blanket she knitted for the dogs, and she is the main person who walks them. Having discovered this, Sasha begs constantly to go to the palace and romp with them.

One day Catherine announced, "Since they seem to love you as much as me, Sashenka, I promise you one of Sir Tom's puppies when that time comes."

After that, Sasha asked nightly, "Will the puppies be at the palace now?"

Then one night last week Igor arrived home with a well-trained, smaller dog with whom Sasha can cuddle, sleep, and walk until Sir Tom and Duchess become parents.

"Are you sure about this?" I asked Igor after our son goes to bed. "Her Majesty's dogs are a bit unruly, to the point of jumping on her writing hand and causing smudges and ink blots. Can you imagine if the puppy gets loose in your workshop? Let alone a second dog—a puppy, no less—in a year or so?"

When the topic turns naturally to the dog again tonight, Igor once more dismisses my worry. "The puppy seems to be accustomed to his leash already. Plus, he might provide some security in case—"

"In case of what? Of criminals?" I'm seldom afraid with Igor at my side, and lock my arm playfully in his.

"In case someone tries to steal my family away from me," he laughs, his granite eyes now back to the sparkling smoky quartz I remember.

Then, suddenly sobering, he adds, "I lost the earliest years with my son, and I must make up for that by spoiling him as much as I can. And protecting him."

"How about spoiling your wife?"

"That too, my sweet," he says, pausing on the Neva embankment and taking me in his arms. "Just remember what they say in the tales my father used to tell me: 'Love is a golden vessel; it bends but never breaks.'"

Somehow, I don't think our golden vessel will break ever again.

THE END

AUTHOR'S NOTES

ACCURACY: As mentioned at the end of Book One, progress on such a venture inevitably is slowed by contradictions in scholarly sources for chronologies and dates, details, dignitaries in attendance at important events, etc. Inconsistencies of a numerical nature abound, as well, such as the number of boats accompanying Catherine on the 1767 Volga voyage. Here I also had to make judgment calls, weighing not only my own knowledge about ports of call (gleaned by personal research trips up and down the mid and lower Volga), but my research into Catherine herself. One biographer, who sadly has proved rather misogynistic in his commentary at various points, insists that Catherine was terrified on the river.

I chose to balance this out with her reactions to other situations throughout the previous 38 years and her consistently courageous attitude in much riskier circumstances.

In another instance, three renowned historians disagree about who initially suggested that the fleet of ships be sent to the Mediterranean during the Turkish-Russian war. In this case, I decided the information was not relevant to the novel and omitted it rather than make an error.

The early scenes with Catherine's son Paul also contradict each other. One biographer claims that the empress did not leave Paul's bedside for an entire week during his illness just after the coronation. In this case, I opted not to portray this, as it seemed out of character.

Any errors are my own or some combination of mine and those of other biographers. I frequently do take creative license in imagining various conversations that involve real historical figures (see below).

DATES: Unlike much of the world at that time, Russia retained its use of the original Julian calendar rather than the Gregorian calendar. Thus, as much as possible, I rely on the Julian calendar, referred to in sources as the Old Style (OS) for all dates in the book. That means that during Catherine's lifetime, Russia was 11 days behind other nations. Many other authors do rely on Gregorian dates, referred to as New Style (NS), or a mix of the two. When you encounter dates in those particular sources you may need to subtract 11 days.

CHARACTERS: Nearly all the characters in Catherine's world and life (including her ministers and her lover Grigory

Orlov) are based on actual people, while those in Maria's life (Anya, Igor, Aunt Gina, Aunt Roberta, Tatiana, Alyona, etc.) are fictional.

AUTHENTICITY: In other fictionalized biographies and at least one satirical TV series, many authors and scriptwriters pick and choose, often grossly altering facts and/or timelines for the sake of the plot. This is something I rigorously attempt to avoid. I remain determined in this series to ensure authenticity in details known about Catherine II's life from reliable available sources, and regret any mistakes that may slip by. Most incidents and many of the conversations retold here actually took place. Once again, the aid of so much available information, documentation, and correspondence on her life and between her and others enabled me to quote Catherine directly in some dialogue.

One scene I had to imagine was Catherine's meeting with Mikhail Lomonosov in 1764, succumbing to the temptation to put some credence in an 1884 portrait by Fedorov envisioning that visit. Elizabeth tended to underestimate the man's greatness and the importance of his contributions to science and language, though I believe that Catherine did not. Had he not died of drink shortly thereafter, unappreciated in his own time, perhaps Russian history might have unfolded differently. It was only early in the twentieth century that the significance of many of his experiments and theories were valued and known.

PETER III: As noted at the end of Book One, the portrayal of Peter III is more negative than some scholars (especially in Russia) would prefer. However, I did not rely solely on Catherine's memoirs regarding his childishness, meanness, and ineptitude in so many areas. Plenty of evidence exists to back this up, most notably correspondence, writings, and reports by other witnesses and diplomats from throughout Europe who met and observed him. Perhaps given time he might have become a tolerable emperor, but certainly Catherine's seizure of the throne resulted in primarily positive changes and developments in Russia.

Peter III's death remains one of the murkiest and most disputed ones in world history. Most scholars can agree on two things: one, that he was in fact murdered (the circumstances remain wrapped in a mystery), and secondly, that Catherine most likely had no role in the murder's planning or execution. Perhaps my favorite summation comes from Vincent Cronin, who argues, "Of her being involved in the murder directly or indirectly, there is not a particle of evidence, while the evidence against it is plentiful."

IVAN VI: As for the death of Ivan VI (presumptive heir to the crown who, as a child, was dethroned by Empress Elizabeth and assassinated early in Catherine's reign), the entire truth may never be known. Yet the trial of the accused usurper has left historians copious piles of notes and testimonies. Should anyone else have shared the blame? Some scholars suspect Panin could've influenced the two guards—exasperated with their solitary duty—who committed the actual murder.

Other biographers, such as Edward Arthur Brayley Hodgetts, argue that Catherine could not have instigated the crime: "The half-witted Mirovitch, with his open and unconcealed hatred of Catherine, his limited circle, his poverty and helplessness, was too obviously a maniac to have been employed as an instrument by so cautious and shrewd a woman as Catherine always proved herself. To have had such a man tried, and to have exposed herself to the risk of his blabbing out the whole story from sheer stupidity or vain gloriousness, was a risk which it is incredible that Catherine should have run when there were so many other more effective and less public means of doing away with the frail and imbecilic prisoner."

SPELLING/NAMES: The spellings of names of actual persons and places always present problems in the transliteration of Russian. Once again, I chose not to try to follow a specific one religiously, opting to go either with the most familiar or recognizable versions or those that seemed to me to be closest to the Russian (as well as German and Polish) spellings. Readers often complain about the difficulty of following along with names when reading books set in Russia. That is primarily due to Russians' habit of using a middle name (known as a patronymic) that identifies their fathers. Thus Igor Igorevich (son of Igor), Grigory Grigorevich (son of Grigory), and Maria Sergeievna (daughter of Sergei) appear frequently.

Russians, like most of the world, also use nicknames (Masha for Maria, Lana for Svetlana, Katinka for Ekaterina/Catherine, Sasha for Alexander). When referring to children, they may use a diminutive such as Ivanushka (Ivan) much as other languages might refer to Daniel as Dan or Danny when he is young.

CROWN JEWELS: Catherine's crown jewels (incidentally, the gem atop the crown turns out to be red spinel rather than ruby) were utilized by all Romanov rulers who followed her through the end of the tsarist era. It and the scepter (later containing the famous Orlov Diamond) can be seen in the Moscow Kremlin's Diamond Fund exhibit. A Catherine the Great emerald cameo similar to the one Igor creates does exist. No records remain as to the name of the jeweler who crafted it. As noted throughout, cameos on gemstones were a favorite of the rich during this entire period in Russia.

RUMORS/MYTHS/LIES: Finally, it bears repeating what I said at the end of Book One: for the first forty-plus years of her life, Catherine took only three lovers (four if you believe that she ever slept with Peter). Hence the promiscuity and rumors of bestiality attributed to her especially in her later life are lacking in evidence, not to mention logic, mathematics, and the detailed documentation of her life. She did take several additional lovers in later years after her long-term relationship with Potemkin (after the events of this book) but lovers documented throughout her entire lifetime of sixty-seven years appear to total roughly twelve to fifteen.

These salacious stories began circulating during and just after the French Revolution that she opposed so strongly. Alas, throughout history it has been far from unusual for powerful women with equally powerful or resentful enemies to face discreditation through scandalous, reprehensible, and fabricated rumors (i.e. Elizabeth I, Marie Antoinette, Alexandra II, Eleanor of Aquitaine). In Catherine's case, despite ruling an empire already accustomed to females on the throne, she reigned when most European powers strongly opposed this idea. The long ban on female rule in the Hapsburg Empire had been softened only recently when Charles II passed a law that his daughter Maria Theresa could share the throne with her husband and later her son. But as Susan Jaques points out, "Gender . . . was a huge problem [for Catherine] in Europe, where she was caricatured as licentious and a regicide."

GRATITUDE: Lastly, I am grateful to the authors whose words and insight I quoted in most of the epigraphs preceding the Catherine chapters, as well as dear friends and Russian historical experts who read over final drafts. Particular thanks go Sue and Eila McMillin, as well as my partner Raymond.

THE RUSSIAN-UKRAINIAN WAR/CURRENT CON-TROVERSY: *In the Shadows* and *Out of the Shadows* are works of historical fiction, requiring nearly 13 years of research. Thus the subject matter and setting are neither intended to take a stand on the war that began in 2022, nor to endorse Putin's regime. Nor do the novels aim to support imperialism by recounting it in history. People need to make up their own minds on issues such as whether violent wars justify the banning, censorship, or destruction of Russian or Ukrainian historical, cultural, and academic figures in an attempt to erase each other's culture.

Since the war began, statues of Catherine the Great have been toppled or removed in Ukraine (including in cities which she founded later in her reign), as have those of the scientist Mikhail Lomonosov. More than 30 monuments to Alexander Pushkin—the renowned poet and central figure in Russian literature—also have met their demise. Meanwhile, Russia has been accused of appropriating thousands of priceless artifacts from occupied areas of Ukraine (considered by some to be a war crime).

Throughout the international community, the issue of "canceling a culture" for political and post-colonial reasons remains controversial. Few people thoroughly understand Ukraine's history, its struggles to survive, the history of Russia banning Ukrainian culture, and the high stakes involved. My hope is that my readers might find themselves more informed about just a fraction of the region's complexity by learning more about Catherine II despite her current vilified status in some countries.

The following are the main sources read & consulted while researching this novel:

Alexander, John T. *Catherine the Great: Life and Legend.* NY: Oxford University Press, 1989.

Almedingen, E. M. *Catherine the Great.: A Portrait.* London: Hutchinson, 1963.

Anisimov, Evgeni V. *Five Empresses: Court Life in Eighteenth-Century Russia.* Trans. Kathleen Carroll. Westport, CT: Praeger Publishers, 2004.

Anthony, Katharine. *Catherine the Great.* Garden City, NY: Garden City Publishing, 1925.

Catherine the Great: Selected Letters. Trans. Andrew Kahn and Kelsey Rubin-Detlev. NY: Oxford University Press, 2018.

Chekhonin, Oleg and Svetlana Chekhoninina. *Oranienbaum.* St. Petersburg: Prepress Kitezh Art Publishers, 2006.

Cone, Polly, Editor. *Treasures From the Kremlin.* Moscow: State Museums of the Moscow Kremlin: 1979.

Cronin, Vincent. *Catherine Empress of All the Russias: An Intimate Biography.* London: William Collins Sons & Co.,1978.

Dixon. Simon. *Catherine the Great.* NY: HarperCollins, 2009.

---. *Catherine the Great: Profile in Power.* Harlow: Longman, 2001.

Erickson, Carolly. *Great Catherine: The Life of Catherine the Great, Empress of Russia.* NY: St. Martin's Griffin, 1994.

Garrard, J. G., Ed. *The Eighteenth Century in Russia.* Oxford: Clarendon Press, 1973.

Grey, Ian. *Catherine the Great*. Philadelphia, Lippincott, 1962.

Haslip, Joan. *Catherine the Great: A Biography*. Toronto: Longman, 1977. 1st American Edition.

Hodgetts, Edward Arthur Brayley. 1859-1932. *The Life of Catherine the Great of Russia*. London: Methuen & Co. Ltd, 1914. Archived "Empress of All Russia." (July 2013). <http:www.catherinethegreat.org> (09 July 2024)

---. "Catherine the Great." http://www.catherinethegreat.org

Jaques, Susan. *The Empress of Art: Catherine the Great and the Transformation of Russia*. NY: Pegasus Books, 2016.

Kaus, Gina. *Catherine: The Portrait of An Empress*. Trans. from German by June Head. NY: Viking Press, 1935. The Literary Guild edition.

Kelly, Laurence, Ed. *A Traveller's Companion to St. Petersburg*. NU: Interlink1981. Reprint 2003.

Kennett et al. *In the Russian Style*. Edited by Jacqueline Onassis. NY: MJF Books, 1976.

Kochan, Miriam. *Life in Russia Under Catherine the Great*. NY: G. P. Putnam's Sons, 1969.

Lawrence, John. *A History of Russia*, 7th Ed. NY: Meridian, 1993.

Lentin, Antony. *Russia in the Eighteenth Century: From Peter the Great to Catherine the Great (1696-1796)*. London: Heinemann Educational Books, 1973.

Madariaga, Isabel De. *Catherine the Great*. New Haven: Yale University Press, 1990.

---. "Catherine the Great: A Personal View. *History Today* 51.11 (Nov. 2001): 45-51.

---. *Catherine the Great: A Short History*. Yale University Press, 1990.

---. *Russia in the Age of Catherine the Great*. New Haven, Yale University Press, 1981.

Mason, Mary Willan. "The Treasures of Catherine the Great from the State Hermitage Museum St. Petersburg." *Antiques & Collecting Magazine* 106, no. 3, 62.

Massie, Robert K. *Catherine the Great: Portrait of an Empress*. NY: Random House, 2011.

Massie, Suzanne. *Land of the Firebird: The Beauty of Old Russia*. NY: Touchstone, 1980.

Montefiore, Simon Sebag. *The Romanovs 1613-1918*. Knopf, 2016.

Oldenbourg, Zoe. *Catherine the Great*. NY: Pantheon, 1965.

Palmer, Alan. *Russia in War and Peace*. NY: Macmillan Co., 1972.

Piotrovski, Mikhail B., Ed. *Treasures of Catherine the Great*. London: Thames and Hudson, 2000.

Pipes, Richard. *Russia Under the Old Regime*. New York, Scribner's, 1974.

Proskurina, Vera. *Creating the Empress: Politics and Poetry in the Age of Catherine II*. Boston: Academic Studies Press, 2011.

Radishchev, Alexander. *A Journey from St. Petersburg to Moscow*. Trans. Leo Wiener. Cambridge, MA: Harvard University Press, 1958.

Riasanovsky, Nicholas V. *A History of Russia*, 4th ed. NY: Oxford University Press, 1984.

Romanov, Catherine. *The Memoirs of Catherine the Great.* Trans. Mark Cruse and Hilde Hoogenboom. NY: Modern Library, 2005.

Rounding, Virginia. *Catherine the Great: Love, Sex, and Power.* NY: St. Martin's Press, 2006.

Troyat, Henri. *Catherine the Great.* Trans. Joan Pinkham. NY: E. P. Dutton, 1980.

---. *Catherine the Great.* Reprint. London: Phoenix Press, 2000.

Van Der Post, Laurens. *A View of All the Russias.* NY: William, Morrow: 1964.

Waliszewski, Kasimierz. *The Romance of an Empress.* New York: D. Appleton and Company, 1894. Trans. from French 1905. Reprinted 1968.

Zwingle, Erla. "Catherine the Great." *National Geographic* 194, No. 3 (September 1998). 94-117.

Suggested Discussion Questions for Book Clubs (Note: Spoilers!)

1. Do Maria's actions when she finally discovers the statue that brought her to the past eighteen years earlier seem realistic? Believable? If you were in her position, would you have done the same thing she did?

2. What are your thoughts about Grigory and Catherine's relationship? Disregarding anything you may have read that takes place years later, do you think Catherine makes the right decision by keeping him as her lover?

3. There are fewer sex scenes in Book Two than in Book One. Did you appreciate that or regret their omission?

What might be the author's reasoning for leaving some out?

4. The narrator(s) use a lot of celestial imagery (descriptions of and references to sky, stars, and planets, directly or indirectly). Provide a few examples. What do these add to the narrative?

5. Once again gemstones play an important role in both main characters' lives. In what way does this enhance the text, the plot, the characters, etc.?

6. Did you notice times when the Maria and the Catherine chapters work together, reinforce an image, play off one another, or compare/contrast the two women's personalities?

7. Find examples of instances where the italicized epigraphs preceding chapters written in Catherine's point of view enhance your understanding of the character. Do they accomplish anything else? What—if anything— would the novel lose if these quotations were eliminated?

8. Do you believe that Catherine was innocent of Peter III's and/or Ivan VI's fates? Why or why not?

9. In addition to the title, the motif of shadows permeates the text. In what ways do you find that to be true?

10. How did you feel about the chapters that take place in the present? Where did you find the narrator's reactions realistic or unrealistic? What might you have done differently than Maria?

11. Is Aunt Roberta's reaction to Maria's return believable? And later, did her decision surprise you?

Above paintings (all in oil): Eriksen, Vigilius. *Portrait of Catherine II in Guard's Uniform on Her Horse Brilliant.* circa 1778, State Russian Museum, Saint Petersburg, Russia. Torelli, Stefano. *Coronation Portrait of Catherine II.* 1763-66, State Russian Museum, Saint Petersburg, Russia. (age 33) Antropov, Alexei. *Portrait of Catherine II of Russia.* 1763, Tretyakov Gallery, Moscow, Russia.

About The Author

Judith Rypma's background includes publication of over 200 short stories, poems, and poetry collections. *Out of the Shadows* is her fifth novel (see beginning of book for titles.)

The author's love affair with Russia started after she read Peter Massie's *Nicholas and Alexandra* in high school. She made her first visits to the former Soviet Union in the early 1980s, followed by well over a dozen trips to an emerging Russian Federation. In the meantime, she earned a degree in Russian Studies and has lectured on Russian topics in St. Petersburg and in the U.S. She has authored numerous articles about Russia, taught its literature, and organized study abroad tours to St. Petersburg sponsored by Western Michigan University, where she is an associate professor emerita.

Check out her website at **http://www.rypmabooks. com**

This novel constitutes a sequel (Book Two). Book One—*In the Shadows with Catherine the Great*—explores Catherine's first 32 years leading up to her coup. It also covers Maria's portal into the past and her evolving relationships with Catherine and Igor. It is not necessarily required to read Book One in order to follow Book Two.

Made in United States
North Haven, CT
08 April 2025

67745457R00228